Death at THE DAY LILY CAFÉ

Also by Wendy Sand Eckel

Murder at Barclay Meadow

Death at THE DAY LILY CAFÉ

WENDY SAND ECKEL

MINOTAUR BOOKS
A THOMAS DUNNE BOOK

This is a work of fiction. All of the characters, organizations, and events portrayed in this novel are either products of the author's imagination or are used fictitiously.

A THOMAS DUNNE BOOK FOR MINOTAUR BOOKS.
An imprint of St. Martin's Publishing Group.

www.thomasdunnebooks.com
www.minotaurbooks.com

Library of Congress Cataloging-in-Publication Data

Names: Eckel, Wendy Sand, author.
Title: Death at the Day Lily Café: a mystery / Wendy Sand Eckel.
Description: First edition. | New York: Minotaur Books, 2016. | "A Thomas Dunne book."
Identifiers: LCCN 2016001441|ISBN 9781250058614 (hardcover) | ISBN 9781466862944 (ebook)
Subjects: LCSH: Women detectives—Fiction. | Murder—Investigation—Fiction. | BISAC: FICTION / Mystery & Detective / Women Sleuths. | GSAFD: Mystery fiction.
Classification: LCC PS3605.C553 D43 2016 | DDC 813/.6—dc23
LC record available at http://lccn.loc.gov/2016001441

Our books may be purchased in bulk for promotional, educational, or business use. Please contact your local bookseller or the Macmillan Corporate and Premium Sales Department at 1-800-221-7945, extension 5442, or by e-mail at MacmillanSpecialMarkets@macmillan.com.

First Edition: July 2016

10 9 8 7 6 5 4 3 2 1

To Elizabeth and Madeline, with love

A symbol of birth and humility, the lily reminds us that our good deeds do not need to be known by others. It is helping someone that gives us the greatest reward.

When you have only two pennies left in the world, buy a loaf of bread with one, and a lily with the other.

—CHINESE PROVERB

Death at THE DAY LILY CAFÉ

One

The Day Lily Café

Join us Thursday for our Grand Opening. Enjoy a complimentary cinnamon muffin with any coffee purchase. Open for breakfast and lunch, 7:00–3:00.

167 people like this.

VIEW ALL 17 COMMENTS

Annie Hart

Yay Mom!!!!!! I'm so proud. :)

Tony Ricci

Good job, princess, but for crying out loud, stop giving away free stuff

Janice Tilghman
Way to go, Rose Red. Way cool.

Mr. Miele's high-pitched beep signaled the first batch of French roast had finished brewing. I cinched my robe and trotted down the narrow stairs of the two-hundred-year-old farm house that had been bequeathed to me by my beloved Aunt Charlotte. The breaking dawn lightened the sky to navy blue, bringing the shapes of the various objects in my kitchen into focus. The glowing green clock of my treasured coffee bistro read 5:00. Boot stomps on the front steps announced Tyler's arrival. After removing two mugs from hooks under the cabinet, I rolled my shoulders back and smiled. I'd done it. I opened a café, and Tyler and I had the organic produce to provision it. I was looking forward to seeing him. He had been swamped with the farm lately, and I spent all day, every day planning menus, prepping, and shopping for the best ingredients I could find—ideally local and organic. As a result, Tyler and I only saw each other for a brief shared coffee in the morning and an exhausted hi/good-bye in the evening.

We first met the day he appeared in the lane leading to my new residence, visibly annoyed at my neglect of the property for the previous two years and anxious to get the fields working again. But over the past year and a half, he had become a dear and trusted companion.

"Just in time." I spun around, a wide grin on my face. "I've been so nervous I couldn't sleep."

"That's understandable," he said, and accepted the mug. Early morning sunlight streamed in the window, irradiating his emerald eyes. His hair was freshly washed, the sandy blond contrasting with his tanned skin.

"We did this together. You and me."

He walked over to the sugar canister. "That's not really true." He pulled open the silverware drawer.

"Sure it is," I said. "You grow most of the produce. You help me with the flowers and herbs. And what about the eggs? All of them come from our own free-range, fat, happy chickens."

"Speaking of chickens." He turned to face me but avoided my eyes. "A hawk got one yesterday. I tried to stop it."

"And?"

"I was too late."

"Oh no. How awful." I gripped my mug tighter. "Which one? It wasn't Scheherazade, I hope."

Tyler shook his head. "I told you not to name them."

"I can't help it. They have such distinct personalities." I searched his face. "It was her, wasn't it?"

"Nope. It was one of the bantams. Mick Jagger set off the alarm by squawking his heart out. He was trying to protect his hens."

"I didn't know roosters did that." I set my coffee cup on the counter. "See? Chickens are amazing. Thus they deserve names."

Tyler peered into the bread basket. "You don't happen to have any extra muffins, do you?"

"Those are my trials from yesterday, so please, help yourself. I think they came out pretty good. Did you ever eat cinnamon toast as a kid?"

"The best."

"That was my inspiration." I removed a plate from the cabinet and arranged the muffins in a circle. "Will the hawk come back?"

"For certain." He sipped his coffee. "It's probably out there right now."

I suppressed a shiver. "Oh, I almost forgot. I have something for you." I tugged my robe tighter around my waist, and walked over to the table. I unfolded a T-shirt and held it up for him to see. "Ta-da!" The tee was a deep forest green with small white letters in the upper left-hand corner that read:

BARCLAY MEADOW

AN ORGANIC SUSTAINABLE FARM

I flipped it over. The same words, only in a larger font, spread across the back. "Do you like it? I ordered a couple. And I got a few for me, too."

Tyler smiled. "I do, actually. Good color."

"It will go nicely with your eyes."

"I would have been better off not knowing that." Tyler took the shirt from my hands, finished his coffee, and set the mug in the sink. He turned around, his face animated in a rare smile. "Good luck today. You've worked hard. You deserve to have this success."

"Thank you." My heart skipped around in my chest. "You know that means the world to me, coming from you."

He lingered a moment and then headed toward the front door. There was no chocolate Lab following him today. Dickens, getting on in years, now waited for Tyler under the shade of a sycamore tree.

I hurried up the narrow, creaky stairwell. I hung my robe on a hook and slipped into a white blouse, short black skirt, and my favorite pair of wedge heels. Once I had fluffed my hair and added a little makeup, I clasped my mother's pearls around my neck. I raised my eyes to the ceiling and, as I always did when I put on the pearls, said, "Miss you, Mom. Every day, all day." I gave my watchful cat a little pat and was on my way at last.

Two

A dense mist rose from the Cardigan River as I drove into town. Despite my best efforts, I was running late. I scrolled through the contacts on my hands-free phone menu, careful to keep an eye on a pair of cyclists weaving along the road in front of me, and clicked on Glenn's number.

"Rosalie, where are you? People are already reading the menu outside."

"I'm on my way," I said. "Have you started the coffee?"

"Of course," Glenn said. I felt instantly soothed by his calm, confident tone. He was my path to Zen.

"There are a couple of bikers in the road in front of me. They must think we Eastern Shore folks have nothing better to do."

"Careful," Glenn said, "you're starting to sound like a native. And I think they prefer the term *cyclists*."

"Has Custer put in the first batch of muffins?"

"The aroma of that cinnamon is making me salivate."

"Thank you, Glenn. I don't know what I would do without you."

"No need to find out. All right, dear. Crystal is setting the tables. She's doing some fancy thing with the napkins. It looks pretty good. Be safe, and remember to share the road."

I ended the call and exhaled a deep breath in an attempt to calm my nerves. I was relieved my employees were ready to start the day. So far I had three: my cook and dishwasher, Custer Wells, Tyler's wayward nephew who had needed a job; and two wait staff—Crystal Sterling, a young woman who was taking an extended break from her fine-arts education at John Adams College, and my best friend, Glenn, who at the age of seventy-two was able to keep orders in his head, soothe ruffled feathers, and pour a cup of West African blend without spilling a drop.

I stared at the cyclists, willing them to turn. That was a lot of spandex. A little too much information for my taste. One of them pointed to a farmhouse. The other wobbled as he turned to look at it. I eased off the accelerator. At least the fog was lifting. A lazy flock of Canada geese flew in a low *V* over the river, their out-of-sync honks piercing the quiet. I sank my teeth into my lower lip. I seemed to be the only one in a hurry this morning.

When the cyclists finally turned down a side road, I gunned the engine—but instantly slammed on the brakes when I noticed Sheriff Wilgus's cruiser idling on the berm. I had slowed to the posted twenty-five miles per hour by the time I passed him. He was scowling, a radar gun at the ready. I gave him a little wave and rounded the corner into town.

THREE

The windows of the Day Lily Café glowed like sun-kissed tangerines in the early morning light as I drove past the front of the restaurant. The café was tucked in a row of storefronts on Main Street, not far from the park in the center of town and just around the corner from Birdie's Shoe Store. Two large white window boxes flanked the glass door, filled with an assortment of fragrant herbs. Royal blue awnings piped in white flapped in a gentle breeze. I continued down Main Street and turned into the alley, toward my parking spot behind the café.

"I'm here . . ." I called as I passed Custer's motorcycle and pushed open the door. He had his head out a window, the small butt of a cigarette tight between his fingers.

"Custer, please, how many times have I told you to go all the way outside to smoke?"

"I just needed a couple of puffs." He stubbed out the butt on the windowsill and shoved it in his front pocket. "You're late."

"I know. Don't forget to wash your hands."

"Yes, boss."

I ignored his sarcasm and tied a short turquoise apron behind my back. "Have you started the potato cakes?"

He shook his head as he lathered his hands. "Too soon."

I studied him. Today would be a test of us all, individually and as a team. Although we had done a cold-open a few weeks ago in order to work out any kinks, I'd chosen Memorial Day weekend for our grand opening. Cardigan would be overrun with tourists from DC, Philly, and Maryland's Western Shore on the opposite side of Chesapeake Bay.

> I watched as Custer tossed a paper towel into the trash as if it were a basketball. At twenty-four, he was illegally handsome, with chiseled features not unlike his uncle Tyler. Thick brown hair jutted out of a black-and-white bandana tied around the top of his head. His eyes were mesmerizing, with light-colored irises centered in a pool of deep green.

"You going to be okay?" I said.

"I could use a few eggs."

"Oh my gosh. They're still in the trunk. Here." I tossed him my car keys.

A smile crept up his face as he looked down at the keys cradled in his palm. I drove a sporty red Mercedes convertible, a fortieth-birthday gift from my now ex-husband, and had never felt comfortable in it.

"Don't get any ideas." I put my hands on my hips. "You know, Custer, Tyler won't tell me why you needed this job so desperately. But he did say something about a probation officer."

"Nobody was wronged. Nothing got stolen." He closed his fingers over the keys. "I guess that's all you need to know."

I watched him walk out the door. With his good looks and sassy attitude, Custer could very well be Tyler's son and not his nephew. Maybe Tyler had a few secrets of his own.

I picked up my belongings, pushed through the swivel doors, and stopped as a wave of happiness washed over me. The room glowed, its ocher-tinted walls as warm and inviting as a Tuscan hillside. The tables sported turquoise-and-white floral cloths with small white toppers, and the honey-colored wood floors shone in the light streaming in the front windows.

"Hello, my dear," Glenn said. He approached wearing our standard uniform: black slacks, crisp white shirt, and his own turquoise apron around his waist, with pockets to accommodate order pads, tips, and straws. "Glad you could make it," he said, and winked.

"Today of all days." I smiled. "Thanks for getting things started." I set a bucketful of fresh flowers onto the dark marble counter, which hosted a row of eight high-backed chairs. Two industrial-sized Miele coffee systems sparkled along the wall, ready for action. I lifted a snowy white peony out of the bucket. Water clung to its stem, and the flower had recently burst open into a display of velvety petals.

"I swear, Glenn, between gathering eggs, snipping herbs, and cutting flowers, I'm lucky I got here when I did. Oh, and did I mention the rooster who is in need of a sleeping aid?"

"Mick Jagger?"

"The one and only. Although Tyler often calls him *stud muffin*. Same difference, I guess."

Glenn chuckled as he pulled two more flowers out of the

bucket. "You're here now, and I'm looking forward to the morning." He smiled over at me. "It's going to be the best debut this town has ever seen." Glenn snipped the stems and dropped several more peonies into a glass vase.

Crystal emerged from the ladies room, tucked her cloth bag under the counter, and walked over to us. Her black slacks sat low on her hips. A long, honey brown braid hung down her back, exposing an intricate Celtic tattoo encircling the back of her ear.

"Hi, sweetie," I said. "Are you ready for the big day?"

"I'm cool." She cocked her head. "You all right?"

"Never been better."

At twenty-six, Crystal had translucent skin and dark eyes that she adorned with thick navy liner. She clutched the chunk of golden amber she wore around her neck, smoothing it with her thumb. "I just got a weird feeling. Is everything okay?"

"Oh my goodness, yes." I patted her arm. "I'm sorry I was late. I think I'm still a little frazzled." I glanced at the clock. Ten minutes to opening. "You ready for our big day?"

"Rosalie." Glenn nudged my arm. "Doris Bird is at the door."

I followed his gaze. Doris, proprietor of Birdie's Shoe Store and a dear friend who had helped me out more than once, including bailing me out of jail last year, had her hands cupped around her eyes, peering in at us. An uncharacteristic frown was set hard on her face. "Oh my," I said, and hurried over to let her in.

Four

Glenn fetched Doris a cup of coffee while I escorted her to the counter. She perched on one of the high chairs at the bar and gazed around as if to orient herself.

"Doris," I said, "what's happened?"

She pushed her thick glasses up her nose. "I brought you your paper." She handed me the *Washington Post*. "I figured you wouldn't have time to pick it up today."

"Thank you." I set it aside. "Who's watching the store?"

"My granddaughter, Ellie Sue. She can't work the credit card machine yet, but she can count money pretty good."

Glenn set a steaming cup of coffee in front of her. "Doris," he said, "you seem upset."

She nodded and gazed over at me. "I need your help, Miss Rosalie. My baby sister, Lori, is in a heap of trouble, and you're the first person I thought of. You did such a good job figuring out who killed that college girl last year, I thought maybe you could help us."

Glenn and I exchanged a knowing look. Crystal hummed while she folded napkins, but I knew she was listening. "What kind of trouble?" I said.

She looked down at her lap and tugged her printed dress over her knees. "CJ, her husband of thirty-one years, was killed night before last." She looked up, her forehead lined with worry.

"Oh," I said. "I'm so sorry." Out of the corner of my eye I saw Crystal frantically sliding a finger across her neck, signaling me to cut the conversation short.

"I can't imagine who could do such a thing." Doris frowned. "Problem is the sheriff has decided Lori is the one who killed him."

"And you're certain she didn't?" Glenn said.

Doris looked surprised at Glenn's question. "She says she didn't. I mean, I believe her, of course. Lori is a lamb. She never even raised a hand to swat at a fly."

"It's seven o'clock," Crystal sang. "And we have customers."

Doris pushed herself off the stool. "I won't keep you. I know this is your big day." Her eyes darted around. I had never seen her so nervous. "I'll be sending folks over here. I have a stack of your menus on the counter."

"Doris—" I took her hand in mine. "I have no idea how I can be of help to you, but that doesn't mean I won't try."

"Rosalie . . ." Glenn said, narrowing his eyes in a warning look.

I wasn't sure if Glenn was concerned about me neglecting the café or getting into trouble, or maybe both, but I felt indebted to Doris for all she had done to help me over the past year. "Can we get together after I close?" I said. "Oh, and let me pour your coffee into a paper cup so you can take it back to the store."

"I don't suppose you would go to Lori's house with me? The sheriff let her go late last night, but she's still pretty upset."

"All right," I said, trying to ignore the million things I would need to do once we closed at three.

"Welcome to the Day Lily Café," I heard Crystal say. She led a young couple over to the table in the corner by the windows.

"How did he die?" I said as we walked to the door.

"Shotgun to the chest. Close range." Doris lifted a hand to the tight gray curls framing her head and stepped gingerly outside.

Glenn watched her go. "Well, that would certainly do it."

FIVE

By ten o'clock we had a line forming outside and I was hustling, making coffee, wiping down tables, and seating customers. Glenn and Crystal were busy taking orders, and for a moment I stopped and took in the scene. A mother with a child in a high chair was placing sliced cantaloupe on the tray. The father played peek-a-boo with her, and the child giggled so hard I thought she would topple out of the chair. Two tanned couples—who looked to be boaters based on their preppy clothes and deck shoes—were sipping coffee and smiling, their breakfasts recent history. I took pride in their spotless plates, practically licked clean. I noticed a woman I vaguely recognized at a table bobbing a tea bag up and down. I placed her at around sixty-five or maybe a little older. Muffin crumbs dotted her plate. She had a grin on her face even though she was alone. And then I realized her eyes were following Glenn.

Glenn approached. Sweat dotted his brow and hairline. "Table six has been waiting a while for their orders. How is Custer keeping up?"

"I'll check. Do you need anything else?"

"Two lattes and a double espresso."

"I'm on it." I pushed through the swivel doors as Custer slid a tray of potato cakes into the oven. Several plates sat under the warming lights. "Table six?"

"Yes, boss." He closed the oven door.

I exhaled, realizing I'd been holding my breath, worried Custer wasn't up to the task. "Three specials?"

"Yes, boss." Custer wiped his hands on his already-soiled apron.

"I don't suppose I could bring you some coffee?"

"Yes . . ."

"Got it," I interrupted. I placed one of the plates on my forearm and held the other two in my hands. I admired the china I had special ordered—bone white with a scalloped edge and a delicate orange day lily hand painted at the top. Custer had arranged the food perfectly: a triangle of omelet filled with applewood-smoked cheddar, scallions, and fresh oregano in the center, surrounded by a wedge of cantaloupe topped with blueberries and crème fraîche, a thick slice of buttered whole-grain bread, and a toasted potato cake.

"Beautiful, Custer," I said. "You are very good at what you do."

He hesitated, looking confused, as if he wasn't sure what to do with the praise I had just offered. I decided to give him time to let it sift in and headed out the door. After delivering the specials to table six, I turned around, and there was my Annie.

"Mom!"

"You're here."

"Of course I'm here."

I smoothed her hair. "Aren't you supposed to be at Jenna's picnic?"

"That can wait." Annie perched on a chair at the bar and pulled an iPad from her tote. "Besides, I don't want to stay at Dad's this weekend."

"Why not?" I said, trying to quell the ember of anger in my gut. What had Ed done this time?

Annie avoided my eyes. "Dad is entertaining."

I started Glenn's coffee orders. "What's she like?"

Annie opened her iPad. "Well, she's skinnier than the last one, if you can believe it. She spends most of her time smoking weed on the back deck." Annie typed in her passcode. "That's probably the only thing that doesn't annoy me." She kept her eyes on the screen.

I decided against a follow-up question in response to that last comment. "Do you want something to eat?"

"Not right now. I'm here because you're doing a lousy job with your Facebook fan page. Today is *huge*." She tapped on the screen, bringing it to life. "You should be posting hourly updates, synced with tweets and Instagram pics."

She tucked a strand of her dark shiny hair behind an ear. Annie was my only child and had just finished her second year at

Duke. Last summer she had lived with her father in order to be closer to her friends. I had missed her terribly, and was thrilled when she chose to live with me this summer. When Ed and I first separated, Annie hated the fact that I moved to Cardigan. But as time went by, she began to grow as attached to the people and the pace of life here as I had.

"Okay . . ." She looked up at me, her wide brown eyes bright with enthusiasm. "I'll start by taking some photos." She pulled her phone out of her back pocket and looked around the room. "Do you think I could ask Glenn to stand next to the chalkboard with the specials written on it?"

"You don't waste any time."

"We don't *have* time, Mom." She gave me a peck on the cheek and strode over to Glenn. They embraced, and my heart warmed. Lifting up her iPhone, she clicked a photo of Glenn, scanned the room, and asked Crystal to stand by the coffee station.

She continued taking more photos, including one of me in front of the restaurant, a plated special, and a fabulous close-up of a vase of peonies.

"How's the kitchen?" Annie said. "I wouldn't mind taking some pics back there."

"Custer is working away. My guess is he's very photogenic, so have at it. Oh, and be sure to tell him you're my daughter."

"Since when have I ever had to do that? Everyone says we're twins." Annie backed through the swinging doors.

I cleaned off several tables and seated three more waiting parties. I looked out at the sun-soaked day. The streets were crowded with people on this holiday weekend. Parents with strollers, loved ones pushing wheelchairs, and couples holding hands, all heading to the park where booths and canvas tents were set up selling crafts and local fare.

Crystal approached, tucking a check pad into her pocket.

"That man at table one ordered a double of sausage and bacon. That's it."

"Must be doing the no carb thing. Be sure to tell him the sausage is homemade here in Devon County."

"Already did. You seem better," she said matter-of-factly. "Must be because your kid is here. You're different when she's around. It's like you're complete or something."

"Wow," I said. "That's exactly how it feels." I shook my head in amazement.

"Except there's no love interest," Crystal added. "That could be the last missing piece." She started to walk away but paused. "I hate those missing pieces, don't you?"

Glenn stopped on his way to the water pitcher. "How are the muffins holding up? That woman over there has eaten three and she hasn't ordered any food yet."

I glanced at the table. It was the smiling woman. "She looks familiar."

"I think her name is Gretchen. She owns a bed-and-breakfast just outside of town." Glenn squinted at her. "She's on the smart-growth committee."

"She's eaten three muffins? Maybe Tony was right. He posted on my fan page that I shouldn't give away free stuff."

"Yes, I think he is exactly right." He brushed his hair from his forehead. "Live and learn." He shrugged his shoulders and headed toward the kitchen, passing Annie as he went through the door.

"I'm heading out, Mom," Annie said. "I'm going home to get to work on your page. I'll be back later."

Her face was flushed. I placed my palm on her cheek. "You're warm. It's pretty hot back in the kitchen, isn't it?"

"Um, yes, Mother. It is *very* hot back there." She tucked her iPad under her arm and half-skipped out the door.

SIX

By eleven thirty the breakfast crowd had slowed, allowing us to start the lunch prep. I changed out the menus, filled the coffee machines, and wiped down the counter. Despite my excitement about our opening, worry for Doris and her sister nagged at me. I wanted to help them. And I felt deeply indebted to Doris. I just hoped I could find the time.

I went back to the kitchen to check on Custer. "We're switching to lunch now," I said. "Time to start the pizzas."

He was whistling as he rolled up several basil leaves and sliced them into small slivers. He looked over his shoulder at the counter. Five pizzas were ready to go, topped with halved cherry tomatoes, basil, and fresh burrata cheese.

"Did you brush the crust with garlic and olive oil?"

"Yes, boss."

"Nice. Is everything going okay back here?"

"Never better." He went back to whistling. The tune sounded familiar. "Brown-Eyed Girl"? I had no idea someone so young could be a Van Morrison fan. More basil unfurled on the cutting board, and he sprinkled them on a pizza.

When I returned to the dining room, Crystal was sweeping the tablecloths with a small brush while Glenn carried a stack of dirty dishes. His tortoiseshell glasses were askew, and his ordinarily neatly combed silver hair had fallen onto his forehead.

"Why don't you rest," I said. "I've got table three right here. They're our last breakfast group."

"Rosalie, I'm fine."

"Sit," I said, and gave him a stern look.

He set the dishes in the washtub and eased himself onto a

chair. He rubbed the small of his back. "Apparently you are insisting."

I wiped my hands on a towel and went to work at Mr. Miele II. The espresso squeezed out of the machine with a hot hiss. I topped the cup with lemon zest and slid it over to Glenn.

"How did you know?"

"It's my thing. Sort of like a coffee whisperer."

Glenn chuckled as he stirred a small spoonful of rock-crystal sugar into the cup. "You're going to help Doris, aren't you?"

"I don't have a choice, Glenn. I could never leave that dear woman in such a predicament."

"How are you at juggling?" Glenn set the spoon on a napkin and lifted the small espresso cup with his thumb and index finger.

"Maybe if I had someone to help me." I gave him a sideways glance.

"Hmm." He took a small sip. "If you just asked me a question, I believe the answer is yes."

"Coming through . . ." a loud voice called from the doorway.

I looked up to see Janice Tilghman charging toward us.

"Snow White," I said.

Janice perched on the seat next to Glenn and dropped a large Coach bag onto the counter. We had been playmates as children when I visited Aunt Charlotte during the summer. Janice came from a wealthy Eastern Shore family, as did her husband. She had opened her arms and home to me last year when I had been feeling as lost and alien as E.T.

"Chocolate," she said.

"Brownie or espresso bar?"

"Both." She glanced over at Glenn. "It's an emergency." She eyed his espresso. "I thought you were getting a liquor license, Rose Red."

I placed the pastries on a small glass plate and set it in front of her. "I've already got it. But I need a mixologist and/or a sommelier before I can expand our hours to include evenings. I don't know the first thing about making cocktails, let alone selecting a wine list."

"You could slip a bottle of Jack under the counter," Janice said as she bit into the brownie.

"One of these little concoctions may help," Glenn said, raising his cup.

"What is it?"

"Italian-style espresso," I said. "Would you like one?"

"Yes. Could you slip a Valium in there, too? Oh, and how about a shot of estrogen."

"Maybe you should make her an espresstrogen," Glenn said, trying to suppress a smile.

Janice nudged Glenn's arm. "Good one." She took another bite of the brownie. "Did you make these?"

"Kevin Davenport stopped by when I was getting ready to open a few weeks ago and offered to provide me with pastries. I tried one and about fainted."

"I love that guy." Janice looked over at Glenn. "He and his boyfriend, Jake Willows, are the first gay couple to last in Devon County. At least so far. But they're pretty dug in."

"You don't say?" Glenn said. "And so many people I know here are forward thinking." Glenn sipped his coffee. "I guess it only takes a few."

"Oh, we're moving forward," Janice said. "Unfortunately, it's at the pace of a sloth."

"So, tell me," I said as I started the next espresso, "what's going on with you, girlfriend?"

"Perimenopause." She pushed her hair from her face. A few damp strands clung to her forehead.

"Sounds bad."

She peered over at Glenn. "Is this too much information?"

He shook his head. "Sounds like you need to vent."

She pointed at Glenn with her thumb. "Was that a play on words?"

Crystal strolled over and stood next to Janice. "I suggest a berry tincture."

"A what?" Janice wrinkled her nose. "What's a tincture? Sounds painful."

"It's like an extract, but it's made with alcohol." She leaned in and peered into Janice's eyes. "You'll need to mix it with some black cohosh." Crystal crossed her arms.

"Well—" Janice reared back from Crystal's intense gaze. "I like the alcohol part. Vodka?"

"That will work. Hold out your arm—straight out, and keep it steady." Janice did as she was told. "Now see if you can resist when I push down on it." Crystal pushed, and Janice's arm collapsed into her lap.

"Whoa," I said.

"So what does that indicate?" Glenn said.

"Are you depressed?" Crystal asked Janice.

"Crystal," I said. "That's not really—"

"I cry for no reason. Just this morning I was doing the dishes and watching Fox News, and all of a sudden I started bawling like a baby."

"There's the reason," Glenn said into his cup.

"Maybe you need a dose of NPR," I said.

"St. John's wort, then," Crystal said. "Add a teaspoon of that." She looked around the room. Table three was finishing up. "Do you mind if I take a little break?"

"Of course not, sweetie," I said. "It's been a big morning."

When the espresso was finished brewing, I set the cup in front of Janice. Only crumbs remained on her plate.

"I see where you're looking," Janice said, sounding indignant. "I was a size six before all this started." She straightened. "Don't judge me until you've walked in my wide pants."

"Not judging."

"You'll see when it happens to you." She shook her head. "I'm hungry all the time and hotter than Hades. My butt is getting so big I'm going to change my name to Jan-ass."

"Oh, honey," I said. "Be easy on yourself."

"Maybe Crystal will help," Glenn said. "I might see what she can do for my knees." He stretched out a leg and massaged his kneecap.

Custer shuffled through the door separating the kitchen from the restaurant, shoelaces untied, holding a Day Lily Café coffee mug. "I need a refill."

"Are you working here, Custer?" Janice had a concerned scowl on her face.

"Back in the sweatbox."

"Ceiling fans," she said. "I've installed one in every room. Trevor had the down comforter over him last night because I had the AC set to sixty-four. The fan was spinning so fast his comb-over was flapping against the pillow."

"I don't suppose I can have that last brownie?" Custer said.

Janice hopped up. "I'll fight you for it."

"Whoa." He held up his palms. "It's all yours."

"Are you sick of the muffins, Custer?" I said. "What about a scone?"

"I think I should let Miss Janice have it."

"I only need chocolate."

"Hey," Custer said, "is this belt okay?" We all stared as Custer lifted his chef's jacket. A white canvas belt looped through his jeans, which hung low on his trim hips. The edge of his plaid boxers peeked out just below a rippled set of abdominal muscles. I blushed instantly at the sight of his rock-hard stomach and the vertical line of dark hair disappearing into his pants.

"It's a nice belt," I said quickly, and looked away. "I'm certainly glad you're wearing it."

Janice continued to stare.

"But do guys wear white belts anymore?" Custer let his shirt drop.

"It's fine, Custer." I cleared my throat.

"Okay, good," he said. "Annie and I are hanging out tonight."

"Annie?" I swallowed hard. "*Really*?" I wadded a table napkin in my fist and squeezed.

"Yeah." He sized me up. "*She* asked *me*." Custer turned and walked with purpose back to the kitchen.

"Holy Mother of God, did he really just show us that?" Janice said.

I nodded slowly. "Uh-huh."

"Talk about eye candy."

"Well," Glenn said. "The boy certainly takes care of his body."

"I knew it was a good idea for you to open this place," Janice said. "I feel better already."

I stared at the door Custer had just disappeared through. "Those six-pack abs, which are on probation, I might add, are hanging out with my daughter tonight." I crossed my arms. "Do *you* know why he's on probation?"

"Absolutely." Janice shrugged. "Isn't it obvious?"

"Tell me," I said.

"Outlaw abs."

SEVEN

Birdie's Shoe Store was a Cardigan institution. The shop was housed in a narrow, declining building with peeling letters on the front glass. The carpet was threadbare and the plastic molded chairs had begun to crack, but none of that mattered to the customers. In addition to a few shoes, the store was home to a wide variety of newspapers, magazines, penny candy, and most important, Doris's friendly face. She was as reliable as the atomic clock, and her presence behind that counter was reassuring to more people than just me. Which was why it surprised me when she hopped off her stool and met me on the stoop. The CLOSED sign thudded against the door.

"Where's Ellie Sue?"

"I sent her home." Doris clutched her handbag. "Seems she's not as good with numbers as I thought."

Doris had already started down the sidewalk. I hurried to catch up. "Where does Lori live?"

She stopped abruptly. "Just outside of town, on Route Thirty-five." She looked down at my shoes. "You've been on your feet all day. I don't know what I was thinking. I walk to work. If I need to go anywhere else, my Betsy drives me."

"Come on," I said. "My car is around the corner."

Doris looked as out of place in my cherry red Mercedes as I often felt. She didn't bother with her seat belt, and after thirty chimes (I counted), the warning stopped. She pointed the way instead of telling me the street names. In Cardigan, people were more likely to give you directions by saying "two doors down from Doc Fisher's house" than an address. The problem for a newcomer like me was that Doc Fisher died twenty years ago, and I hadn't a clue where he once lived.

Loose gravel crackled under the tires as we drove down the long lane leading to Lori's house. The road ended at a pale yellow, aluminum-sided split-level.

A variety of barking dogs immediately surrounded me as I tried to climb out of my car. A German shepherd began to lick my shoes enthusiastically. "I can't imagine how I must smell after serving food all day." I shut the door, thinking my car looked even more ludicrous on this humble property.

Doris waited on the porch, hand on the door. "Sit," she commanded the dogs, and they immediately sat in unison, their tails thumping on the floorboards. I followed Doris into the house and was met with the smell of home-baked cookies. Despite the long day I'd spent at the café, my mouth watered.

I stood in the foyer and admired the marble tile beneath my feet. It looked Italian and glistened like polished glass.

Lori appeared and extended her hand. "You must be Rosalie," she said, and smiled. "I'm Lori Fiddler. I'm pleased to make your acquaintance." She was several inches shorter with a slighter stature than Doris, but she had the same wide blue eyes and kind smile. I had always guessed that Doris was in her mid-sixties, but her sister appeared at least ten years younger, probably more. Shoeless, she wore a neat white blouse over a pressed pair of blue jeans. Her feet were dry and cracked, but her toenails were polished salmon pink.

"Come into the kitchen," she said. "I made tea."

Doris followed her sister. "You don't look like you spent most of the night at the sheriff's department."

"I was in the shower for at least an hour when I got home last night."

"I get that," I said, stepping into the kitchen. The small room was scrubbed clean. Despite the metal cabinets and chipped Formica counters, it was warm and inviting. A faded gingham cloth covered the table, and three waiting teacups surrounded a plate of chocolate chip cookies. I looked down at the floor. This one was solid red oak. "Lori, your floors are beautiful."

"That's what Carl James does . . ." She stopped and placed a hand over her heart. She looked at Doris. "I have to say *did*, now, don't I? That's what Carl James *did*." She turned her gaze to me. "Flooring. That was his trade." Lori shook her head and slid into a chair. "He refinished our bedroom floor about a week before he died. It had always been an old pea-green carpet. He and his worker were up there banging around for days." She gave Doris a pained expression. "I still can't believe he's never going to walk through the front door again."

Doris patted her sister's hand and helped herself to a cookie.

"Those cookies smell delicious," I said.

"After my shower," Lori said, "I didn't know what to do with myself, so I decided to bake. For who, I'm not exactly sure."

"I get that, too." I crossed my legs and leaned back in my chair. "Lori, Doris has asked me to help you. But I'm wondering if you should start with a lawyer."

"I have one. She's legal aid. She was with me while the sheriff asked me questions last night. But she sure didn't say much."

Doris rolled her eyes. "That woman only does it because the court makes her. She has about as much interest in helping you as she does in eatin' tar."

"Doris, you know I can't afford a regular lawyer." Lori looked at me again. "Carl James had a good job working on those new dorms at the college, but just a few weeks ago they sent all the managers home."

"Lori," I said, "why does the sheriff think you killed Carl James? Does he have any evidence?"

"Not that I know of." Lori played with a button on her blouse. "The biggest thing is I don't have an alibi. The time of death was late at night. Around midnight. Who has an alibi when they're sleeping?"

"Too bad they can't question the dogs." Doris picked up her third cookie.

"Where had he gone that night?" I took a small sip of tea.

"He was at the tavern," she said. "At least I think that's where he was."

Doris rolled her eyes. "You know that's where he was. He went there every night."

"Only recently, Doris," Lori said.

"So who could have killed him?" I said. "Did he have any enemies? Or was he in some sort of trouble?"

Doris started to answer for her sister, but Lori placed a hand on her arm to quiet her. "Let me tell you how it was with Carl James and me. You see, we got married right out of high school. I mean, after I got out of high school. Carl James never finished. He was always a charmer. Swept me right off my feet. He did like his Kentucky Gentleman, but he always came straight home from the tavern and was never too drunk to drive. He would bring in the dogs, turn out the lights, and kiss me on the cheek before he crawled into bed."

"That's sweet," I said.

"I believe you mentioned the tavern," Doris said. "If Rosalie is going to help us, maybe you should stop sugar-coating everything and tell her something useful."

"I don't know what you want me to say," Lori said. "There was a lot more to him than just a man who liked to go out drinking. Do you know, every morning when I set his coffee in front of him he told me he loved me? And that meeting me was the best day of his life." She smiled at the memory. "And then he would always say he didn't need any sugar in his coffee because I was sweet enough." She clutched the button again. "Please let me grieve, sister of mine. I know you and CJ didn't always see eye to eye, but he was my husband. You and I were both raised to be good to our men."

Doris exhaled a long sigh. Cookie crumbs dotted her dress. "The thing is, Miss Rosalie, I agree with my sister to a point. CJ wasn't a bad man. He was a good provider. And I know he was loyal to Lori here. But see, some folks found him hard to take. I guess that's true for everyone, now, isn't it?"

"Yes, that's for darn sure." I finished my tea and set the cup on the saucer. "Was there anyone in particular who found him disagreeable?"

"Not that I know of." Lori shook her head. "This must have been some sort of accident."

Doris was frowning at Lori. "Honey, he was shot in the chest at close range."

"I'm aware." Lori's eyes drooped. Her hands fell into her lap. "It's just so awful."

"It's tragic," I said. Lori twisted her hands together. A tear trickled down her cheek. I desperately wanted to help her, but so far neither of them was giving me much to work with. "So you said he was at the tavern. I don't know the place."

"It's the Cardigan Tavern," Lori said. "It's on College Avenue. Carl James liked to go there and watch baseball and talk with his friends. Since he got laid off, he went there every night, like Doris said. It was fine by me. It was better than having him sulk around here. You see, Carl James hated being idle. He liked to work. And he was very good at what he did."

"I can see that just looking around your home."

Lori smiled, but her lips trembled into a grimace.

I hesitated, unsure how much more she could take. "Who found him, Lori, and where?"

"A young couple walking their dog yesterday morning.

They found him in a lacrosse field and . . ." She covered her mouth.

"I'm sorry, Lori, but I have just one more question. Had you reported him missing?"

She shook her head. Her hand dropped into her lap. "I never knew. The sheriff's call woke me up. That's when I noticed he had never come to bed."

"Okay, honey," Doris said, and rubbed her sister's arm. "I can see you're spent. Rosalie and I will be going now so you can get some rest. You okay?"

"I'm okay. And Butch is coming by later."

"What's *he* doing in town?" Doris said, a scowl set hard on her face.

"He was Carl James's best friend." She brushed a wet strand of hair off her forehead. "Of course he would come."

"Who is Butch?" I said.

"Butch Wells." Doris shook her head. "Don't you go trusting him, Lori. You're vulnerable right now, and he knows it."

I thanked Lori for the tea and cookies and headed back out to the foyer. Doris stayed behind and whispered with her sister for a moment. I peeked into the small living room and noticed a gun cabinet with three very well-polished shotguns standing upright. I walked over to it. There were four slots. One was empty. I tugged on the knob but the door was locked.

"Ready?" Doris said from behind me. She took in the cabinet. "You think she did it, don't you?"

"No, of course not."

"We are all she has, Miss Rosalie. You and me. CJ was a good enough man, but he had a chip on his shoulder. It's like he always felt the world owed him more than he got. But you and I can't go there. We have to figure out what really happened."

"Agreed," I said. "But I noticed there's a gun missing from this cabinet. You can tell one was here not long ago, because the shape is outlined by dust."

"So you *do* think she did it."

"That's not what I'm suggesting. Maybe someone took it in order to frame Lori." I studied the tall cabinet. "But how would they get inside?"

"That's easy." Doris reached up and found a key on top of the cabinet. She held it out to me.

"But who would know it was there?"

Doris shook her head. "Everyone keeps their key exactly there. Little ones can't reach. Grown-ups don't forget."

"But they would have to find a way inside the house."

"Front door," Doris said matter-of-factly.

"That's right. No one locks their doors on the Eastern Shore." I frowned. "Doris, does Lori have any children?"

"Yeah. Just one. But Jamie couldn't have done it. He works in Delaware. He's a police officer. And a good one at that."

"I wasn't accusing him, either. Just asking questions." I tucked my arm through Doris's and started for the door. "The key to conducting an investigation is not jumping to conclusions. First you have to gather evidence. And then you let the evidence point you in the right direction." We stepped out into the sunlight, and I fished my sunglasses out of my bag. "And the missing shotgun could be significant." I let go of her arm so she could walk around to the other side of the car. "If someone took that shotgun, maybe they had a vendetta against Lori." I slid into the car. "We'll have to find out if the sheriff has the murder weapon."

As Doris and I drove away, the dogs chasing us most of the way down the lane, I said, "Tell me about your family, Doris. Did you have other siblings?"

"No. It was just me and Lori." The seat belt signal was almost finished. "After me, my mama had trouble getting pregnant. It took her a while before she could conceive again, plus a miscarriage in between. And Lori was always small. My daddy used to call her his little runt."

"Do you mind if I ask what kind of childhood you and Lori had?"

Doris thought for a moment. "We had a good mama, but she was always tired. She worked hard cleaning houses, and then she had to come home and take care of us. I think plain old living just pooped her out."

"What about your father?"

"Let me tell you this: The way I see it, when women get hitched at a young age they either marry their fathers or the opposite of their fathers. And Lori married our father. I loved my daddy, but he was a lot like CJ, thinking he got the short end of the stick." She looked over at me. "When you think like that, no one can ever make you happy no matter how hard they try."

"That's some truth." I eased off the gas as we entered the town limits. "What about you? Did you marry your father?"

"Opposite." She nodded stiffly and stared ahead. "I've always had an independent nature. So I got out of that house as fast as I could and started working. I married my Charlie after I opened the store. He helped me out some, but he was just as happy sitting in a chair behind the counter talking with folks. He was a gentle, good man." She smiled. "He could always find something to be happy about, even if it was as simple as sharing a cold beer." She clutched her hands together. "We had a good run at marriage. I sure do miss him now that he's gone."

When I stopped in front of Doris's house, I turned in my seat to face her. "Lori mentioned Butch Wells. Is he related to Tyler? Distant cousin, maybe?"

She gripped her purse with one hand, the other on the door handle. "Butch is Tyler's older brother."

• • •

As I at last headed home, I wondered . . . who had I married? My father or the opposite of him? He was a farmer, which was very unlike Ed, and led a simple life, preferring quiet and certainty over excitement and surprises. He expected his coffee to be strong, his food piping hot, and my mother to deliver a frosty Budweiser to him every evening before supper. The only change he welcomed was that of the seasons because, after all, in rural Virginia, that was certain, too.

But my father never seemed to know what to do with me. Sometimes I wondered if he wished they'd stopped having children after my brother. Oliver would have been enough for him, I think. I was certainly the opposite of my father. I loved surprise parties and fairy tales and skipping. And I had never been comfortable with silence. I spent afternoons in the barn chattering away at the cows, naming each one, making them queens and princesses pining over unrequited love. But my need to fill the airwaves would cause my father's ears to stretch back like an annoyed cat's. Funny, I thought as I turned into my drive, I never thought much about my father.

I parked my car and killed the engine. I was exhausted and in need of a shower, and my brain was beginning to hurt. I climbed out of the car and started toward the house, but stopped when an eerie feeling prickled my scalp. Someone was watching me. I looked around. Dusk had settled, casting a gray pall over the house and its surroundings. I walked over to the chicken coop but didn't notice anything out of the ordinary. Then I looked up. I froze when my eyes met the steely, unwavering gaze of a hawk, its razor-edged talons gripped tight around a sycamore limb.

EIGHT

The next morning I cracked open the door to Annie's room and peered in. One arm was draped over her forehead; the other clutched our cat, who gazed at me with a contented look. He winked a few times and settled his chin on Annie's hip. My adopted cat had originally been named Sweetie Pie, but after just one day on the farm and seven dead goldfinches under his belt, Tyler renamed him Sweeney Todd. Annie and I had reluctantly agreed to the name change, but had shortened his name to Todd. An odd name for a cat, but he seemed content with whatever we called him. Just as long as we called him.

Annie looked younger than her twenty-one years in slumber, a peaceful expression on her face, her cheeks tinted a bright pink. I was curious about her evening with Custer. But she had already completed two independent years in college; I had no business telling her who she could or couldn't date. I squeezed the knob and left the door slightly ajar.

After an early shower, I immediately began my tasks. I was not going to be late to the café again. Once I was properly groomed, I headed downstairs and into the kitchen, picked up a flower basket, and went out to the garden to gather herbs for the day's menu.

I opened the front door and almost tripped over Scheherazade, my favorite chicken. She was huddled on the coir doormat. Her black-and-white feathers were puffed out, making her look twice her normal size. I scooped her up, just as Tyler taught me, holding her close to my body like a football. She pecked at the buttons on my blouse and eventually laid her head against my chest.

"Sherry," I said, "why are you trying to come into the house?"

I carried her toward the coop. "You have a brand-new house of your own."

I found Tyler standing amid the chickens while they pecked at the grass. He held a rifle in one hand.

"Are you going to shoot the hawk?" I said as I neared.

He shook his head. "Not legal."

"Are you going to shoot the chickens then?" I gave him a small smile.

"I'm just letting them free range before I put them back in the coop." He eyed Scheherazade. "Where did you find her?"

"Huddled on the stoop." I set her down, and she lingered at my feet. "I saw the hawk last night when I got home. I think the chickens are scared."

"Affirmative." Tyler scanned the clump of sycamores.

His jeans were snug around his slender frame and he was wearing his new Barclay Meadow T-shirt. "You look nice today."

Tyler didn't respond. When he finally looked at me, he said, "We're down a few eggs. This hawk situation is having some consequences."

"Is there anything we can do?"

"I'm new at this." He gripped the barrel of the rifle with both hands. "I'm realizing something, now that you've got the café. I never thought I'd say this, but I need some help around here."

Our eyes met. "Of course," I said. "Whatever you need."

"Thank you." He stepped closer. He was inches from my face. He smelled clean and fresh, like a sheet dried in the sun. He lifted his hand. "You got a little toothpaste on your chin," he said, and wiped it away with his thumb.

The Day Lily was quiet, reminding me of a still-life oil painting. Shafts of light warmed the wood floors. Everything was neatly stored and stacked, ready for a new day. I looked from table to table, remembering the voices and faces from yesterday.

I unlocked the front door and went out to sweep the steps. I stood on the sidewalk and gazed up at the largest window. Delicate gold letters that read THE DAY LILY CAFÉ arced on the glass. Beneath, in a smaller font, were the words WHOLESOME, LOCAL, ORGANIC FARE.

The window boxes were filled with herbs so their scents would lure customers inside. Unlike the herbs I grew at the farm, I allowed these to flower. Once an herb has flowered, the leaves taste bitter. But in my window boxes, the chives hosted puffs of purples and the thyme had burst into delicate yellow flowers. As I pinched off the tops of the basil, a peppery anise-like aroma met my nose.

The day was warming up quickly, the air thick with moisture. Cicadas hummed in a nearby tree. I began to sweep but stopped when I noticed Doris headed toward me.

"Morning," I called to her.

She held out a sheet of paper. "Lori made a list of people who might have had it in for CJ."

"Oh, good," I said, and looked down at it. The names had been written by an unsteady hand in a felt pen that had smeared in spots. "Do you know any of these people?"

"A few." She crossed her arms. "You'll find most of them at the tavern. They're regulars."

I read through the names. My head shot back up. "Sheriff Wilgus?"

She stared down at the papers. "I don't know why she wrote his name down. Joe may be a pill, but he isn't about to go killing someone, no matter how mad he gets."

"So I wonder why she put his name on the list."

Doris shrugged her shoulders. "He's always hated CJ, but that goes way back. And maybe Lori is mad at him for keeping her at the jail so long." Doris sunk her hands into the pockets of her cotton dress.

"I'll do some Googling as soon as I get a chance. Would you like some coffee? I can put it in a to-go cup again."

"No thanks. I've been away from the store enough lately. And you can't make money if you aren't there to take it. But thank you just the same." She shielded her eyes and gazed up at the window. "I knew this café was what you were meant to do." She looked back at me. "If you don't mind me saying so, I think I knew it before you did."

I laughed. "I don't think, I *know* it. And thank you. I am very happy doing what I love."

"Miss Rosalie, Lori and I are going to try and scrape some money together for you. We talked about it yesterday."

"Oh, Doris, my goodness gracious. I would no sooner take your money than jump off the Bay Bridge." I placed my hand over my stomach. "Just saying that makes me woozy. But listen, I don't even know if I can help you, but I'm going to try. My reward will be knowing your sister is safe." I gave her a warm smile. "I appreciate the opportunity to return the favor. I've felt indebted to you for quite some time."

She hesitated. "All right. At least for now."

Glenn strolled down the sidewalk. "Well, if it isn't the two loveliest ladies I've seen today."

Doris rolled her eyes. "We're probably the only ladies you've seen today, and you know it."

Glenn chuckled. "How is your sister holding up, Doris?"

"Better now that we have Rosalie on the team."

Glenn smiled. "And as I told Rosalie yesterday, if you want me to add my two cents, I'd be happy to help."

I was surprised to see tears welling in Doris's eyes. "This town is a better place now that you two are in it." She turned quickly and started down the sidewalk. She shook her head as she walked. "I swear," she muttered, "it's like the world has turned upside down."

NINE

Crystal was seated at the bar, dipping a tea bag in and out of a cup.

"Good morning, sunshine," I said.

Glenn whistled softly as he began setting water glasses on each table.

"Hey," Crystal said. She was hunched over her cup, elbows on the bar.

I rubbed her back. "Did yesterday wear you out?"

"Let's just say waking up isn't the easiest thing I do each day."

I noticed a face at the door and hurried over to let Kevin, my pastry maker, into the café. He carried a large, white cardboard box in his hands as proudly as if it were a coronation crown.

"Special delivery," he sang as he headed for the bar. "Hey, Crys. Hard night?"

"Do I look that bad? I'm just waiting for the caffeine to kick in. It's a process, and it takes a little time."

"You look gorgeous, as always. And I'm digging this." He pointed at the tattoo behind her ear. "What's it mean?"

"It's a Celtic shield," she said. "For protection."

"Sweet," Kevin said.

Crystal smiled. A compliment from Kevin would brighten anyone's day. He had excellent taste and always stepped out in crisp, pressed clothing. Today he wore a pink oxford, its sleeves rolled up to his elbows; a spotless pair of white pants; and a pastel plaid belt. Designer sunglasses dangled from a leather loop around his neck.

Kevin was in a relationship with Jake, a professor at John Adams College, the school located in the heart of Cardigan. Kevin had several occupations, running an interior design business and making confections being just two. A lot of people in Cardigan did the same. There was only so much money to be made and only so many people to do the work that needed to be done.

"What did you bring me today?" I peered into the box.

"Definitely more espresso bars. They sure went fast."

"Janice is going through perimenopause."

"JJ? The poor dear." He placed his palm on his chest. "I'll bring more if I get some time. And is our lovely sheriff still crushing on the scones?"

"Two a day."

"He's going to get chubby." Kevin opened my pastry case and began stacking the treats. "Oh, say, Crys, how's my aura today?" He straightened his spine and turned to face her. "I've got a meeting with the building committee at the college. I'm putting in a bid to do the interior design of the new dorms."

She narrowed her eyes. "Good. It's a bright royal blue."

"And that means?" Kevin waited expectantly.

"Opportunities are coming."

"Yay!" Kevin clapped. "Blue is my favorite color."

"Morning, Kevin," Glenn said. "I'm going to do my best to stay away from those brownies."

"I don't know how any of you do it, working here. All this delicious food, unlimited coffee, and those muffins. I'd be spinning in circles like I just had an IV of Red Bull."

Glenn shook his head. "It isn't easy."

"Okay," Crystal said as she stood. "There it is. Caffeine jolt. My eyes are open wider already."

"Good," Glenn said. "Let's start the day. Egg bake is our special. Do you have the description handy?"

"Menu insert," I said, picking up a stack of small cards. I read the top one. "Egg bakes. Roasted veggies, black olives, fresh mozzarella, and tomato sauce in a ramekin, with a baked egg on top. It's served with a slice of honeydew topped with basil-infused cream and a small arugula salad with shaved parmesan and a lemon olive oil dressing." I looked up. "Crystal, could you write the special on the chalkboard? You have such beautiful handwriting."

"All of that?" she said with a bewildered look on her face.

"Just write *roasted vegetable egg bake* and add the sides."

"I'm drooling," Kevin said as he folded up the empty box.

"We should all get together sometime, Kevin." I poured him a to-go cup of coffee and slipped it into a cardboard sleeve.

"I like the sound of that," Glenn said. "Not to invite myself, of course."

"Yes, we should definitely do that." Kevin picked up his cup.

"Good luck with your meeting," I said.

"Okay, toodle-loo, everyone." Kevin waved as he walked toward the door.

"Say," Glenn said, "is Custer here?"

I looked over at him. "I certainly hope so. He had a late night."

"How do you know that?"

"He was hanging out with Annie."

Glenn eyed me over the top of his glasses. "That worries you, doesn't it?"

"I'm not sure. Do you think it should?"

"He's doing a fabulous job so far. You've given him a chance working here. I admire you for that."

I crossed my arms. "But, Glenn, it's my Annie."

"All right, mother hen." Glenn smiled. "You go on and worry. I won't try to stop you."

"We have a customer," Crystal called from the chalkboard. Glenn turned toward the door and stopped abruptly. Gretchen, dressed in a breezy floral dress, waited patiently on the stoop.

I nudged Glenn. "It's the woman from yesterday. Gretchen, right?"

"It is." He crossed his arms. "We agreed. No free muffins today."

"That's correct. Nothing is free except coffee refills. Glenn, she seems very pleasant. Do you think she came back to see you?"

"I'm not on the menu," Glenn said as he continued toward the door.

I found Custer slicing the honeydew. A tray of egg bakes sat prepared and ready for the oven.

"Ciao," he said without looking up.

"Everything all right?"

"Always."

"Did you have fun last night?"

He looked up and narrowed those gemstone eyes. "You know, boss, I think it's better if I keep my private life exactly that."

"Exactly what?"

"Private."

"Oh." I felt flustered. Was he right? But he was with my Annie. He continued to gaze at me. "Okay," I said. "I will try to respect that. But it's an awfully small town. And families don't come any tinier than mine."

"And I will respect that."

I picked up the bowl of thickened cream and began scooping

small dollops onto the honeydew. "Do you come from a big family, Custer?"

"Plenty big."

"And Tyler is your uncle on your father's side?"

"Yes. Why are you so interested?"

"Just curious. Doris said something about fathers yesterday and I've been thinking about mine. I used to drive him crazy. He thought I talked too much." I set the honeydew slices on a tray. "Hard to believe, right? Anyway, after supper he would go out on the front porch and smoke a pipe. He would sit still, just listening to the crickets chirp. The only movement was the whir of the ceiling fan to keep the mosquitos away." I stared off, remembering the scent of pipe smoke, the glow when he puffed on the stem. "I would sit with him on the swing every chance I got. I would tell him made-up stories about animals and ogres, and when I ran out of things to say I'd push the swing with my sneaker. Now I think about those memories and wonder if all I was doing was disrupting his solitude."

Custer stopped slicing and looked up at me, his eyebrows dipped together. "So we're talking here, is that it?"

I hesitated, trying to understand his meaning. "Yes. At least, I hope so."

"First of all, I don't want to think about my father." He pointed the knife at me as he spoke. "He's not worth the time. But I will tell you a little of what I think about family. You see, kids are a barometer for what's really going on. When they feel something isn't right, they act out. Some kids get into trouble, like starting a fight with a sibling. Others, well, maybe they start chattering like you did, you know, as a distraction from the real trouble."

"Trouble?" I cocked my head. "I never thought of it that way."

"And some kids . . ." His eyes darkened. "They might pick fights with one parent so he leaves the other parent alone."

"Okay." I nodded. "I understand." I brushed my hair back from my face. "Custer? Is your father's name Butch?"

"It is." Custer's knuckles whitened around the knife handle. "And that's all you need to know about him."

Ten

Not long after the doors opened, the café was bustling. Glenn and Crystal had learned a lot yesterday and now moved about the room like Fred and Ginger. Custer had established a routine of his own, and the food was coming out of the kitchen in a timely fashion. I was busy making espressos when Glenn sidled up to me. "You have a customer." I peeked around him and there was Sheriff Wilgus seated at the bar.

"Sheriff," I said.

"Hart." The sheriff's uniform was open at the collar. He placed his felt hat gingerly on the counter. "Get to work on time yesterday?" He watched as I poured coffee into a to-go cup. "I could have given you a ticket."

"But you didn't."

"I will next time."

Since the day I'd discovered Megan Johnston's body on the banks of my property over a year ago, Joe Wilgus and I shared a prickly relationship. My investigation had more than irked him; in fact, it exposed a nest of corruption and led him into AA. He was still sober but now struggled with an insatiable craving for sweets. I was not surprised to see him in the café. He had come in every day we'd been open and ordered two iced maple scones and a black coffee to go.

The sheriff was a handsome man in a rugged sort of way. He was in his early fifties and had a thick head of dark hair that he sculpted into a pompadour of sorts. It wasn't hard for me to rankle him, and I knew I got under his skin. I would venture a guess it still nagged at him that I had uncovered a murder he'd tried very hard to ignore.

"The usual?"

He didn't bother to respond. As I picked up the pastries with a piece of tissue paper, Custer approached with an empty mug in his hand. He stopped and took in the sheriff. Joe Wilgus lifted his head slowly and locked eyes with him. I glanced over at Custer. He looked away and fidgeted with his cup. I filled it quickly, and he disappeared through the swinging door.

The sheriff shifted his weight. "That delinquent ever tell you he got fired from his last job?"

"You mean Custer?"

"Who else was just standing here?" He fixed the plastic lid onto his cup. "Well? Did he tell you?"

I hesitated, tempted to lie, but I was terrible at it. "No," I said. "He didn't tell me."

The sheriff stared at the door. "I'll be back." He stood and headed for the kitchen.

"You can't—" I rushed to the door but jumped back when it swung toward me. I heard muffled voices and tried to make out what they were saying. The sheriff was speaking angrily to Custer.

"That looks dangerous," Glenn said. "What if someone comes out of the kitchen?"

I put my index finger to my lips.

Glenn frowned and said in a loud whisper, "I need a latte."

I froze when I heard the sheriff's voice again. "You know anything about him getting shot?"

"He's talking about CJ," I whispered back. "He's asking Custer what he knows." I jumped back when the door burst open. The sheriff strode over to the bar and picked up his bag and cup.

"So, Sheriff Wilgus, you're actually conducting an investigation this time?" I crossed my arms.

He pointed a finger at me. "You mind your own business, Hart."

"I was just wondering why you would question Custer if you're so certain it was Lori who killed CJ?"

"How do you . . . ?" He shook his head in disgust. "I asked him because I don't trust him. And neither should you." He placed his hat on his head. "I *am* conducting an investigation. And I am going to prove Lori Fiddler killed her husband in cold blood. That make you happy, Hart?"

"No," I said. "It's all a horrible tragedy, if you ask me."

"Nobody *is* asking you. And if I hear you've been nosing around again, you will learn the true meaning of misery."

I watched him go. Muscle memory sent a vibration of fear through me. So, I thought, it's me versus the lawman again.

ELEVEN

Dream big, my mother used to say. I know it's not the most original of encouragements, but I took it to heart. She had died very quickly after a breast cancer diagnosis five years previously. I missed her every day. But I knew she was with me. On warm summer evenings I could feel her sweet breath on the back of my neck; I could hear her whisper in the trees, telling me to be strong and know I was loved. I could smell her perfume when I wandered through my rose garden and feel her touch when my hands were deep in a mound of bread dough. I learned my love of cooking—or nourishing, as she called it—from her. She was the heart of my family, and our farm was where everyone gathered for the holidays or, sometimes, for no reason at all.

And now I hoped to create a gathering place of my own. When I designed the layout of the café, I made certain there would be room for at least eight bar chairs under the marble counter. Once I figured out how to stock my liquor, beer, and wine, I hoped people would stop in to catch a Ravens or an Orioles game on the flat-screen TV behind the bar. But until then, it was where we sat the overflow.

A ruddy-faced man was my first customer to be seated at the bar that day.

"Hello, missy," he said with an Eastern Shore twang.

"Hello," I said. "Welcome to the Day Lily Café."

He leaned back and crossed his hands over his sizable stomach. "Everybody's been telling me how good the grub is here, so I thought I'd come in and see for myself."

"You just made my day." I set a place mat and menu in front of him.

Glenn approached with a wide grin. He extended his hand to the man and said, "Jackson. What a pleasure to see you here."

"Commissioner," he said, and shook Glenn's hand. "How many jobs do you have, anyway?"

"I wear too many hats. But don't we all?" Glenn said. "Have you met Rosalie?"

"Not officially."

"It's nice to meet you," I said.

"Likewise. Jackson Crawford's the name."

"Thanks for stopping in." I smiled.

"I've been looking forward to coming here ever since you put up the sign. I didn't think I'd have the time, but it appears now I have loads of it."

"Coffee?" I said.

Jackson nodded. "Black, please." He picked up the mug as soon as I set it down in front of him. I watched as he took a large gulp. "Say, that's a good brew. Nice and strong."

"Rosalie is an excellent barista," Glenn said. "Jackson, if you don't mind me asking, why aren't you at work over at the college? Aren't you managing the construction of the new dorm?"

For the first time since he entered the café, Jackson's smile faded. "They laid off all the contractors. Brought in some folks from away."

"But why?" I said. "Did something happen?"

"Oh yeah. Somebody stole a bunch of money from the construction site. Only the foremen and contractors were allowed in the trailer where they kept the cash, and only if the CFO was in there. So until someone fesses up, we are all forbidden from the site."

I thought about what Lori had said, how CJ had been tense since he was laid off. He must have been a contractor, too. I wondered if there was some sort of connection. Money had been stolen, and a man had been shot. Glenn studied me. No one knew me better than he did, and I would guess he was making the connection as well. "I should get back to work," he said, and gave me a surreptitious wink.

"Would you like to order breakfast, Jackson?"

"Yes, ma'am. You know, I may not look like it"—he paused and looked down at his round belly—"or maybe I do. But I consider myself to be sort of a foodie." He smacked a hand on the menu. "I'm not even going to open this. You just bring me the best you got."

"How about the special?"

"I'm in your hands. And I can't think of a better place I'd rather be."

I typed Jackson's order into the computer and delivered food to several tables. Gretchen was still seated, with an empty plate before her. At least she ordered, I thought. She was reading the *Post* and sipping tea. I was curious to get to know her. And I admired any woman who was drawn to Glenn's quality. "Would you like some dessert?" I said.

She looked up at me with warm, honey brown eyes. "That sounds tempting."

I was caught off guard by her British accent. Now I was even more curious.

She laced her fingers together and rested her hands on the table. "But I don't want to overstay my welcome."

"Then why don't you come and sit at the bar? I'll have Glenn bring your check to you there."

"Oh, that would be lovely." Gretchen tucked her paper under her arm, picked up her handbag and teacup, and stood. "I'll just have a little nosh." She wrinkled up her nose and smiled. I watched as she walked to the bar and perched on the stool next to Jackson.

"What is she doing?" Glenn stood next to me.

"Having a nosh," I said, and grinned.

"She's eating something *else*?" Glenn shook his head. "How does she stay so slender? The woman eats volumes."

"I like her eyes. They're very kind."

When I returned to the bar, Gretchen and Jackson were deep in discussion about Devon County's smart-growth plan. "I went to the meeting last night," Gretchen said. "The farm behind my inn is for sale. There's a development company that wants to put in a senior housing development."

"As much as I'd like to get in on the construction side of it," Jackson said after draining his coffee, "they can go build it somewhere else. We need to preserve this county as best we can."

"I was hoping to talk to Mr. Breckinridge about it." Gretchen's feet dangled from the high stool. Her posture was perfect.

Crystal appeared by my side. She studied Jackson. "You know, there's a lotion at the natural food store that is good for rosacea."

"Crystal!" I said.

"Oh, blimey." Gretchen covered her mouth and tittered.

"Is that right?" Jackson said. "Well, there's no denying it. I drink some coffee or a glass of bourbon, and my face gets red as a beet."

"The lotion is made from emu oil." She scratched her nose. Her rounded nails sported black polish. "You also might have a food allergy, probably to dairy."

"Hang on," Jackson said. "Did you say *emu* oil?" He shook his head. "And there's no way I'm giving up dairy. Everything tastes better with a slab of cheese, and that's a fact."

"Agreed," Gretchen said. "Or a dollop of sour cream."

Crystal tucked a loose strand of hair behind her ear. "It might also be yeast."

"Okay, well, thanks for your help, Crystal," I said, feeling my own face start to redden in embarrassment. "Do you need something, sweetie?"

"Nope. I'm good." Crystal spun around and headed into the kitchen.

Once she was out of earshot I said, "I'm so sorry, Jackson. Crystal is a lovely young woman, but I'm finding she has a few boundary issues."

"No offense taken."

"Perhaps she could use a three-second delay," Gretchen said, and nibbled on a brownie.

"Let me at least go get your breakfast," I said, and followed Crystal into the kitchen. Several specials were waiting under the heat lamps. Pride puffed out my chest. The egg bake was in a medium-sized oval ramekin, the melon at an angle with the basil cream dripping down the sides, and the small mound of salad made it a perfect triangle. Custer had rimmed the outer edges with more basil cream slashed with filigrees.

"Everything looks perfect, Custer. Are you sure you weren't a chef in your previous job?"

"I'm sure," he said as he loaded a dish tray.

Crystal picked up her order and backed through the door.

"So what was your last job?"

He stopped loading and looked at me, a frown turning down his lips. "Why do you want to know that?"

"Just curious. It's good to get to know you better, is all. I mean, we are all working in close quarters. And I hope we will be for a long time."

Custer hesitated. "I was in construction. Helping over at the college."

"I see. So what sort of work? Drywall? Cement?"

"Floors." He turned away and picked up an egg. "Problem is, my old boss is dead now."

TWELVE

By four p.m., our chores were finished and it was time to go home. Glenn untied his apron as he approached. "So what do you think about the stolen money?"

"You mean do I think there's a connection with CJ's murder?"

"That's exactly what I'm asking." He wadded his apron and stuffed it in a nylon bag I was going to drop off at the laundry.

"I thought I might wander over to the campus and see what's up," I said. "Do you think they'll still be working on a Friday afternoon?"

"Someone will be there. I think they are in a bit of a rush. They've promised those rooms to incoming students this fall. It must be pure chaos with all the contractors being laid off." Glenn rubbed his chin. "It seems so harsh to blame everyone. I remember my mother doing that. Make us all stand in line until one of us confessed to the infraction."

"As I recall, President Carmichael is still at the helm."

"Yes, that he is. You know, I haven't seen anything about it in the paper. Seems like that would be headline news."

I put my own apron in the bag and cinched the string. "I haven't had a chance to read the paper in weeks." I propped the bag against the bar.

"Never underestimate the power of the written word." Glenn smiled. "So, my dear, do you have a theory?"

I rested my elbows on the bar. "Nothing to clear Lori, but I think there could be a connection with CJ's murder. If CJ had something to do with the stolen money, and if it's as much cash as Jackson suggested, it might have motivated someone to go after it and him." I checked the clock. "I better head over there. I want to get home before Annie goes out."

"Custer again?"

I nodded. "It's good for a daughter to look into her mother's eyes before she goes out with a boy, don't you think? Especially one as mysterious as our Custer."

"You have always been able to convey a great deal with those brown eyes." Glenn thought for a moment. "But you're also very good at concealing what you're thinking. That's a true talent. No wonder Doris asked you to help her."

"What about you, Glenn? Plans for tonight?"

"Oh yes. Big plans. First I'm going to take a long shower, then watch the news. Then read all of my papers and probably fall asleep while doing it. Then . . ."

"Glenn, maybe you should think about going out. Maybe a movie with someone from Waterside Village. If everyone is over fifty-five, there must be plenty of widows."

"Yes." His brow furrowed. "They bring me casseroles."

I smiled. "Well?"

"I like my life, Rosalie. And now we have another investigation. Let's focus our attention back on that, shall we?"

After parking my car in a visitor's spot on campus, I made my way to the construction site. I was still in my white blouse and black skirt, but I slipped into a pair of low-heeled sandals. I had no idea who I might meet, but as my mother said when I went on my first job interview, don't give them a reason to not like you.

I glossed my lips and fluffed my hair as I walked. A large steel skeleton of a building appeared once I passed the stately red-brick student center. Several pickups were parked haphazardly near the site. Large Dumpsters surrounded the structure like shrubbery. I made my way around to the side and finally spied a double-wide trailer.

My heels sank in the loose gravel. I slowed my gait. The afternoon sun baked down on everything in its path, and I swore even the trees overhead were panting. I walked up to the door and read a large sign. Bold letters read: KEEP OUT. EMPLOYEES OF CHESAPEAKE DEVELOPMENT COMPANY ONLY. A heavy bolt and padlock secured the door.

"You need a hard hat, ma'am," a voice said from behind me. I turned around and faced a young, very muscular man in a white T-shirt with suspenders holding up his khaki pants. His boots were massive. He knocked on his yellow helmet. "You need one of these."

"I'm sorry. I was just looking for someone," I said. "His name is Jackson Crawford." I pulled a parcel wrapped in aluminum foil out of my bag. "He owns Crawford and Sons construction. He loves the muffins I serve at the café. I promised I would drop some by. Have you seen him?"

"Not for a while," the man said. "He was laid off with all the other local owners. Sorry, I don't mean to be rude, but I really don't want one of those beams slipping loose from that crane up there and bashing in your skull. So I'm going to have to ask you to be on your way."

I took a few steps back. "But why was Jackson laid off? I don't understand. It looks as if you still have a lot of work to do."

He put his hands on his hips and shook his head. "Ya think?"

"The students will be here before you know it. Right? Why lay people off?" I shielded my eyes and looked up at him. He was very tall.

"We're busting our asses. I've been working twelve-hour days. Barely have time to eat."

"That's a lot. Say, I don't suppose you'd like a blueberry muffin?"

He considered my offer. "Actually, I was about to head over to Birdie's for a couple of candy bars. So, yeah, I'll take one if they're as good as you say they are."

"Let's go over to that bench away from the cranes. I'm a little concerned about my head."

He followed and sat down after me. The bench shuddered from his weight. I unwrapped the foil and pulled a napkin from my bag. I placed three muffins on it and held them out to him. He was such a large man, eating just one would be as satisfying as a Chiclet.

He took a bite and chewed. "I see why Jackson likes you stopping by." He peeled off the rest of the paper wrapper and finished the first muffin.

"Thanks. I'm also trying to drum up interest in the café." I crossed my ankles. "I'm Rosalie, by the way."

He brushed his hand on his pants. "Name's Calvin." He grimaced. "Please call me Cal. My old man is Calvin, and I'd like to keep it that way."

I hugged my tote. "So, Cal, why did everyone get laid off? Did something happen?"

"Oh yeah. You could say that. Like a big lump of cash got stolen out of the trailer. Only people allowed in there are the foremen so they can get their payroll. And the only time they can go in is if the CFO is in there. Rest of the time it's padlocked."

"So why pay them in cash?"

He peeled the paper from another muffin. "The cash is for the day laborers. We bring in all kinds of extra guys and pay them on a daily basis. They're not on any payroll. When we start the drywall, landscaping, ductwork, all that kind of big stuff, we bring in temporary workers."

"Why not cut them a check?"

"You ask a lot of questions." His eyebrows dipped. "Let me just say this. Most of them don't have bank accounts. You can use your imagination to figure out why."

"I see. But how can you be so sure it was a foreman? Was the lock broken?"

He shook his head as he chewed. "Whoever it was must have memorized the combination. We changed it every week, but this guy got in there anyway. Boss has an alarm on there now."

"Good idea." I thought for a moment. "Couldn't it have been someone from within your company?"

He laughed and wrapped the napkin around the last of the muffin cups. "Only one guy allowed to do payroll. He protects that money like it's his firstborn. And he is none too happy that a whole lot of it is gone."

I looked up at him. "How much is a lot, Cal?"

"We think the guy got away with over five hundred K." He smiled at me. "Sound like a lot to you?"

Thirteen

I drove down the lane to my home with the convertible top down, a warm breeze ruffling my hair. I was exhausted but exhilarated as I reflected on another successful day. The lunch crowd had been even bigger than breakfast, and the special—falafel sandwiches, herbed red potatoes, and a Greek salad—had been a big hit.

Dappled sunlight streaked through the canopy of tall cedar limbs over the drive, and I took in the scent of freshly mown grass. I slowed my breathing and reminded myself to savor this moment—my café had opened, and people showed up. A lot of people. And they liked it. Not to mention I just managed to glean some valuable information from a strapping young construction worker. I couldn't wait to tell Glenn. I forgot how compelling it was to work toward righting a wrong.

Later, refreshed from a shower, I was looking forward to putting my feet up and having one glass of wine to celebrate a successful day. I slipped into a tank and a pair of shorts and toddled downstairs, my wet hair already spiraling into ringlets. As I passed by the front door I noticed Tyler perched on the stoop. Oh, good, I thought. I could use a Tyler fix.

"Hey," I said as I opened the door. I was startled to see a woman seated next to him.

Tyler looked over his shoulder. "There you are. This is Bini."

I stepped onto the stoop. "Bini?"

She stood and turned to face me. Small in stature, she looked to be in her early forties. She wore a white ribbed tank and snug-fitting denim shorts. Her biceps were defined, her hair in a short, easy-to-maintain cut. She was cute in a petite, rugged sort of way, with small hazel eyes that were fixed on mine. She switched a sweating bottle of National Bohemian beer to her left hand and held out her right. "Bini Katz."

I extended mine, and she gave it a very firm shake. "Hi, Bini. It's nice to meet you."

"Bini started working here today." Tyler looked over his shoulder. "Beer?"

"Oh," I said, relieved he wasn't on a date. "You're going to help out around here?" I closed the door behind me and sat next to Tyler on the steps. "That's so great. And, yes, please. A beer sounds perfect."

He popped off the cap and handed it to me. My first sip made a glugging sound as it funneled through the long neck of the brown bottle. I wiped my mouth with the back of my hand. "So what did you two do today?"

"I mainly showed her the ropes," Tyler said. "But Bini has already proved her worth."

"And you, Bini?" I leaned forward and looked past Tyler so I could see her face. "Did you have a nice first day?"

"Yep," she said, staring ahead.

I looked around and realized the Volvo was gone. "Annie must be out."

"She's meeting Custer in town," Bini said. "There's some live music in the square tonight."

"Oh. Okay. Thanks for letting me know, Bini." I sat back and took a longer sip, trying not to feel weird that Bini Katz knew where my daughter was before I did.

Tyler opened the cooler, popped off another cap, and handed it to Bini. She accepted it without a word. She didn't even have to ask. No wonder Tyler hired Bini. Unlike me, she seemed perfectly content with his minimalist approach to conversation. I tried to gather my thoughts. Was I feeling jealous? That's what it was. But why? Bini had already helped Tyler. They'd probably known each other for years.

Be a grown-up, Rosalie. "I'm really glad you're working here, Bini. Tyler needs some help with the farm, now that we have the chickens and the café is occupying so much of my time."

"Say, Ty," Bini said, "There's been a Butch sighting."

"Yeah, I heard." Tyler drained his beer and reached for another.

"I heard that, too," I said. I set my beer down and hugged my knees. "Custer's father, right? Are you close with your brother?"

"I wouldn't say that." Tyler dangled his beer between his knees. He took a swig and continued to stare ahead. Bini mirrored his every movement. She took another sip of beer as well and held it the same way. No one spoke for several minutes. We all seemed to be staring down the lane at nothing.

"So, are we waiting for someone?" I said. "Godot, perhaps?" I laughed a little at my own wit, but they remained silent.

Despite the lack of conversation, I realized there was a cacophony coming from the side of the house. "What is that racket?" I stood and headed around the corner of the house toward the chicken coop.

I stopped in my tracks. Hundreds of crows filled the towering sycamore trees. They squawked and chattered, crowding onto several platform bird feeders that had suddenly appeared in my yard like mushrooms after a rain. I shivered at the number of flapping wings and sharp beaks, feeling as if I were in an Alfred Hitchcock movie.

I hurried back around the house. "Tyler, have you seen this?"

"They've been here most of the day," he said, finally making eye contact.

I smiled instinctively when our eyes met. He had the loveliest vivid green eyes I'd ever seen.

"The birdseed worked," Bini said.

Tyler stood and walked over to me. "They've gone through four sacks already." Bini appeared behind us a few seconds later.

"Birdseed?"

"Crows will keep the hawk away," Bini said.

"But they're huge. Are you sure they're not ravens?"

"They are common crows," Bini said. "Technically a raven is in the crow family. But if you'd ever seen one, you'd know these aren't ravens."

I turned to look at her. "I have seen a raven. It's the mascot at Ravens football games. It wears a little black jacket with a purple *B* on it. And I'm telling you, those birds are just as big." I turned back toward the crows. "Are they at least keeping the hawk away?"

"No sign of it," Tyler said.

"It won't come around," Bini said. "Not with the crows."

"But what about the garden?" I said. "Won't they eat the herbs and vegetables? Isn't that why farmers have scarecrows? To keep the crows *away* from the fields?"

"I didn't expect this many," Tyler said.

"Crows eat insects," Bini said. "They can help the fields."

"Except we're feeding them crack instead," Tyler said under his breath.

"Will they eat the chickens?" I said.

Bini shook her head. "Won't happen. Besides, the crows are here for the seed."

"Exactly," Tyler said. He pulled his cap lower on his forehead.

"But they're carnivorous, right? I've seen them eating roadkill."

"They're omnivores," Bini said. "So, sure, you'd see that. And they're very smart. They can count to five." She glanced over at the coop. "They might steal an egg or two."

I looked up into the trees. I didn't like the thought that they were smart. And unlike the sweet trill of songbirds, the crows' call was atonal, a squawk that hurt my ears. "Where are the chickens? Why aren't they free ranging?"

"They're still spooked from the hawk." Tyler looked over at me. "What's your breakfast special tomorrow?"

"A frittata. Why?"

He looked back at the crows. "The chickens still aren't laying a whole lot of eggs."

"What chicken could lay an egg when these crows are out here getting ready to attack?"

"There was an eagle eyeing the hawk when he grabbed the chicken," Tyler said. "I'm a little worried it will be back, with or without crows."

"So the eagle would eat the crows?" A shiver trembled down my spine. "I feel like I'm in *Jurassic Park*."

"Won't happen," Bini said. "Not enough room for an eagle to land. A hawk can drop from the sky, but an eagle has to glide in like an airplane." She held out her hand, palm side down, and had it come in for a landing.

"The eagle was most likely here to steal the chicken from the hawk," Tyler said. "Eagles are scavengers. They take prey from other birds all the time, hawks, osprey, even blue herons, just 'cause they're bigger and stronger."

"Well, isn't it appropriate the eagle is our country's symbol," I said.

"Love it or leave it," Bini said.

My mouth fell open. "Back to the eggs. A frittata requires a lot of them. Plus I'll need more for the à la carte menu. I'm serving a feta and chive omelet."

"Sounds pretty good," Tyler said.

"You'll have eggs." Bini sounded as if she would lay them herself.

Just then the flock took flight and headed right for us. One flew so low I could feel it in my hair. "Oh!" I cried, and lost my balance. Tyler grabbed my arm, and my beer bottle flew out of my hand. Bini caught it midair. It spewed foam. She handed it to me, shook the overflow from her hand, and walked away. I felt the top of my head, wondering if I'd been scratched. "Tyler?"

"Well, at least there's no hawk." He frowned, his tanned forehead deeply furrowed. "Bini got us this far. Maybe the chickens will be out tomorrow. It's like you said, they're smart. They should know the difference between friend and foe."

Fourteen

Once Tyler and Bini left for the day, I made a cup of tea and sat at my desk. I acknowledged the warning in my gut about Tyler's new workmate. We'll be okay, I thought. I'll have to pay more attention. Maybe Bini's expertise will help Tyler.

No life was without chaos or disappointments, but if you had something to ground you, it was all bearable. Creating a sustainable, organic farm grounded Tyler. The Day Lily did the same for me.

And yet Tyler was a big part of my new life. We were companions; we shared the farm, coffee, pets. And now he had someone new to accompany him. "Oof," I said aloud, placing my hands over my stomach. I felt completely and utterly clueless about what to do. Maybe I had been taking him for granted. I'd been so focused on the café, and now I had another investigation.

All I knew was I couldn't let what we'd created slip away, no matter what, and maybe who, filled our time.

I finished my tea and decided to look over Lori's list. I scanned the page, but Sheriff Wilgus's name stared back at me as if he were waving his arms around for me to pick him. But why had Lori added him to the list? Doris said the sheriff and CJ had always hated each other, so their animosity must have originated a long time ago. But what was the cause, exactly?

I logged on to Facebook and typed Lori's name in the search box. There must not have been a lot of Lori Fiddlers on social media, because her face popped right up. I sent her a friend request and visited her timeline to see if any of her public information would be helpful.

I studied her list of friends, scrolling through a myriad of photos of people accompanied by family pets or in silly poses with a best friend. Nothing suspicious. Her own photos were fairly generic, too. Lots of pictures of her son, Jamie, in his uniform, graduating from the police academy, Lori's arm around his shoulder. There was a photo of her new bedroom floor. It really was beautiful. There must be something helpful here, I thought. I propped my chin on my hand. Her profile said she'd gone to Devon County schools. I assumed Joe Wilgus had, too. His family lived in Cardigan for generations. Lori and the sheriff could easily be the same age. Had their feud started in high school?

I sat straighter in my chair, my humming nerves telling me I stumbled onto something. I noticed my friend icon had a notification. *Lori Fiddler has accepted your friend request.* That was fast. I checked the clock. It was only seven. I messaged her.

Any chance I could stop in and see you this evening? I won't stay long.

OK.

On my way. Btw, do you still have your high school yearbooks?

As I drove over to Lori's, I thought about what I was undertaking. Again. I wondered if I was making a mistake, agreeing to help Doris. Would it distract me from the farm and café? And what about Annie and her new relationship? I hadn't seen her tonight. No eye contact.

I was certainly a curious person. And I did love a good puzzle. But it was more than that. In Lori's case, as in Megan's, I felt an obligation to people who had been victimized to root out the truth. I'd questioned my motivations then, too. But one year after Megan's killer was found guilty and sent to prison for life, Corinne Johnston, Megan's mother, wrote me a note thanking me for discovering what happened to her daughter. Having the killer behind bars had helped her grieve in peace. And although she would never be the same—what mother could?—she believed my solving the crime had enabled her to continue living.

When I arrived at Lori's, I switched off the engine and attempted to get out of my car. A black Lab's massive paws were on my door and he was trying with some success to duck his boxy head through the open window. "Sit," I said in a less-than-convincing voice. He leaned in and slurped my ear. After checking to ensure he hadn't swallowed my pearl earring, I forced open the door. Five wagging tails thrashed my legs, and I almost tripped over a yipping Yorkshire terrier.

I noticed a shiny red Camaro parked next to Lori's van as I walked, doing my best to avoid stepping on tails and paws. I looked up to see Lori at the screen door. "Sorry about the welcoming committee," she said. "I think they are a little attention starved now that Carl James is gone." She opened the door a crack. "Sit," she said, and all five dogs simultaneously perched on their hindquarters.

"They're just enthusiastic," I said. "I may need a navigation system to get to your door, but I actually love dogs. Please don't worry about them."

She opened the door wider, and I stepped inside.

"Let's go out to the screened porch," she said. "I hate being in this house ever since Carl James died."

The porch looked out onto a densely wooded lot, the setting sun barely peeking through the trees. Plants on stands and in a variety of pots lined the floor. A hodgepodge of dog beds, some held together with strips of duct tape, were piled in the corner. The musty scent of wet fur lingered in the humid air.

We sat on an old wood-framed sofa. A small lamp lit the room, its yellow bulb giving everything a jaundiced tint. She was dressed in a housecoat. Her hair was piled on top of her head and some sort of heavy cream glazed her face.

"Lori, do you have a job to go back to?" I turned to face her.

She shrugged. "I clean houses." She smoothed the cotton smock over her knees. "I think my clients understand I need time to grieve."

The dogs discovered us and began lunging at the door. I noticed several rips in the screen and wondered if they would eventually burst through.

"Sit," she said again. Their bottoms hit the grass.

"You can let them in," I said. "I don't mind."

"No. They will overwhelm you. I know there are a lot of them. But they just sort of accumulated. I have no idea where the Yorkie came from. I think someone dropped her off because they knew we'd take care of her."

"It's really nice that you do. The Devon County shelter is overflowing." I studied her face. "How are you, Lori?"

She eyed me. "I think I see him sometimes, in the shadows of this house. And when I go to bed I can smell the faint scent of his cigar." She gripped her hands together. "It's as if he's haunting me."

"He lived here," I said. "This was his home. And you anchored him. Maybe he isn't quite ready to leave you."

"Is that how it works? If so," she said, shivering, "I don't like it one bit."

"I don't really know how it works." I rested my elbow on the back of the sofa. "But maybe he's trying to help you figure out who really killed him."

"Well, I'm not listening, so he can go on to the afterlife." She stared out at the darkening night. "Why did you want my yearbooks?"

"I was just wondering if you and Joe Wilgus went to school together."

"How did you know that?" She looked over at me and frowned.

"Well, you appear to be about the same age, and according to Doris, his dislike of CJ started a long time ago." I shrugged. "It just made sense that it could have started in high school."

"Wow," she said, eyes wide. "My sister is right. You're good at this."

"How good?"

"I'll show you." She went inside the house and returned with a stack of three books. She sat down and opened one. The aged, gray cloth was topped with faded blue letters that read, *Devon County High School, The Blue Herons, 1981*. The corners had begun to curve inward. She flipped through the pages until she came to one titled *Homecoming*. She slid it onto my lap. "I was crowned my senior year."

I looked down at a photo of Lori in a sparkling tiara, a bouquet of long-stemmed roses in her arms, standing on the fifty-yard line grinning hard. Her arm was looped through a tall football player's, a helmet tucked under his other arm, his knees dirty from the first half. "You're lovely."

Lori leaned over and peered down at the photograph. "I wasn't bad back then. But it's just Devon County." She laughed a little. "It doesn't take much to become homecoming queen when there aren't many girls to choose from."

"You would have stood out at any high school." I studied the picture. "Your date is very handsome."

She looked up at me. "You mean you don't recognize him?"

I glanced back at the picture. Dark thick hair. Longer, though, not a pompadour. I already knew before I read the caption: *Crowned queen, Lori Westcott, and her escort, Joey Wilgus.*

"He was the quarterback," she said. "We went to prom together that year. You should see what he wrote next to my senior picture. He always believed we would marry one day."

I looked over at her. "So where does CJ fit in?" I folded my hands atop the open book and waited for her to form her response. An owl hooted eerily in the distance.

"Carl James started coming over to my house that spring. He had quit high school and was making a lot of money learning the flooring trade. He bought a big old convertible and kept coaxing me out for rides. Joey and I were going steady, but he was applying to the community college and I never wanted to bother with more education. I didn't like school. I mean, I liked the social stuff. But studying gave me a headache. Sometimes I think I have some sort of learning disability, you know? But teachers didn't really pay attention to that back then.

"Anyway, I felt like Joey was distracted, focusing on his future and all." She exhaled. "I found out I was pregnant right after prom." She combed her hair back from her face. "Carl James was so persuasive. I couldn't resist him." She peered over at me as if to check my reaction.

"What happened when you told Joe?"

"Oh." she shivered. "He was so angry I thought he would explode right there. And then he went after Carl James. The way I heard it, the fight was brutal. They both ended up with broken noses. Carl James said Joey pulled out a knife at some point and they finally stopped. The cops said they didn't find a knife on either one of them, but one of the cops was probably Joey's dad."

My mind was reeling. "And so you and CJ got married? Did you have the baby?"

"Yes." She clenched her hands into fists. "I was so sure it was Carl James's baby. But then Jamie was a month premature."

"What are you saying?"

"Jamie weighted nine pounds six ounces. Nothing preemie about him."

"So . . ." I placed a hand on my forehead then looked up at her. "Could Jamie be the sheriff's baby?"

"Shush," she said, with her index finger over her lips. "Jamie is home for the funeral. He's upstairs in his bedroom."

"I see."

"Anyway," she said in a softer voice. "I never breathed a word to Carl James that Joe and I had been intimate."

"So how did the sheriff react when you got married?"

"He's hated me ever since. I don't know what he thought about the baby. But one day when Jamie was in high school he said the sheriff pulled him over for speeding. He hadn't been, of course. He said Joe just stared at him. Hard. Then told him to get on his way."

"So maybe he does know."

"I don't even know, Rosalie. Don't you see? Either one of them could be Jamie's daddy. But how could I go and break Carl James's heart when I wasn't even sure? It would have ruined all of our lives. And I didn't think it was worth it. I still don't."

"So that's why he's coming down so hard on you. Because you broke his heart."

She placed both palms on her cheeks. "I've certainly made a mess of my life."

"We all do, don't we? By the time we hit our age, that is. Too much room for error."

Lori placed the stack of yearbooks on a nearby table, the top one still open to the homecoming page. Her eyebrows dipped as she gazed out at the night. "He isn't going to stop until he gets his way. He's a very stubborn man."

"Lori, is there a chance CJ might have stolen a little money? Did you see any indication of that?"

"What?" Her eyes shot over to mine. "Why would you ask me that?"

"That's why CJ got laid off. Someone stole some money from the work site. He didn't tell you?"

She hesitated and blinked a few times, avoiding my gaze. "No," she said. "He was very upset about his job. Look, Rosalie, you're a dear for working on this tonight, but it's been a long day and I'm past spent."

"Okay." I placed my hand over hers. "We probably both need to get some sleep."

We stood and headed for the door. The dogs were on alert. As we passed through the house I heard the deep pounding of hard-rock music coming from the second floor.

"I swear he sees me. You know I can't sleep in our bedroom? I hear things." She reached the door. "I've been sleeping on the sofa with the dogs at my feet. They're restless, too." She leveled her eyes with mine. "I didn't kill him. You know that, don't you?"

"I'm certainly trying to prove you didn't. And the best way to do that is to figure out who did." I started out the door but stopped. "Lori, was CJ ever, well, violent with you?"

"Lord, no." Her eyes filled with tears. "He treated me as if I was a prize he won but never deserved."

"How was he with Jamie?"

She stared down at her feet. "Okay." She looked up again. "Carl James believed in discipline and responsibility. Jamie started working with him when he was thirteen. He learned the business pretty quickly."

"But he didn't follow in his father's footsteps?"

"No. And I think that irked Carl James, if you must know. He believed Jamie didn't think his father's profession was good enough. And then when Jamie decided to be a cop, well, Carl James never really got over that. It was a deep, deep hurt."

"Thank you, Lori. This has been helpful." I lifted my hair and fanned the back of my neck. "You think you'll be able to get some sleep?"

"The doctor gave me some Xanax. I took one a little bit ago. I think I'll take another one now."

I glanced up the stairs. "How is Jamie handling his father's death?"

"Other than his mother being blamed for it, he's handling it very well."

FIFTEEN

I occupied myself while waiting up for Annie as long as my eyes would stay open, but eventually I climbed into bed. I patted the comforter, encouraging Todd to join me. He leapt onto the pillow next to my head and began kneading it with his paws. Todd originally belonged to Megan, the girl who was murdered last year. Her mother couldn't bear to look at the cat after she lost her only child. I liked having him in my life. And I felt as if I was still helping Megan in some way by taking care of him.

As I stroked his fur, I thought back to the summers I spent here at the farm with Aunt Charlotte as a child. There was almost always a jigsaw puzzle in progress on a card table in the living room. We would sit around it in the evenings listening to opera, Broadway musicals, or simply the bullfrogs belting out their ballads through the open windows.

We would unfailingly begin the puzzles by sorting the edge pieces from the rest and connect the border. Once the perimeter was completed, Aunt Charlotte would let me pick which section I wanted to attack. While I would routinely select the cat in the basket or the house with a stream of smoke rising from the chimney, she would offer to start with the monochromatic sky. Of course, she chose those sections because they were the most difficult. While I matched an eye to another green eye and part of a nose, she would be studying the shapes of the pieces, the number of prongs and flat sides, trying one and then another. As a mother, I now realized what she was doing. The best way to hold my interest was for me to experience success.

Puzzles. And now I had another one before me. Doris was convinced her sister was innocent. And I had promised to prove it. Unlike Megan, who had been new to Cardigan and relatively unknown, CJ had been a town fixture. Maybe it would be easier this time. Or maybe not.

I checked the clock. Still no Annie. I worried Custer was somehow involved in CJ's death. He had been working for CJ right around the time the money was stolen. And then he was fired. Custer was a young man with layers of history that he protected fiercely. And now he had inserted himself into Annie's life.

I wondered about his father, Butch. Neither Custer nor Tyler seemed pleased to learn he was in town. But it made sense for Butch to be here if he was in fact CJ's best friend.

Todd had stopped purring. He lay on his back, stretched out, paws in the air. I stared up at the cracks in the plaster. The front door clicked shut. I sat up and switched on the bedside lamp. Todd and I listened, ears forward, for Annie's soft footsteps. I saw her shadow pass by the door and called out her name.

She stopped and peered in. "You're up?"

"Just sitting here thinking."

She stepped inside. "You have to get up so early, Mom. I can't believe you are still awake."

I patted the bed next to me. "Come and sit."

"You sure?"

"Uh, *yeah*."

Annie trotted over and jumped on the bed, sending Todd a few inches into the air. She scooped him up and buried her face in his thick Maine Coon fur. She was wearing a short madras plaid skirt, a turquoise tank, and a headband. Annie had never been big on makeup or spending time on her very thick hair, but somehow she always managed to look cute and pulled together.

"How was your date?"

"We're just hanging out, Mom. I think it's too soon to call it a date."

"But you like him."

"Oh, well, there's that. For sure."

"He's certainly good-looking."

"A lot of guys are good-looking. I swam that race a year ago. Now I want some depth. Someone who actually likes to talk about real stuff."

My heart did a little dance: I was proud of who Annie was, yet worried she was attracted to Custer's depth—the same depth that had just been concerning me. I wondered if she knew he was on probation. "What do you talk about?"

"Everything. It's so cool. Did you know he reads Lao Tzu? It helps him a lot."

"Well, that proves he's related to Tyler."

Annie kicked off her flip-flops and tucked her legs under the comforter. "Do you like him, Mom?"

"Of course. I mean, what I know of him. Does he ever talk about his family?"

"Not really. I met one of his sisters tonight. She's only sixteen, but she seemed okay. A little on the shy side, but Custer was nice to her. He didn't, like, pretend he didn't know her or anything."

"Did he kiss you?"

"Mother!"

"Sorry," I said. "That just slipped out."

"Do you and Tyler kiss?"

"*Tyler*? Annie, why would you ask me that? Of course we don't kiss. We're business partners."

"But you want to," she said, and slid further under the comforter.

My face warmed. "Subject change. Have you talked to your father lately?"

"Nope." She picked at a cuticle.

"Are you going to see him anytime soon?"

"He hasn't asked."

"Annie," I said, my tone more serious. "What do you make of your relationship with him?"

"I think I'm tired of being the only one doing any work. He could come out here to see me, you know. But I always have to go to him. So I'm staying put. If he wants to see me, he can ask."

"But don't you miss him?"

"Honestly? I miss how things used to be with him. But I know for sure he doesn't miss me. When I'm around he acts like he doesn't know what to say to me. He asks me a bunch of stilted questions, and then when he runs out of stuff to say he claps his hands together like a talk-show host signaling the monologue is over."

"What can I do to help?"

"That's the thing, Mom, you aren't there to help. So he doesn't know what to say. I don't think you realize how much you managed our relationship. But you would if you saw us now." She sat up and climbed out of bed. "Anyway, I'll let you sleep and dream of Tyler."

"Annie!"

She giggled and darted out of the room, flip-flops in hand.

I switched off the light and snuggled under the covers. Maybe I had married my father.

SIXTEEN

Carl James Fiddler's funeral was held on a cloudy Tuesday morning. It was not well attended.

Glenn and I sat toward the rear of the Baptist church. For our first few months, the Day Lily would only be open Thursday through Sunday, allowing me time to plan menus, provision the restaurant, and catch my breath. And after our grand-opening weekend, our three-day respite would allow Glenn and me to focus on the investigation.

I was grateful to have Glenn's help again. Although the investigation into Megan's death had begun as my obsession, I later gained the help of three dear friends. Glenn was the first to sign on. Then Tony Ricci insisted on being included. Tony, who was now happily in love, lived in Wilmington, Delaware. Sue Ling, a young Korean American woman, was the fourth in our detective group. She'd moved back to California, finished her memoir, and had already signed on with a literary agency. I'd read the manuscript in one day. It screamed bestseller.

I watched as Lori and Doris sat down in the first row of pews. A young man in the dress blues of a police officer was next to her. "That must be Jamie," I whispered to Glenn. "I want to meet him before he goes back to Dover."

Glenn narrowed his eyes and nodded.

The casket was closed with a modest bouquet of flowers fastened on top. The preacher cleared his throat. He was an older gentleman who had already begun to perspire. He patted his forehead with a folded handkerchief as he began his eulogy. CJ must not have been a regular churchgoer, because this man didn't seem to know him. There were no personal stories or mentions of his character. Instead the preacher relied on the funeral boilerplate, stating that CJ was in a better place, that Jesus had already welcomed him to heaven, and his family would join him when their time came. Jamie shifted in his seat at that last remark.

Lori listened intently. Maybe hearing that CJ was already in heaven and no longer haunting her house was a welcomed relief. I scanned the crowd, wondering if the murderer was seated among the congregants. Pale light filtered through the stained-glass windows, but it was still dark inside the small church. The pew was hard and creaked every time Glenn or I adjusted our position. I was relieved no one volunteered to speak when the minister offered the invitation. The service was over in exactly eleven minutes.

As we waited for Doris outside, Glenn said, "Well, that was shorter than a Las Vegas wedding."

"And about as sentimental," I said.

"Look," Glenn said. "Here comes Doris."

The air was thick with humidity. Doris's gray curls were tight around her head and she breathed heavily as she lumbered toward us. "Did you find a seat in that crowd?"

"It was certainly sparsely attended," Glenn said. "How is Lori?"

Doris scowled. "She seems fine. Do you know she painted her kitchen this weekend? The sheriff is trying to lock her up and throw away the key, and she's painting her kitchen sunflower yellow."

"I've never asked you this," I said, "but will Lori be okay financially? Did CJ have life insurance?"

"Why do you want to know that, Rosalie?" Doris said, still scowling. She huffed out a sigh. "Yes. There's a life-insurance policy." She removed a handkerchief embroidered with pale blue thread from her bag. "I suppose you heard, then."

"Heard what?"

"They found the murder weapon."

"And?" Glenn said.

"It's the shotgun from Lori's cabinet. It was in a Dumpster on the college campus."

"Any prints?" Glenn said.

"Yup. Somebody tried to wipe it clean, but whoever it was did a lousy job. Sheriff said the perp was in a hurry."

"Could he ID any of them?" I said.

"Yes. Lori's, of course. I don't think he even bothered to look for any others."

I noticed tears welling in her eyes. "Doris, are you all right?"

"No, I'm not." She held the handkerchief to her nose. "I'm scared, Miss Rosalie." A tear escaped down her cheek. She looked from me to Glenn and back to me. "I'm worried she might have done it."

"You think she might have killed CJ?" Glenn said. "What's happened to change your mind?"

"I feel like I don't even know her anymore. And she's always been impulsive. That's how she ended up pregnant in the first place."

"Let's sit down." I looped my arm through Doris's and guided her over to a nearby bench. We sat together and Glenn knelt in front of us.

Doris dabbed at her eyes. "Lori says she doesn't know when the gun went missing. She said sometimes CJ kept it in his truck."

"Was he keeping it in the truck before he died?" I said.

"She doesn't remember."

"Lori seemed to love CJ very much. She only says good things about him. Do you know if they argued about anything lately?"

"Lori did seem tense the week before he died. She wasn't returning my phone calls, and when I went over there she was as nervous as a cat." Doris shook her head. "It felt like she was keeping something from me. And Lori never does that. She's an open book."

"If the gun was in his truck, anyone could have used it," I said. "Maybe whoever killed him was at the tavern the night he died. There are so many possibilities. Don't give up on your sister yet. Okay?"

"I'm just so scared. I hate believing she could have done something so awful, but once I get a thought, I can't shake it." Doris checked her watch. "I've got to get going. My Betsy is driving us home. We got a few family members coming over." Doris nudged her glasses higher up on her nose. "I think Lori has made about ten dozen cookies. And she invited that Butch Wells over, too." Doris wadded the handkerchief tight in her fist and stood. "She shouldn't be socializing with that man. He's nothing but trouble."

"We'll figure this out, Doris," Glenn said. "The sooner the better."

"That's right." I gave Doris a quick hug and she started back to the church. Once she was a out of earshot, I fanned myself with my program and said to Glenn, "Do you have plans this evening?"

"What do you have in mind?"

"Want to get a cold one at the Cardigan Tavern?"

SEVENTEEN

Despite the blazing evening sun, the tavern was cool and dark inside. Lingering scents of spilled beer and mildewed carpet lurked in the air. Glenn and I were a little overdressed. He was in creased khakis and a starched shirt, and I was still in my sleeveless black dress and pumps. Glenn placed his hand on my back and guided me toward the bar.

Regardless of the odor, the tavern appeared to be clean and well kept. The only other bar I'd been to in Cardigan was Joey's, a place in the center of town with comfortable seating and live music. This watering hole appealed to a different clientele; my guess was these patrons were less focused on being entertained. The reason they came to the Cardigan Tavern was to drink.

A flat-screen TV was tuned to a Baltimore station. The manager of the Orioles was giving an interview. They were playing the Red Sox that night. I liked tuning back in to the world on the days the café was closed.

Glenn and I perched on adjacent barstools. I looped my purse around a hook under the counter.

"So what exactly do you hope to learn tonight, Rosalie? You don't expect the sheriff to show up, do you?"

"I certainly hope not. He's supposed to be sober." I folded my hands together and rested them on the bar. "CJ was a regular at this place. My guess is someone here may know something." I looked around the room. "Time for some sleuthing, Glenn."

"I like the sound of that."

The bartender, a middle-aged man in a black T-shirt, approached while drying a glass. His head was shaved clean and shone as if it had been polished. He wore wire-rimmed glasses, and a square patch of facial hair had been sculpted under his bottom lip. Intricate tattoo sleeves adorned his arms. "How can I do ya?"

"I would very much like a cocktail," Glenn said eagerly. It must have been pretty obvious to the bartender that neither of us got out much.

I studied the beer taps. "How's the Blue Point toasted lager?"

"Wanna taste?" He flipped the tap, filled a small glass, and set it in front of me.

"Oh my. That's delish. I'll have one of those."

"I'll have a martooni," Glenn said. "With three olives, please."

I giggled. "Glenn!"

"When they're good that's what you call them." Glenn's grin was wide, his eyes dancing with delight. "And stirred, please, not shaken." He turned to face me. "Shaking can water it down."

"The man knows his martinis." The bartender returned Glenn's smile. "I'm guessing Bombay Sapphire?"

"Perfect," Glenn said.

"Are you the owner?" I said.

"Name's Chuck. Work here six nights a week, so I might as well be. Owner lives in Florida."

Once Chuck had walked away, Glenn swiveled in his barstool to face me. "This was an excellent idea, my dear."

"Agreed. Didn't I suggest to you the other day that you should get out more?" I studied our surroundings. Two men were playing a vintage pinball machine. An image of Fonzie and three well-endowed women adorned the back wall. An equal number of men and women were seated at the bar. Some were in pairs, others alone with a drink before them next to a cell phone. Most looked as if they'd just finished a day of hard work. Or maybe a month. "I've never been here before, Glenn. I like bars."

"An undiscovered treasure. Want to play pinball?"

"We are here on a mission. We both need to focus. And I have a feeling Chuck is our man."

A few minutes later, Chuck set our drinks down on cardboard squares advertising Heineken. After toasting Glenn, I sipped the frosty beer. "Chuck," I said, and took another sip. "This is very good. Where's it brewed?"

"Craft brewery on Long Island. Do you know Kevin and Jake?"

"I do. Kevin makes my confections. I just opened the Day Lily Café. You should stop in some time."

"I heard about that place. You're getting some good reviews."

"So why did you ask us about Kevin and Jake?" Glenn said.

"They're regular customers. They like the pinball machine, and Jake is a big sports fan. Anyway, they told me about Blue Point and asked if I could stock it. Now it's a bestseller." He wiped down the bar.

"I know Kevin, but I haven't met Jake yet," Glenn said.

"Good guy. Used to be the captain of the John Adams lacrosse team. Now he's the coach. His biceps are as big as tree trunks," Chuck said. "And he's got to be at least six-three. Wouldn't you say so?"

"He's very fit. And super good-looking."

"You weren't going to hear me say that." Chuck rolled his eyes. "I like that Jake and Kevin are part of this town. And they make it better, you know, like telling me about Blue Point."

"I totally agree," I said.

"How's your martini, sir?"

Glenn smacked his lips. "Perfectamente."

I laughed again while Chuck walked over to another customer. "I love craft beers. Glenn, I need to do some research. We could install beer taps at the café."

"And maybe offer some gin."

"Something tells me our productivity is about to decline."

"There is certainly a danger of that."

Chuck returned with a bowl of popcorn. "I've seen you folks around, but I apologize for not knowing your names."

"I'm Rosalie, and this is Glenn." I scooped out a handful of popcorn. "We're new by Cardigan standards."

"We went to CJ Fiddler's funeral this morning," Glenn said. "Did you know him?"

"Always sat right there." Chuck pointed to a seat at the corner of the bar. "Anybody show up at the service?"

"Not many."

"But you did?" he said.

"We're friends with Doris and Lori," I said. "I never met CJ. What kind of man was he?"

"He was all right. Always paid his bill. Didn't hit on anyone's wife. Sometimes he got a little loud, but who doesn't in a bar?"

"Did he ever get into an argument?" I wiped my hands on a napkin.

"A few times. But I try to keep things copacetic in here. See that sign over there?"

I followed his gaze. A large piece of poster board was pasted on the wall over the tequila. "No politics, no religion, no problems," I read aloud. "I like that."

"Do people follow it?" Glenn said.

"For the most part. But being in a bar tends to loosen inhibitions."

"So CJ kept to himself?" I said.

"You see, I'm a bartender. People tell me things. I see things. But if I go blabbing what I know, it's bad for business. But I'll give you this—something was eating at CJ a few days before his death. He was drinking harder and staying longer." Chuck noticed a customer waving to get his attention. "How about another round?"

Glenn lifted his glass and said, "That would be terrific." Once Chuck was out of earshot, Glenn leaned toward me and said, "You driving?"

"Can't you walk home from here?"

"After two martinis, that may not be the case. Thus the question."

"I'm at your service." I finished my beer. "I don't know if we're going to learn much from Chuck."

"We know CJ was acting funny. I wonder why," Glenn said.

"Losing his job? The money?"

Glenn pulled an olive off his toothpick and popped it in his mouth. "We know those are possibilities. But that doesn't tell us who killed him."

I looked around the room. "Do you recognize anyone?"

Glenn dropped the toothpick into his empty glass. "A few. The woman with the purple tips on her hair delivers my mail."

"Do you know her? I mean, enough to ask her about CJ?"

"I can certainly try. She likes to talk, that's for sure."

Chuck returned with our drinks. "You know, you two seemed interested in CJ." He rested his elbows on the bar. "There was one incident that really stayed with me. It wasn't too long ago, but it just seemed so out of character for a guy like CJ."

I curled my toes inside my shoes, willing him to continue.

"What was that?" Glenn sipped his new martini.

"Remember how I was telling you about Kevin and Jake

liking the pinball machine? Well, they usually come in on the weekends, so they never ran into CJ. But I guess Jake won a pretty big tournament, so they stopped in for a Blue Point to celebrate. They were having a good time, and the whole place was enjoying them. That kind of energy is contagious, you know?"

"What happened, Chuck?" I said.

"I never knew CJ was homophobic. But he got riled up. He drank too much and started making comments like telling them not to use the men's room. Everybody tensed up, and then he said something pretty foul to Kevin. Jake got mad, really mad, and told him to take it outside."

"Good lord," Glenn said. "I didn't realize people still said that sort of thing."

Chuck laughed. "Sure they do."

"Did they get in a fight?" I clutched my glass.

"I don't really know what happened. But Jake came back in alone. I could see he was upset. His face was red, and his jaw was clenched. But he sat next to Kevin and apologized to the crowd. Then he slapped down his credit card and bought a round for the house."

EIGHTEEN

The next morning I made my way to the kitchen freshly showered and dressed. It was Wednesday, and the café wouldn't reopen until the next day. I was looking forward to catching up with Tyler. I had an idea for a soup shooter we could serve and wanted to see if he knew someone local who could sell us some asparagus.

I was surprised to see every light downstairs ablaze. When

I rounded the corner Bini was at the stove wearing lime green rubber gloves. "Good morning," I said as I made my way to Mr. Miele.

"Hey," she said without looking up.

I filled my mug and turned to see what she was doing. I watched as she scrubbed my stovetop, putting her full body weight, such as it was, into her efforts.

"What are you doing, Bini?"

"You had some serious buildup under your burners."

"Why are you cleaning my kitchen?"

"Tyler said you both need help." She turned around. She was wearing another snug ribbed tank, the same cutoff shorts, and work boots. "When I got here this morning the kitchen was pretty messy. And then you were sleeping in so late, I thought I'd better clean it."

I glanced at the clock. It was just now 7:00 a.m. "I had an idea for a recipe last night. I was trying out a few versions." I sipped my coffee. "After being at the café all weekend, doing the dishes last night would have felt like a busman's holiday." I smiled. "You know, like when someone who cleans houses all day doesn't have the drive to vacuum her own carpet."

Bini frowned. "I don't really understand what you just said."

"Well, thank you for cleaning my stove. We should get you a Barclay Meadow T-shirt. Are you an extra small?"

"Most of me is, but they're usually too tight around my biceps."

I failed to prevent my eyebrows from rising. "A small, then." I topped off my coffee and headed outside to find Tyler. I had a pretty good idea where he would be.

When Tyler had first suggested we raise chickens in order to create a certifiably sustainable farm, I had balked at the idea. I always thought chickens were stupid and messy. At least they were treated that way on the farm where I grew up. Ours were truly free range, with no fencing or coop. They would just flap around in the barn eating whatever they could find until my father was hungry for a roasted chicken dinner. To him, farm animals existed to serve man, and he raised his children to hold the same belief. At least he tried. Sensing his only daughter's inclinations, he informed my mother early on that *Charlotte's Web* would be banned from the house. So of course, knowing I was forbidden to read it, I headed for the fiction section of the elementary school library and looked up E. B. White the first chance I got.

But my chickens were living the good life. At least they had been, until the hawk came along. Tyler had built a charming house for them, with white siding and forest green shutters to match the main house. They had comfortable nests and he kept the coop immaculate, composting their waste to use as fertilizer in the fields. He built a cistern on the roof that gathered rain and emptied out into their watering trough. Their fencing was movable so that Tyler could rotate their ranging area. Sometimes he had them near the garden to eat the insects and dig up weeds, and other times he let them roam free in the grass and shrubs.

The sun was rising quickly, already scorching the air. I rounded the corner and heard a hammer pounding in the barn. There was no sign of the chickens. Despite Tyler's admonitions, I had grown attached to them. I had named each one, which was easy because their personalities were so distinct. They had free range, and so did I.

We had Mick Jagger, the strutting rooster of course; Katy Perry, a brightly colored hen who loved the sound of her own voice; and Eleanor Roosevelt, a proud matriarch who herded the smaller hens. And they definitely weren't stupid. That was something else Tyler taught me. Farm animals were focused on their flocks and herds, not on what humans would like them to do. In order to get a chicken to do what you want, you have to act like a fellow chicken.

Tyler emerged from the shed pulling a massive square of wire fencing framed in balsa wood. "Hey," he said.

"No crows?" I sipped my coffee.

"We stopped feeding them. Too expensive. Plus they made a heck of a mess."

I always found myself smiling a lot when I was with Tyler. His presence just made me happy. And he was a worker. Perspiration stains were already appearing under his extra-large Barclay Meadow T-shirt, and he had a dusting of sawdust on his jeans.

"Can I let the chickens out?"

Tyler scanned the sky. "I think so. If we're both out here, I doubt the hawk would take the risk."

I opened the door to the coop and called to the chickens. The first to emerge was Scheherazade. I was partial to her. She was sweet and exotic and very observant of the dynamics of her flock. But Tyler had a special fondness for Chicken Little, a petite Ohio Buckeye with dark reddish-brown feathers who was fiercely independent and one of the hardest-working egg layers in the coop.

"Are you going to put that screen over the free-range fencing?"

"I think it will work. Bini has another idea, but in the meantime this will keep them safe."

"Can I make us lunch today?" I shielded my eyes as the sun blazed through the trees.

"That—"

"Say, Ty." Bini walked toward us as she tucked her cell phone into her back pocket. "I just heard from Jason at Great Neck Farm. I've got a group together to meet today about forming a co-op. Jason also wants to talk about maybe starting a CSA. Pizza Hut at twelve."

Pizza Hut? I thought. My competition?

"Thanks, Bin. Say, while you're here, can you help me put this screen over the fencing?"

Bini hoisted one end of the ungainly screen.

"Can I help?"

"We got it." Bini eyes were focused on Tyler's back. She heaved the screen up on her shoulder and they walked in sync.

Once they had settled it on the fence, I said, "What's a CSA?"

Bini looked at me as if I had grown a second head. "You live on a farm and you don't know?"

"Community supported agriculture," Tyler said. "I'd like to get us to biodynamic before we start talking about that." He studied the fence. "I think we need to shift it a little. Ready?"

Feeling useless, I went over to Dickens, who was panting under a tree. I brought his water bowl closer, and he lapped it up eagerly. CSA? Biodynamic? I sat down next to Dickens and scratched his ears. I watched as Tyler and Bini adjusted the screen. Bini brushed her hands on her jeans. Her muscles were tight and defined. I stopped scratching when I felt something. "Tyler," I called, "there's a lump behind Dickens' ear."

"Probably just a tick bite or a fatty deposit," Bini said.

I explored the skin under Dickens's velvety ears. "It's hard, though. Not soft like a fatty deposit."

"Labs get lumpy," Bini said without making eye contact.

Although I realized Bini was trying to prove her worth, I hoped we would reach a place where it didn't always come at the cost of making me appear ignorant. I wanted to tell her I had grown up with Labs, my favorite being a yellow one I'd named

Pancakes. But it was pointless. Besides, she was helping Tyler. My job was to make her to feel welcome on the farm. And I was actually looking forward to admiring the stovetop. I hadn't scrubbed it since I first moved in.

"Hey, Bin," Tyler said, "you ready to take the tractor tour? I want to show you what I was talking about yesterday."

"Tyler?" I called.

He stopped and faced me. "Yeah?"

"Can you find me some asparagus?"

"I'll ask the guys at lunch." He started to walk.

"And Tyler?"

"Yeah?"

"I have some time today. I could take Dickens to the vet. Just to be safe."

Bini stared hard at Tyler. He looked from her to me. I kept stroking Dickens and tossed a wad of brown fluff into the grass. "That's a generous offer," Tyler said, "but I'll take him. He's due to go anyway." He started to walk toward the tractor but stopped. "Maybe you could pick me up some Frontline."

I cajoled Dickens to follow me into the kitchen. It was too hot a day for him to be under the tree pining for Tyler. And it wasn't a good idea for me, either. After munching on a biscuit, Dickens galumphed onto the cool wood floor with a loud exhale of breath.

My phone beeped and I slid my finger over the bottom. Glenn:

At Birdie's. Jamie is here with Doris. Don't you need your paper?

NINETEEN

I found Glenn seated in one of the plastic chairs at Birdie's next to a tall man in his early thirties dressed in jeans and a polo shirt with the collar popped. His face was tanned, his thick dark hair neatly combed.

"Hello, Doris," I said.

She introduced me to her nephew. I extended my hand and said, "It's nice to meet you, Jamie. I'm very sorry about your father."

"Thank you," he said in a polite voice. "I still can't believe it happened." He gazed up at me. "You were out at my house the other night. You and my mom were looking at her high school yearbooks." He cocked his head. "Why was that?"

I could feel Glenn's eyes on me. "Glenn and I are helping your mom. I just thought there might be a clue there." I shrugged. "But we came up short." I walked over to the counter. "I brought muffins," I said. "Double chocolate. Always a crowd pleaser."

"Oh, I've missed these muffins," Doris said.

I peeled back the cloth napkin I had placed over the basket and held it out to Doris. "They were a big hit at the café on Sunday."

Doris selected a muffin, and I walked over to Jamie and Glenn. Glenn removed one, but Jamie shook his head. "No, thanks." He patted his stomach. "The force likes us to stay in shape."

"You worried about gaining a pound or two?" Crumbs dotted Doris's lips. "These muffins are worth it."

Jamie smiled. "You've been trying to fatten me up my whole life."

Doris perched on the stool behind the counter. "Jamie's only going to be around for one more night. He's got to get back to work."

"I'll be home next time I get a few days off. Aunt Doris acts like I'm never around."

"How'd you get that tan?" Doris said. "You been to the beach?"

"Okay, so I don't come home every time I have a few days off."

"Well," Doris said, "the sooner the better. Your mom has lost her senses." Doris slid my paper over to me on the glass counter.

"Thanks. Do you know Tyler and our new employee are eating at Pizza Hut?"

"If you want to compete with the chains," Doris said, "you're gonna have to open more than four days a week, Miss Rosalie. I get folks in here asking me why you aren't."

"I'm working on it. There's only the four of us." I brushed my hair from my face. "I think we all need a few days to recover—right, Glenn?"

"I'm doing just fine. Say, I didn't know you and Tyler hired someone. Who is he?"

"*She* is Bini Katz. Do you know her, Doris?"

"I know her." Doris folded her arms. "Something is off with her. She's not so good with people."

"Really?" I said. "I thought it was just me."

"I don't know what it is, but she's awkward. Always has been."

I considered her words.

"Jamie," Glenn said, "we haven't really come up with a plausible suspect yet. Do you have any idea who could have done such a horrible thing?"

"My mom didn't kill my father." Jamie cracked his knuckles. Ten loud pops. "The sheriff has no business accusing her."

"Being a police officer, you must have a lot of questions,"

Glenn said. "Too bad you can't help the sheriff out with his investigation."

"I think it's best I stay out of it," Jamie said, and placed his hands on his thighs, his knees spread wide apart.

"Maybe you could help Rosalie and Glenn," Doris said. "Glenn asked if you have an idea who might have done this."

"My dad worked hard," Jamie said. "He was good at what he did. But it sure irked him when one of his customers didn't appreciate the quality of his work. I was with him one time when this woman didn't want to pay him the full amount. So he got down on his knees and showed her how the kick guard was joined just right. He kept pointing stuff out until she told him to shut up and wrote the check."

"Not all of his clients were that easy," Doris said.

"Oh yeah." Jamie nodded. "But it's hard getting paid around here. You do the work and then folks decide they don't want to part with their money. And then you see them in church on Sunday and you think, what the . . . ?"

"Is there someone specific who comes to mind?" Glenn said.

"Not really. But Dad used to do projects with that guy Jackson Crawford. You know, Crawford and Sons Construction? They didn't always see eye to eye." Jamie laughed and shook his head. "And then the next thing you know they're hanging at the tavern together making bets on a Ravens game."

"I hope you don't mind my asking," I said, "but did your dad carry one of his shotguns in his truck?"

Jamie stopped fidgeting and grew still. "Only when we went hunting."

"Is there a gun rack?" Glenn said.

Jamie shook his head. "He kept it under the seat."

"No alibi, and now the shotgun that nobody knew was there," Doris said. "What's your mom doing today? She back at work?"

Jamie clenched his hands together. "Butch is over there. That's why I came here." I looked from Doris to Jamie and back to Doris. I gave her a questioning look, and she just shook her head. I thought about what Custer had said the other day, that a child is the barometer for the health of the family. My guess was Jamie held secrets as tight as his clenched hands.

"Jamie is coming to my house tonight," Doris said, apparently anxious to change the subject. "I'm making him spaghetti and meatballs, and then we're going to play *Call of Duty*. Ain't that right, Jamie?"

"That's right," he said. "And you will probably kick my butt." He smiled at his aunt. It was a nice, warm smile.

"You play video games, Doris?" I said.

"Sometimes I feel the need to blow something up. Jamie and I have been blowing things up for many years."

I folded my paper. I knew there were things Doris wanted me to know that shouldn't be aired in front of Jamie. Or maybe she didn't want me to know. She seemed very protective of her nephew. I caught Glenn's eye. We were going to need to talk. "Well, I have work to do. I'm trying a new recipe. Asparagus soup shooters. What do you think? I'll serve them as a breakfast appetizer. Maybe lunch, too. I thought it would be refreshing in this heat."

"Not for free, I hope," Glenn said.

"Been there, done that. Now I just have to find me some asparagus. Seems my provisioner has other things on his mind." The bell on the door jingled behind me as I exited the store.

I walked toward my car and noticed the sheriff's cruiser idling along Main Street. I bent down and peered in the window. The sheriff was staring ahead, the air-conditioning blasting a part through his hair. I rapped on the glass.

He sat for a moment and finally buzzed down his window.

"You didn't put any money in the meter." I flashed him a smile.

"What do you want, Hart?" he said, his expression deadpan.

"I have some scones at the café. I'll make you a cup of coffee, too."

"I thought you were closed."

"I am. But I put the scones in the fridge. They'll be fresh as a daisy." I straightened. "Meet you there."

I headed toward the café, hoping he would follow. Sure enough, I heard the gears shift into park and the engine go silent. I left the door open and flipped on the lights. I was already starting the coffee when he walked tentatively into the room.

"I have half a mind to be nervous about this."

"Just supporting our local law enforcement. Have a seat."

He perched on a chair.

"Be right back," I said, and fetched the scones.

When I returned, the sheriff was looking out the front door. Jamie stood at the bottom of the steps on the sidewalk, hands on his hips, gazing in at the sheriff. I stood stock still. Jamie stared hard, eyes narrowed to slits, jaw set. The sheriff looked away, and after a moment Jamie turned and continued down the sidewalk.

Sheriff Wilgus cleared his throat. "I'll take it to go."

"No problem. But we'll have to wait for the coffee to finish." I drummed my fingers on the counter. "How well do you know Jamie Fiddler?"

The sheriff shrugged. "Not well."

"He's very handsome," I said and dropped the scones into a thin white bag. "Good hair."

"I don't notice that kind of thing."

I folded the top of the bag. "Did he ever get into any trouble?"

"I said I don't really know the boy." He stood up and hitched up his belt.

I hesitated. He wasn't nibbling. And maybe Lori was right. Maybe there were secrets that didn't need to be aired. "Jamie didn't look too happy with you."

"Maybe he isn't happy with his mother for shooting his father."

"Maybe he thinks you're picking on her unnecessarily," I said.

"Speaking of his illustrious mother, seems she's living it up since she got rid of her ball and chain."

"Painting her kitchen is living it up?"

"She painted her kitchen?"

I pressed my lips together. I wanted to get information out of him, not offer what I knew. "What do you mean by living it up?"

"She's been seen at the tavern with Butch Wells. Her husband's body ain't even cold yet." He lifted his chin. "Sound like a grieving widow to you?"

"She said Butch was CJ's best friend. Maybe he's just helping her with her grief."

"Ha! The only time he comes around is when he wants something."

"Sheriff, where exactly was CJ's body found? I know it was in a lacrosse field, but where exactly?"

"The one that backs up to the tavern."

"Do you think someone moved the body, or was he killed in the field?"

"She shot him right there in the field and left him for dead." He scowled. "I knew you had a reason for this. What the heck do you care whether or not Lori Fiddler shot her husband? If you were from here, you'd know everyone expected her to do it twenty years ago."

"You know why." I crossed my arms and leaned back against

the counter. "Doris Bird. She's beside herself with worry for her sister."

"Tell me something I don't know. Doris has tried to set her sister straight her whole life. But she's a lost cause, and something tells me Doris Bird knows it." He gathered up a stack of artificial sweetener packets. "You ever know people who just can't help but make bad decisions even if they know it's the devil telling them to do it? Kinda like Judas? That's Lori Fiddler. Delayed gratification. That's what I'm talking about. She doesn't know what it means. She's like a pigeon following a trail of bread crumbs until she realizes she's in the middle of the road. Then bam. Tire hits her."

"My goodness. You've thought about this before."

"Look, Hart. You don't know jack. Got it? You're from away. It will take you years to even try to piece any of this together. But a guy like me? I saw it coming."

"You're right. I don't know. But you sure seem to. Did you go to school together? Is that how you know her so well?"

He pursed his lips, snatched up the bag, and pushed the chair out of his way with a hard squeak. "Leopards don't change their spots."

I exhaled a sigh. "I guess that's true for you and me, too. Here we are again, arguing about a murder."

"That ain't happening again. No way, no how." He picked up his hat. "Once I put this together, Mrs. Fiddler is going to jail. Now, you got that coffee?"

I filled a cup with a steaming Gold Coast blend. "Maybe you're just doing your job, but it almost seems as if you have a vendetta against Lori." I popped on the top and handed it to him.

"The only vendetta I have is she killed her husband. I think that's reason enough. I'm the sheriff, in case you hadn't noticed. And I don't take kindly to murderers in my town." He fixed his hat on his head. "Nor do I take kindly to people interfering with police business."

"She sure is pretty," I said, and drew a circle on the counter with my index finger. "Has she always been that pretty?"

"Pretty? Maybe you should look a little deeper. You won't like what you see."

I watched as the sheriff turned and exited the café in six heavy steps.

TWENTY

After accepting a delivery and trying out a few salad recipes for Thursday's lunch, I headed home with the top down. I drove slowly, preoccupied with thoughts about families. They were complicated systems, and one dysfunctional member could have a devastating impact on the rest. I hadn't learned enough about CJ to know what kind of father he had been. And yet Chuck's description of CJ's interaction with Jake and Kevin revealed a high level of intolerance. I wondered if that was how he raised Jamie—kept him on tight reins, no room for uniqueness. What impact would that have on his son?

My thoughts turned to Ed and Annie. He had been expecting her to visit this past weekend. I wondered if he had missed her, made plans that he was forced to cancel. Although Annie might not have realized it yet, the growing distance between them could do harm. I squeezed the steering wheel, wondering if I should call Ed. While raising Annie, I was the one who read the parenting books and advice columns. I consulted with other mothers at play groups and sporting events. I remember sharing my thoughts and ideas with Ed about the best way to raise Annie. And he seemed comfortable with me taking the lead. I certainly never left the discipline to him. It was never *wait until your father gets home*. I wanted Ed's arrival in the evening to be pleasant and warm, something we all looked forward to.

But that had all changed. Although I'd read every book I could find about children and divorce, my attempts to share my newfound knowledge with Ed fell flat. And now it was up to Ed to work out their differences without my intervention. But what about Annie? The divorce was devastating to her. And now she was in a relationship with a deep and guarded young man. Was she drawn to him because he was damaged in some way by his family life? Did Annie see them as kindred spirits, both wounded soldiers?

My divorce took my breath away for many months. It was as if the story of my life had been rewritten. While I had been dreaming of our retirement, Ed was dreaming of a thirty-year-old wispy blonde. And yet my anger with Ed had cooled. I was breathing again and living my life. My new, unexpected life. I had healed in many ways. But had Annie?

I clicked the phone icon on my steering wheel and scrolled down to Ed's number. I listened to one ring tone but quickly ended the call. Give it some time, I thought. Ed will miss Annie on his own. My involvement may cause even more distance. Come on, Ed, you're blowing this.

TWENTY-ONE

On Thursday morning the four Day Lily employees held a staff meeting. We were all in uniform, seated at a table as we drank our morning beverages. Custer wore his black bandana around his head and white chef's jacket, and Crystal's customary braid trailed down her back. Glenn was bright eyed and eager to start the weekend.

"First of all, does anyone have any suggestions or comments after last week?" I said.

"I think you should put the egg bake on the regular menu," Glenn said. "That was very popular."

I made a note on a yellow legal pad.

Crystal sipped her tea. "And I think we should take turns checking the bathrooms. The ladies room ran out of toilet paper a couple of times."

"Oh, I had no idea." I made another note. "Why don't I be in charge of that." I set the pen down. "Don't forget to suggest iced coffee. On a day like today it could be very popular. And I can make any of our regular coffee drinks over ice."

"Excellent idea," Glenn said. "How did things go for you, Custer?"

He spun his mug around. "It would be all right by me if the sheriff didn't come back into the kitchen again."

"Agreed," I said. "Okay, so listen to this. Janice suggested I talk to the folks who own the Yellow Labrador, that organic winery the next county over, about supplying us with local wine. And guess what? They have a sparkling wine. So I had a brainstorm." I looked from face to face. "Ready?"

"What?" Crystal said looking puzzled.

"What do you think about a champagne brunch on Sundays?"

"Only brunch? You mean we wouldn't have to switch from breakfast to the lunch menu?" Custer said. "That works for me."

"I love it," Glenn said.

"We would only need to stay open from eight to two, I think. And then maybe we can start opening on Wednesdays.

Eventually," I added. "Not too much change at once." I checked their reaction.

"Means more money for all of us," Crystal said. "Especially with alcohol."

"Agreed. I've also decided to give Custer whatever tips come in at the bar. That okay with all of you?"

Custer looked at me, his mouth open a little.

"Maybe we could have pitchers of Bloody Marys," I said. "But I'll need a good recipe. Something to make it unique to the Eastern Shore."

Custer rapped his thumbs on the table. "Old Bay?"

"Oh," I said. "That's a really good idea."

"I wholeheartedly agree." Glenn straightened his posture. "What's our special today?"

"Tomato Benedict. Local ham with a honey mustard hollandaise. I've been working with the bakery on English muffins. These are incredible, if I do say so myself. They're made with buttermilk."

"Sounds delicious," Glenn said.

"Good. The sides are smashed potatoes and a romaine salad with—" I stopped when I heard someone in the kitchen. We all looked at the door and in walked Bini.

"We found you some asparagus." I heard a loud thud behind her, and Tyler appeared through the doorway.

He put his hands on his hips. "There's a lot of asparagus."

"Really? Oh my goodness. What am I going to do with it all?"

"Uh, serve it?" Bini said.

Glenn looked from me to her, eyebrows dipped as he took it all in. He had yet to meet Bini.

"Jeremy over at Bunny Hill Farm had a big load he was happy to sell us now that he's nearing the end of the season," Tyler said. "Deal was we had to buy it all."

I combed my hands through my hair. "Good lord. Well, we can't put it with the special. That's too much green."

"I'm sorry?" Bini said. "What are you talking about?"

"I thought you wanted to make shooters," Tyler said.

"I hadn't heard from you, so I wasn't planning on it today." I looked at Custer. "Can we swing it? I have an idea of how I want to prepare them. Can you start chopping the asparagus and sautéing it with some shallots and butter?"

"Yes, boss."

Tyler towered over his nephew. "Was that sarcasm in your tone?"

I stood. "That's what Custer calls me. And I don't mind a bit."

Tyler rested his hand on Custer's shoulder. "As long as he's respectful."

Custer shrugged out from under Tyler's hand and stood. He shuffled back to the kitchen without saying a word.

"Tyler," I said. "Custer is doing a fabulous job. And he is nothing but respectful to all of us."

Tyler looked at the kitchen door as it swung back and forth, his face lined in thought.

Bini took in the café. "This is a pretty nice place."

I gasped. That was the first kind thing she'd ever said to me. Maybe there was hope for us. "How about some breakfast, you two?"

"No time," Bini said.

I turned when I heard a rap at the door. Doris was clutching my paper. I let her in. She wiped her forehead and set my paper on the counter. "It's in the nineties already. Anyone who doesn't think global warming is real is a fool."

"Coffee?"

"On a day like this?" she frowned.

"Iced coffee, then. How about an iced latte?"

"I'll take one of those," Tyler said.

"Well, okay, me, too," Bini said.

Doris was staring at Tyler. "You hear your brother's back in town?"

"I did," Tyler said.

"Well, he's sniffing around my sister like a dog in heat."

"He must be out of money," Tyler said.

I started the coffees. "Does Custer know?"

"Custer doesn't need to know," Tyler said. "Nothing good would come of him encountering Butch."

I gave Doris her coffee. "But he's your brother." I looked at Tyler, perplexed.

"He may be your brother, but he needs to let Lori be." Doris turned to leave. She brushed past Kevin as he bustled through the door with customary white box.

"You guys are not going to believe what I have here." He walked with purpose to the counter. He was in white shorts, a plaid short-sleeved shirt, and a pale blue bow tie. His arrival was like popping a balloon of tension that had been building in the café with the mention of Butch Wells.

Kevin stopped when he saw me pour a latte into a cup of ice. "Oh, would you look at that. Draw two, bartender." He looked around the room. "Okay, I know little Crys and Glenn. But who are you?"

Bini looked at Kevin and blinked a few times. Tyler stepped toward Kevin and extended his hand. "Tyler Wells. I lease Rosalie's farm. And this is Bini Katz."

"Oh my Lordy. What an awesome name! Bini *Katz*? Oh, that's delicious."

I watched Kevin, appreciating the way he brightened a room. I thought back to what Chuck had told us about his and Jake's encounter with CJ. My heart sank as I imagined how anyone could ever be cruel to such an open and kind person. I wondered how he would tell the story.

Bini was still staring at Kevin, a blank look on her face. "So what did you bring us, Kevin?" I said.

He opened the box. "Key lime bars. Can you stand it? Instead of lemon bars, I made key lime. Is there anything better on a day like today?"

Within seconds, Glenn, Crystal, Tyler, and Bini had all stepped closer to Kevin, crowding to get a glance at the box.

"I feel like a gazelle in a herd of lions," Kevin said, "and it's kind of fun."

"Go ahead and feed them, Kevin," I said. "They're on me."

"I'll bring you some more," he said, and started to pass out the pastries.

Glenn took a bite of the key lime bar. Crumbs dotted his lips. "You need to bring more than just a few."

Once he had distributed the pastries, Kevin walked over to the glass case and began stacking the remaining bars artfully. I envied his ability to make everything he touched more appealing. "Kevin," I said, "remember what I said about getting together sometime? Are you two free this weekend?"

Kevin stopped and frowned. "What are you doing Sunday?"

"Looking forward to having a few days off."

"We'll make dinner. No need to bring anything."

"It's a date," I said. "But I have to bring something. Wine?"

"It will get drunk," he said. "And if all goes as planned, so will I."

I smiled. "Why don't you give me one more key lime bar? I'll take it back to Custer." I set it on a napkin and served up four iced coffees.

I found Custer chopping the asparagus. The scent of shallots cooking in butter whetted my appetite. I noticed four large cartons of asparagus on the floor. I could barely step around them. "Kevin—"

He stopped chopping. "You think I can't hear everything you all say out there?"

"Oh, so you know about the key lime bars?"

"I know about my father," Custer said. "That's why you asked about him the other day, isn't it?"

"He came back for CJ's funeral." I set the napkin next to him. "Are you going to try to see him?"

"Why the hell would I do that?" Custer's face was flushed. Perspiration dotted his upper lip. I had never seen him angry before.

I crossed my arms. "Will he try to see you?"

"Uh, no. But if he comes near my mother—" He stopped, still gripping the knife. He lowered his eyes. His chest lifted and fell. " 'He who knows how to be aggressive, and yet remains patient, becomes a receptacle for all of Nature's lessons.' "

I studied him. "Lao Tzu?"

Custer dropped the knife onto the cutting board. "Thank you for the key lime bar. Now, how do I make this soup?"

TWENTY-TWO

"How do you spell asparagus?" Crystal called from the chalkboard. She had already drawn a small glass and colored it a bright green. "It doesn't look right to me."

Glenn spelled it out while placing coffee mugs and saucers at each table.

"That looks really cute, Crystal," I said, emerging from the kitchen with a tray of shooters.

"So you figured out a recipe?" Glenn said.

"I think so. Want a taste?"

Glenn set the last of the mugs on a table and brought the empty tray over to the bar. "Always," he said with a devilish grin. "Why else do you think I work here?"

"So it's all about the free food?"

He set the tray down on top of the stack. "Free *good* food."

"Grab me one, too," Crystal said as she climbed down from the step stool.

Glenn picked up two small glasses. He handed one to Crystal and they knocked them together. "Oh, this is delicious," Crystal said after taking a sip. "What did you put in here?"

"Shallot, butter, half and half, and Custer suggested a few spices. Warm or cold?"

"I say warm," Glenn said, and finished the glass.

"Agreed," Crystal said. "We're going to sell a lot of these." She spun around on the toe of her Toms shoes. "I'll be back. I need to redo my hair. This humidity is giving me some serious frizz." She untied the piece of raffia she fastened at the end of her braid as she walked.

"Guess what?" I said to Glenn.

"You have news?" Glenn straightened the collar of his white oxford.

"I was thinking it would be good to hear more about what happened to Kevin and Jake at the tavern. You know, to get a better idea of how it occurred. Also to understand CJ's tendencies. He seemed willing to step outside with Jake; doesn't that mean he could have gotten in an altercation with someone else?"

"And how are you going to arrange that?"

"Done." I grinned. "Are you free to go to Kevin and Jake's house for dinner Sunday night?"

"*Hello*, coworkers," Crystal called as she re-braided her hair. "Why am I the only one to ever notice we have patrons?"

"Wouldn't miss it." Glenn walked over to the door and unlocked it. "Welcome to the Day Lily Café," he said as several customers stepped inside. The sun was blazing, the air vibrating. One customer in the first party wore a tank top that already had dark spots under her arms. The cheeks of the small child she removed from a collapsible stroller were cherry red. I escorted them to a table and decided to lower the thermostat a few notches.

The café filled quickly. Not long after we opened the doors, Jackson sat at the bar wearing a Crawford's Construction polo shirt and khaki shorts. "Don't even give me a menu, darlin'." He set his elbows on the bar. "Bring me your special and a hot cup of joe."

"Can I start you with a soup shooter?"

"If you think I'll like it, you don't even have to ask."

When I brought him the soup and coffee, I noticed Gretchen waiting for a table. I motioned her over. "Do you mind sitting at the bar?"

"I'd prefer to," she said as she hopped onto the high chair. She exchanged greetings with Jackson while I set her place.

Jackson's soup glass was already empty. "I'll have another," he said. "And you're going to want one of these too, Gretch." I felt his eyes on me and looked up. "Doesn't Miss Rosalie look extra pretty today?"

My face warmed.

Glenn approached. "Bigger glasses for the shooters next time," he said, looking harried. "That woman over there has had three."

"We can start right now," I said. "We certainly have enough asparagus."

"Hello, Glenn," Gretchen said with a wide grin. "Did you get new spectacles?"

"Why, um, yes," he said as he shoved them higher up his nose. "Yes, I did."

"They make you look exceptionally fetching."

Glenn rolled his shoulders back. "Why, thank you."

"Yes," Jackson said, "quite fetching."

"I hadn't noticed," I said. "But Gretchen's right, they are very nice."

"I honestly don't think they're any different from the pair I had before." He pushed through the kitchen door with a tray in his hand.

"Part the sea, I'm coming through." Janice rounded a party of four waiting for a table and strode up to the bar. She peered in the confections case. "Where are the espresso bars?" she said, slightly out of breath. "Did Custer eat them all?"

"Kevin didn't bring me any today," I said. "The key lime bars are awfully good."

Janice sat down. "I ran from my car to get here. I can't take this heat anymore. I'm going to die. You are all invited to my funeral."

I set a glass of ice water in front of her. She immediately lifted it to her blazing cheek. "You're here again, Jackson? It's a Thursday. Aren't you supposed to be working over at the college?"

Jackson sipped his coffee. "They still aren't letting us back because they haven't found the stolen money."

"So who's building the dorms?" Gretchen asked. "Don't they have to have them finished by the fall?"

"The college has always prided itself on hiring local. But now they've brought in a construction company from Baltimore." He wiped his mouth and dropped his napkin in his lap. "They better figure this out pronto. They're going to tear down that old dorm that was built in the sixties next. And I'm counting on that contract."

"Are they trying to figure out who did it?" Janice said.

"I certainly hope so." Jackson wadded his napkin. "Because if they are waiting for a confession, whoever took it has probably already hit the road."

Custer emerged from the kitchen with a tray of soups. "It's too crowded back there. Can you use these?"

"Absolutely," I said, and smiled. "They are going like hotcakes. I think that little pinch of turmeric you put in there did the trick."

Custer filled his coffee mug and turned to go back to the kitchen. He stopped and looked over at Jackson. Jackson eyed him warily. When he opened his mouth to speak, Custer held up his hand. "Don't waste your breath."

I watched Custer go. Jackson scowled. "Everything all right?" I set glasses of soup before Boone and Gretchen.

Jackson picked his up immediately. "It is now."

"Do you know Custer?"

"He used to work for CJ Fiddler. Got fired right before CJ died." He took a healthy swallow of soup. "Not sure why. He was a pretty good worker."

"He's doing a good job here, too," I said. "Jackson, did you know CJ very well?"

"We've worked a few jobs together. He was pretty quiet except after he'd had a few. You know how some people are totally different when they've been drinking? Like a different personality. That was CJ. All of a sudden he'd be talking like a magpie. Sometimes he was pretty funny. Other times, well, he'd be hard to take."

"He installed the most beautiful marble compass rose in my foyer," Gretchen said. "It's really quite stunning." She lifted her soup shooter. "It's the first thing people remark about."

"Too bad he's dead." Janice licked her finger and dabbed at what remained of her lime bar. "My kitchen needs a new floor."

"Did you see the story on the Baltimore news?" Gretchen said. "They interviewed the sheriff."

"He couldn't stand still," Jackson said. "And he never took off his sunglasses."

"I think he may be right about charging the wife," Janice said. "Lori is close to my age. If I was married to anyone but Trevor, there could be some violence. And I would be declared innocent by reason of hormonal imbalance." Janice scanned the room. "Maybe you didn't hear me say that." She lowered her voice. "I mean, what I was trying to say is Trevor's a good guy. You got that, right?"

Gretchen covered her mouth and giggled. She corrected her posture when Glenn approached the bar.

Glenn sidled up to me while I frothed some milk in a small metal pitcher. "Rosalie," he said, and waited for me to finish. "Do you realize what's happening?"

"Something good?" I glanced up at him.

"Very good." He leaned in. "Don't you see?"

I set two lattes on the bar and faced Glenn. "See what?"

"Look around you and take it in. It's your dream. You've created a gathering place." He beamed. "You have regulars, my dear. And they love it here."

TWENTY-THREE

Although I was tired from the long day, my brain was buzzing and not the least bit interested in turning in. I carried a cup of tea out to the back porch. The tea was a gift from Crystal. She grew the herbs herself in a small garden behind her house. According to Crystal, it was a blend of dandelion and juniper berry for cleansing the kidneys and liver, and cinnamon for taste and just about anything else that ailed you. She hoped we could offer it at the café.

I took a small sip and let the flavors settle in my mouth. After another sip, I was sold. She would have to come up with a brand name. We could even write up a little description for the back of the menu. And maybe we could sell the tea at the café. Better yet, in Layla Parker's lovely gift shop two doors down. It was always good to support neighboring businesses while promoting my own.

I propped my feet on the ottoman and looked out at the night. Fireflies blinked on and off. The sun was a faint memory on the horizon, a thin strip of violet glowing above the distant trees.

Annie was out with Custer again. They had been together every night since they met. Just the thought of Custer caused a tug in my gut. I sipped again. It was clear after this morning that Custer was not the least bit interested in seeing his father. And Tyler barely acknowledged his brother's existence. Who was this man, and how did he impact his son? If he was merely an absentee father, that was one thing, but if he was a father who inflicted harm, that was an entirely different story. I shuddered to think Custer was the one who stole the money. It just didn't fit with his quoting Lao Tzu.

I was looking forward to our dinner with Kevin and Jake. I would have to find a subtle way to ask them about the incident at the tavern. I didn't want to suspect them, but I couldn't leave a stone unturned. And what about the sheriff? Was he Jamie's biological father? I sipped more tea. I wondered if either of them considered it a possibility. If Jamie knew, would he have confronted his father? Fathers. All these thoughts about fathers and the disconnection and dysfunction regarding their offspring triggered thoughts of my own.

A waxing moon illuminated wispy clouds as they drifted past. A fox barked in the distance just as a pattering of rain began to fall. A breeze carrying an earthy scent cooled my skin. My father had loved an evening rain. I would often find him on the porch watching it fall, a warm smile on his face. When I started to talk he would say, *Hush now, little Rosalie. Let's just listen.*

I hugged my knees and tried to visit the memory from a different perspective. Was he trying to get rid of me, or did he want me to share his appreciation of the rain? Maybe it was his form of meditation.

I listened. The drops were heavy as they plopped on the leaves, a precursor to a bigger rain to follow. My father's favorite book was *The Grapes of Wrath*. He read it at least once a year to remind him of his blessings. *This verdant land we are borrowing is a gift from God,* he would say. Although we owned our modest property, in his mind, we were just borrowing it from Earth for a bit.

In the evenings he would often invite my mother to walk around the perimeter of the farm. As in his favorite book, he thought it important to lay eyes on what he owned as often as possible. I accompanied them occasionally, often skipping ahead or getting distracted by bunny nests or a turtle hidden in the grass. Sometimes he would tap me on the shoulder and say, *Lookie there, little Rosalie. See the fruit on those trees? In three days you're going to eat the best peaches and cream you ever tasted.*

I smiled at the memory of those peaches.

My entire family was a little surprised when I got into the University of Virginia. But my guidance counselor explained that the school needed to fill their quota of students who weren't from Northern Virginia, where the better schools were. My father had hoped I would return to our rural roots. But I couldn't wait to leave. I ached for excitement and variety. And when Ed asked me to marry him and move to the DC suburbs, I jumped at the chance.

And so I followed Ed. I loved him and wanted to please him. Unlike my father, Ed appreciated my attention and efforts. It seemed to work for a while. Until it didn't.

TWENTY-FOUR

Sunday's lunch special was based on a meal I'd prepared for one of our suspects last year while searching for Megan Johnston's killer: grilled cheese and a creamy tomato bisque with a small chopped salad on the side. But this was no ordinary grilled cheese. The bread was sliced over an inch thick and was based on Aunt Charlotte's recipe, full of whole grains and seeds. The melted aged cheddar was topped with lettuce, red onion, and fresh tomato, the bread slathered with pesto mayonnaise.

I carried four specials to the last (at least I hoped they were the last) of the two parties remaining in the café. After depositing their plates I returned with a pitcher to fill their water glasses, and my heart warmed at their reaction to the presentation of their food.

I found Glenn behind the bar checking his watch. "Ready to go home soon?" I said.

"Looks like we may get out of here on time. Maybe I'll have a chance to take a nap before we go to Kevin and Jake's."

I began stacking clean mugs on a shelf above the coffeemaker. "Glenn, do you realize Gretchen was here every day this week?"

He leaned back against the bar. His white shirt hosted several stains, and his apron was starting to slip down his hips. "She invited me over to her inn for tea tomorrow."

"Really?" I smiled. "Are you going?"

"I don't think something like that is in the cards for me, Rosalie. I had one great love, and that's enough. I consider myself a lucky man."

I set the last mug on the shelf and faced him. "It's only tea."

"I know what's happening," he said. "She's courting me. I'm not blind."

"She seems like a lovely person. I've really enjoyed her sense of humor these past few days."

"Rosalie, she says things like *poppycock* and *bollocks*." Glenn shook his head.

"That's what Brits do. I happen to love her accent. It makes her sound intelligent."

Glenn peered at me over his glasses, his arms crossed tight. "Perhaps you should be the one going to tea."

"Glenn." I placed my hand on his arm. "Why does that trouble you? I would think it would make you happy."

"I had a good run. That part of my life is over."

"Do you feel it would be a betrayal to Molly if you saw someone else? I find it hard to believe, based on the way you've described her, that she would want you to stop living."

"I am living a very full life." He flashed me a tired smile. "Maybe too full, but I like it just the same."

"You know, Crystal and I had a conversation last week, and I said something about my life being complete now that I had the café. And she asked how it could be if I didn't have love."

"Well, she's in her twenties. That's where she's headed. But you have plenty of love in your life, dear. I believe everyone surrounding you basks in the warmth of your compassion."

"Thank you, Glenn. I hope that's true." I gazed over at him. "But she has a point. Romance is fun. And I think I miss it a little."

Crystal emerged from the kitchen. "Two tables left," she said. "Maybe we should flip the sign?"

I glanced over at the clock. Five minutes. "You know what? I think that's a spectacular idea. Custer must be spent back there."

"Speaking of Custer," Crystal said, "who is that guy in the kitchen with him?"

"It's not the sheriff, is it?" I asked, worry sending a shot of adrenaline through me.

"No." Crystal headed toward the front door. "But Custer doesn't seem too happy."

Glenn and I exchanged a concerned look and started for the kitchen.

I knew who it was immediately. The green eyes. The sandy blond hair. "You must be Butch," I said.

Custer glared at him, hatred smoldering in his eyes.

"Well, look who's here," Butch said. "You must be the boss woman."

"What are you doing here?" Glenn took a protective step closer to Custer.

"This here's my son. And I heard he got himself a pretty good job." His eyes locked on Custer's. "So they let ya out of jail, did they?"

Custer squeezed the spatula in his hand. "I never went to jail, you son of a bitch."

Butch shifted his weight and crossed his arms. "You deserved to. And you and I both know it. I think that lady judge just liked your looks." Butch winked at me. "Takes after his daddy."

"The kitchen is for employees only." Glenn positioned his body between them. "It's part of our insurance policy. So I'm afraid I'm going to have to ask you to leave."

"But I haven't finished talking with my boy. I have some questions I'd like him to answer."

"I got nothin' to say to you," Custer growled.

"Glenn's right about our insurance policy," I said. "So if you don't leave now, I'll have to call the sheriff."

Butch chuckled heartily. "Oh, he's your best buddy now, isn't he, boy? You want her to call Mr. Big Bad Sheriff and tell him I was making trouble for you? You think he'd see it that way?"

I removed my cell from my apron pocket and slid my thumb across the bottom. I looked over at Butch, my eyebrows raised. "You really aren't going to leave on your own?"

He waved his hand at us. "I'm leaving." He pushed open the door. "I'm not through with you, son." He stopped and faced Custer. "Maybe I should ask your mama."

Custer took a menacing step toward his father, but Glenn blocked his way. They jostled a little, and Glenn's glasses tumbled to the ground. Butch let the door slam behind him.

Custer knelt down and picked up Glenn's glasses. "I'm sorry," he said. He walked over to a cabinet and removed a bottle of glass cleaner. After spritzing both lenses, he wiped them clean with a paper towel.

He held them out in his palm. "I'm really sorry."

"No harm," Glenn said as he fixed them back on his nose. "Will you look at that? This is the cleanest they've been all weekend."

"See?" I said. "There's nothing for you to be sorry for."

Custer looked down at his sneakers. "I didn't mean to shove you, Mr. Glenn."

"I might have shoved me, too, if my father was acting that way."

"Crystal has already flipped the sign, Custer," I said. "We're closed. The two remaining tables are finishing up. Why don't you take a break?"

"I could use a cigarette," he said, his voice shaky.

"Maybe I'll carry this out first." Glenn picked up an overstuffed black garbage bag. "I want to make sure there isn't more trash in the alley waiting for you."

Glenn found me at the bar cleaning one of the Mieles. "My heart is still pounding." He smoothed his hair back in place as he sat down. "What on earth do you make of that?"

I placed my palm on my forehead. "What an awful man. Why do you think he came here?"

"Certainly not to have a friendly visit with his son."

"He seemed to want something from Custer." I ran a slow, steady stream of water in the aluminum frothing pitchers. "It all keeps pointing back to the money. If Butch really was CJ's best friend, maybe they were in this together."

Glenn rested his elbows on the counter. "But then he would know where it is. Why bother Custer?"

"Do you think he's okay? Custer, I mean."

Glenn shook his head slowly. "How could anyone be okay with a father like that?"

As I turned down the lane to Barclay Meadow, I noticed Tyler's pickup heading toward me. I pulled over onto the narrow strip of grass next to the cedars to wait for him. I buzzed my window down—it was way too hot for a convertible today—and smiled at him when he stopped. Tyler's window was already open, his elbow jutting out. He was not a big fan of air-conditioning. *When you work outside all day,* he once said, *the artificial coolness can throw off your body's ability to regulate its temperature.*

"Hi," I said. "Working on a Sunday?"

He was freshly showered even though it was only four o'clock. I caught a whiff of his scent. Tyler never wore cologne. Instead he used a sandalwood soap his sister made by hand. I had grown very attached to the now familiar fragrance.

"Just came back to shut down the irrigation."

"How's everything going?"

"Good," he said. "Getting a lot accomplished. Hiring Bini is one of the smartest things I've done in a while."

"I'm really glad, Tyler." My stomach tightened as I realized I had become quite jealous of the time Bini got to spend with him. "I'm off for three days. Maybe we'll have a moment for you to tell me all about it."

"Sounds good. You know, she is one of the hardest-working people I know." His right hand was draped over the wide steering wheel. "I actually have a hard time keeping up with her."

"Really? I find it difficult to believe she works harder than you."

"Damn close. How about you? Good day? You must be spent."

"I am. But we had a very busy weekend. I can't complain about that."

He frowned for a moment. "I hope I didn't upset Custer the other day."

"He seemed fine. Except, Tyler? Your brother stopped in to see him today."

"Oh." He stared ahead.

"You two are very different," I said tentatively.

"Yeah." He huffed out a laugh.

"Tyler, Butch seems like he could cause a lot of trouble. For Custer and whoever else gets in his way."

"He's been doing that his whole life." He looked over at me at last. "Look, Rosalie, I have to run. Bini and I are meeting some guys at the country club for beers. We're making progress on the co-op."

"That's great. I hope the meeting is a success. Coffee tomorrow?"

"At some point during the day. Bini and I sure dug those iced lattes. Catch you on the fly." Dust spit out from under his tires as he drove away. I tried not to focus on the fact that Tyler no longer started his sentences with *I*. It was now *Bini and I*.

Before I could park, I noticed Annie in her Volvo and proceeded to have my second drive-by conversation. She cranked down her window. "Hey, Mom. How did it go today?"

"Really great. But I'm glad it's Sunday night. Where are you off to?"

Annie was in shorts and a halter top, her face framed by a lace headband. "Custer asked me to meet him. He sounded upset." I noticed a tear welling in her eye.

"Annie, what's wrong?"

"Um, well, did Custer say anything today about me?"

I shook my head. "Not a word. Why?"

Her forehead scrunched up. "Are you positive? Because he sounded weird. And I'm worried he doesn't want to hang out with me anymore." She wiped away a tear. "Between Dad and Custer, I feel like no one wants to be around me."

"Oh, honey, I'm positive he didn't say anything like that." I squeezed the steering wheel. "If he's upset, it's more likely something else. It was such a long weekend for him. He has a lot of responsibility, you know. Nothing would work if we didn't have Custer in that kitchen. I hope I'm paying him enough."

Annie gave me a weak smile and the tear trailed along the curve of her cheekbone. She brushed it away and sniffled. "That's nice of you to say."

I lowered my voice. "But don't tell him, okay?"

"Ha-ha." Her face brightened.

"I'm going to Kevin's house for dinner, so don't wait up."

"Oh, I wish I could go. I love Kevin."

"I know, right? Should be fun."

"Okay, Mom, got to run." She blew me a kiss and continued around the circle. I parked the car and shut off the engine. Should I have warned her about Custer's father? Could she somehow get caught in the crossfire? I flopped my head back on the headrest. "Oh, my dear, sweet Annie," I said aloud, "take care of you. In love and—" I shuddered. "And everything else."

TWENTY-FIVE

Many of the houses in Cardigan, from the historic farms to the rows of edifices lining the rivers and creeks, had been built in the eighteenth century. Kevin and Jake were lucky enough to obtain one along one of the widest points on the river, just three short blocks from Birdie's Shoe Store.

I noticed Glenn's Prius and checked my watch. I was right on time. Of course Glenn would be a little early. He took pride in being prompt and dependable, and I cherished that about him.

I had taken a little catnap with Todd and a long, hot shower before I arrived. I climbed out of my car and headed for the front door. It was a sultry evening, the air still thick with lingering moisture from the heat of the day. I had slipped into a sleeveless cotton maxi dress and cinched it with a belt. Knowing Kevin's excellent eye for style, I wanted to look presentably fashionable, so I accessorized with a pair of gladiator sandals and dangly gold earrings.

"Oh, look at you," Kevin said with enthusiasm as he double-kissed my cheeks. "And you smell like a little piece of heaven." He frowned for a moment. "Chanel?"

"How did you know?"

"I know the good ones," he said. "Come in. Glenn and Jake are out on the deck."

As I followed Kevin through the narrow house, I was awed by their jaw-dropping taste. The sparsely decorated rooms were designed in muted greens and grays with a pop of coral or yellow here and there. I was equally impressed by how each room had been designed around a focal point of standout artwork.

When we reached the kitchen the house opened up to a wall of doors and windows overlooking the Cardigan. "Wow," I said. "What a view."

"We barely use the other rooms." Kevin faced me and smiled. "I knew you would appreciate this place. Your café is so fabulous. You've got an eye."

I presented Kevin with a bottle of rosé. "This is from the Yellow Labrador, that winery out on Mallory Road. I'm thinking of serving their wine at the café."

"Rosé is perfect on a hot summer night." He opened a drawer and removed a Rabbit corkscrew. "You and I think along the same lines."

"They also have a sparkling wine. I'm starting a champagne brunch on Sundays. What do you think?"

"In Cardigan?" Kevin placed a hand on his chest. "Finally. We've been driving to Annapolis. I love champagne brunches." The cork squeaked as he pushed down on the lever. "Plated or buffet?"

"Plated. I don't have room for a buffet. Plus I only have Custer, and together we can prepare just so many dishes. We're stretched as it is. Do you think it will fly?"

Kevin filled two wineglasses. The rosé sparkled in the late evening sun hovering just above the horizon, the reflection from the water intensifying its pale pink glow. "Plated is better. I hate having to stand up to get my food. All that jostling makes me tense. And then there's the kid in front of you who picks up the tongs and takes one French fry at a time. And that's the only thing he's eating. *Hello*, parents."

"Exactly."

He handed me a glass and raised his to meet it. "To new friends."

"To new friends," I echoed, and sipped the wine. "Oh my," I said. "I like it. You?"

"It's fabulous. I need to pour one for Jake. He will go buy a case tomorrow." He removed another wineglass from a rack beneath a cabinet. "I made a martini for Glenn, so he is good to go. Why don't you join them. I'll be right out."

I slid open the door, picked up the hem of my dress, and stepped out onto the deck. A pergola framed the space, and a large ceiling fan with rattan teardrop-shaped blades spun lazily. Comfortable outdoor seating was arranged in carefully planned groupings and a coffee table hosted what looked to be a delicious assortment of appetizers: prosciutto-wrapped fresh mozzarella balls, shrimp on ice, bruschetta with various toppings, and an assortment of Mediterranean olives.

"Rosalie," Jake said, and gave me a warm hug, although my face only reached his armpit. "I'm so glad you both could make it on such short notice." Jake was dressed in a tight-fitting black tee, his muscles hard as rocks, and silk khaki pants.

I gave Glenn a quick kiss. He had changed into linen trousers and a pressed shirt. "You look nice," I said.

"A far cry from the mess I was earlier today." He turned to face the river. "What do you think of this view?"

"Absolutely stunning."

Kevin arrived with the bottle and a plate of sliced cheeses. "Rosalie got this from the Yellow Labrador."

Jake accepted the glass and took a healthy sip. He swirled it in his mouth and frowned in thought. "I like it." He sipped again. "No, I love it. We should . . ."

"Get a case?" Kevin said, and winked at me. "What did I tell you?"

"Glenn," I said, "we need to take a road trip out there this week and order some wine. We're ready, right? Can we handle serving wine?"

"After the past two weekends, I think we can handle whatever comes our way."

Kevin leaned in toward Glenn. "Say *kina hora*. Quick."

Glenn looked puzzled. "Why?"

"Just say it," Kevin said.

"Okay, *kina hora*. Now why did I just say that?"

"It's like knocking on wood. Keeps away the evil spirits. When you say something bold like you just did, you want to ensure you didn't jinx yourself."

Jake laughed. "It's a Yiddish thing. Right, Kev? But I think it actually works."

"*Kina hora*," I said. "Just to add my two cents."

Jake set his glass on the table. "I have to check the lamb."

"Lamb?" Glenn patted his stomach. "You've already put out such a spread, how will I have room for dinner?"

"It's light. Lamb lollipops and some roasted veggies."

"Oh my," I said.

"Jake," Kevin said, "I forgot the music." He tapped his palm against the side of his head. "What an idiot. I'll be right back."

Once they had both gone into the house, Glenn and I walked over to the deck railing and looked out at the river. Several sailboats were moored close to a nearby marina, the swift current parting at their hulls.

"This is lovely," I said.

"Yes. What a place they have." After a pleasant silence Glenn asked, "Do you still think about her?"

"Every time I gaze out at this river."

A soft, jazzy riff emanated from a set of outdoor speakers.

"The whole situation was really quite remarkable," Glenn said. "You finding Megan. Searching for her killer. And then figuring it out." He shook his head. "I still can't believe it all happened."

"Who is Megan?" Kevin joined us at the railing. Jake appeared right after him with the rest of the wine and began topping off our glasses.

"It's a long story," I said.

"But it sounds like a good one," Kevin said. "You said something about searching for a killer. I'm beyond intrigued."

"Why don't we sit," Jake said. "The lamb is resting."

We settled into adjacent chairs. I crossed my legs and took a sip of wine. "You sure you want to hear this?"

"You're stalling!" Kevin sang.

"I found a dead body in my marsh grasses last year. The family said she committed suicide and asked the sheriff to close the investigation. But it just didn't seem right, so I decided to look into it. After a long search, Glenn and I, and two of our friends, discovered she had been murdered."

"We may have helped Rosalie," Glenn said, "but she's the one who got the killer to confess."

"That's incredible," Kevin said.

"It was really quite awful," I said. "And she was a lovely girl."

"Who was she?" Jake said.

"A student at the college."

"Wait," Jake said. "I remember this. I heard a rumor that was why Nick Angeles left the school. Everyone was shocked. He was the president's darling."

"I remember Nick," Kevin said. "He was wicked handsome. Did he hit on her? He was a vicious flirt."

"You could say that," I said.

Jake leaned in. "He slept with her, didn't he?"

"Can I plead the Fifth?"

"I knew it." Jake sat back. "What a sleaze. No wonder they got rid of him. I'm pretty sure he lost that big grant of his, too. We have so many excellent teachers, but you get one guy like that and a school could lose its reputation. I hope he's pushing a broom somewhere."

"So, not only did Rosalie solve this crime," Glenn said as he speared a shrimp with a toothpick, "but she's been asked to solve another."

"Get out." Kevin slapped his thigh. "You're a regular Miss Marple."

I looked over at Glenn, admiring his segue. "Doris Bird's sister has been accused of killing her husband. Did you hear about it? Her husband, CJ Fiddler, was shot in the chest two weeks ago." I bumped my knee against Glenn's. This was it. Our opportunity. Way to go, friend.

Jake finished his wine in two gulps. He set the glass down with a thud.

Kevin eyed him warily. "We know about it." He looked back at us. "I mean, it's Cardigan, right? If you don't know something as sensational as that, you're dead." Kevin rubbed his chin. "That didn't come out quite right."

Glenn chuckled. "Well, you certainly have a point. Rosalie and I have been asking a lot of questions. Chuck, the bartender at the Cardigan Tavern, said CJ could get a little mouthy after a few drinks. Isn't that what he said, dear?"

"Yes," I said.

Kevin looked over at Jake. "Can I tell them?"

Jake clenched his jaw. "It's like you said. Nothing is a secret here. Go ahead."

Kevin straightened his spine and looked back at us. "We had a run-in with CJ not long ago. We love the Cardigan Tavern. And Chuck has started stocking our favorite beer.

"We like to go in there on the weekends and watch football or lacrosse or whatever. It's a nice outing for us. And Jake has the highest score on the pinball machine." He smiled at his partner. "We don't get to spend all that much time together, with Jake's teaching and coaching."

"And you ran into CJ at the tavern?" Glenn said.

"Pretty much literally ran into him there," Kevin said and downed the last of his wine.

"I don't know if mouthy is the right word to describe him." Jake fell back into his seat. His eyes darkened. "He's worse. He's a raging bigot."

"Oh my." Glenn sipped his martini. "I don't think I'll like what you're going to say next."

"He was really hateful," Jake continued. "He complained to Chuck that we shouldn't be allowed to use the bathroom. And he kept knocking back shots. We ignored him, but the slurs got worse. Then he said something to Kevin that pushed me past my limit. I won't repeat it."

"I thought CJ would pee his pants when Jake stood up. I don't think he had any idea how fit Jake is. Or how tall."

"It didn't faze him," Jake said. "The words kept flying out of his mouth as if he had a case of unmedicated Tourette's syndrome."

"They took it outside," Kevin said. "Jake still won't tell me what he said to CJ. But Jake came back in alone." Kevin gazed over at him. "Jake's my guy. He stood up for me, and it meant the world to me." He looked back at us. "I don't know that anyone has ever done that for me. I mean, you can imagine the abuse I took in high school." He shrugged. "But you can't change your spots, no matter how hard you push down on the eraser. And believe me, my father sure tried. And then I found Jake, and now our lives are in place. A good place. And I think we have a home here. Cardigan has a reputation for not accepting diversity, but we have made fabulous friends. CJ was the first person to act out." Kevin picked up an olive. "Anyway, listen to me, could someone please hit the pause button?" He chewed and dropped the pit into his hand. "But I will say one more thing: I'm not sorry that CJ guy is dead." He stared off into the distance for a moment. "Is that terrible to say?"

After an exquisite dinner and an even better dessert, Glenn and I walked to our cars, exhausted after the busy weekend. He opened the door for me. "My heart is heavy, Rosalie," he said. "Are you thinking what I'm thinking?"

"I'm trying not to."

"Could he have?"

"To defend the man he loves? Maybe. Who knows what CJ said."

"I don't want to go there." Glenn exhaled a long sigh.

"It was such a lovely evening. I like them both very much. As a couple and as individuals." I pulled my keys from my bag. "You know, Glenn, last year with Megan all of our suspects were strangers. Most of them weren't even from Cardigan. It's different this time. We coexist with these people. Our lives bump together in all kinds of ways."

"Yes, that's true, isn't it?" Glenn smiled. "All right, my dear, maybe we should both sleep on it. Who said small-town life was boring?"

"I'm still waiting for that to be the case." I opened my car door. "Good night, Glenn."

When I spotted Annie's Volvo in the driveway, I allowed the chronic knot of worry in my stomach to relax. She was home.

The house was dark and utterly still. I filled a glass with water and decided to check my e-mail. The glow of my computer screen cast an eerie light over the room. I smiled when a fluffy tail weaved between my legs. I scratched Todd's back while I waited for Safari to open.

A familiar dread passed through me when I saw an e-mail from Ed. The subject line read: Have you kidnapped Annie?

I'm not sure what you're trying to pull, Rose, but I haven't heard from Annie in weeks. We had an agreement that she would spend at least two weekends a month with me. She is being belligerent and disrespectful, and I won't tolerate it. I expect her here next weekend, no excuses. You have always said we should never put Annie in the middle, and now you are using her to sabotage my relationship with her. I honestly thought that kind of behavior was beneath you.

Ed

I combed my hands through my hair and thought of a million different ways to defend myself. But whatever I said would be lost on him. He was determined his view of the situation was the correct one, and I knew from experience he wouldn't budge due to an intense need to be right. I clicked reply and wrote the following:

Annie has a new friend. She is spending all her time with him. And I am afraid an infatuation is something neither of us have any power to influence. In the meantime, please contact Annie directly. I think she would like to know you are missing her, at least.

All best,
Rosalie

I was almost grateful to Ed for pushing me over my limit. I was now officially exhausted and brain-dead enough to go to sleep. I shut down my computer, picked up my water glass, and climbed the stairs. Annie's door was latched, which was unusual for her. She liked to encourage Todd to share her covers. I decided I needed a visual. I gripped the knob and turned it slowly. The door creaked as I eased it open. Light from the hallway cast shadows into the room. I could make out the contour of Annie's body under the covers. Todd let out a meow and preceded me into the room. I bent over to kiss my daughter's forehead but froze when I saw Custer's head nestled against her neck, his face peaceful in deep slumber.

TWENTY-SIX

Annie and Custer were gone when I awoke the next morning. Annie was due at the physical therapy office where she was interning at seven, and apparently Custer had hitched a ride. After stewing for most of the morning and being completely unproductive, I came to the conclusion that I needed a chicken fix.

I grabbed a bag of food scraps I had brought home from the café and headed out to the coop. The hens were inside, cooing and brooding on their nests. Mick Jagger rested in the dirt, although he looked up alertly when I entered. "Hello, ladies," I said. The hens watched me carefully, their heads moving in staccato jerks. I continued out to the fenced-in ranging area. Tyler's chicken wire was fastened over it, protecting them from the hawk.

I sat down in the soft grass and tucked my legs beneath me. I removed some torn bread and a few blueberries from the bag and tossed them into the grass in front of me. Next I took out some waffle pieces and held them in my hand.

"Yoo-hoo," I called. "Sherry . . ."

It took a few moments before Scheherazade peeked her head out of the henhouse. "Look what I brought you." She took a few tentative steps out of the opening and looked up at the sky. Her head darted and twitched. Mick Jagger appeared soon after, standing guard.

"Come on out, Mick." I tossed a piece of waffle toward him. Scheherazade walked over and pecked at it. Crumbs tumbled out of her mouth as she tipped her head back and swallowed. "Good girl," I said. Mick Jagger joined her, and together they pecked and swallowed and moved on to the orange rinds.

"Oh, ladies," I called. "Don't miss out on the fun." I heard movement in the henhouse and, feeling safe thanks to my presence, the hens slowly risked emerging from the coop. I tossed more scraps, and they tentatively began to eat. Mick ate a little more and then proceeded to walk the perimeter of the fence, which was quite a sizable stretch of grass. Tyler had put the fencing around several azaleas and hostas so the chickens could seek cover if they felt threatened again.

Eventually I was surrounded by my dear, sweet chickens. Scheherazade stayed close and allowed me to stroke her feathers. Finally, I thought, you can stretch your skinny legs again.

"I'm not even going to ask what you're doing."

I looked up to see Tyler standing next to the fence, a coffee mug in each hand. "I'm doing what you told me. I'm being a chicken." I patted Scheherazade. "See? I'm showing them it's safe to come out."

"Mind if I join you?"

"Of course not." I scanned the lawn. "Where's Bini?"

"I let her go for the day. She worked all weekend, so I sent her home." He shook his head. "I had to force her, though. She kept saying there was too much to do. You hang around this place long enough and that becomes your mantra."

Tyler walked around to the door of the henhouse and came into the pen. He ducked his head to avoid the wire cover. That was not necessary for me. "They've been spending so much time inside, I need to clean it out in there again," he said. "That'll make it the second time today." He eased himself onto the grass and handed me a coffee mug. He looked into the bag of scraps, found some arugula, and tossed it out to the hens.

Tyler looked down at his right hand. His reattached finger had healed beautifully after he'd severed it with a rusty saw over a year ago.

"Does it ever bother you?"

"I can tell you when it's going to rain." He smiled at me. "I still can't believe you saved it. You are the only reason I still have an index finger on my dominant hand."

"You're welcome." I stroked Sherry, grateful she was calming down. "Tyler?"

He sipped his coffee. "Yes?"

"I need to know more about your brother."

Tyler set the mug on the grass. "I'd prefer you call him Butch. I don't consider him to be my brother."

"What's your relationship with him like?"

"What relationship?"

"Tyler, I know you're not one for elaboration, but what happened to him? He couldn't be any more different from you. Is he like your father?"

"No," Tyler said quickly. "My father was an honest, hardworking man."

"So how did he get to be the way he is? Is it genetic?"

"It's never just the one, is it?" He crossed his ankles and tossed another rind to the hens. "If he resembles anyone, it's my grandfather on my mother's side. The thing is, Butch is a good-looking man." He eyed me. "You may have noticed?"

"He has the Wells eyes. I'll give him that."

"He could charm anybody from the day he learned how to talk. Probably before that. He charmed my mother. And he conned my father."

"And Custer's mother?"

"Sally was smitten. She's about five years younger than Butch and pretty as can be. She's sweet, too. Well, at least she used to be. I think Butch soured her good nature a long time ago. But once she had Custer, Butch didn't want anything to do with her. He left when Custer was three."

"Wow," I said. "You two are like Cain and Abel."

"There's some truth to that. But Butch isn't jealous of me. I'm not even on his radar, and I intend to keep it that way."

"It couldn't have been easy for you growing up. He must have gotten all the attention."

"I don't enjoy a lot of attention. Remember the finger?"

I laughed softly. "Right." The chickens had stopped eating and were squatting on the grass, some nestled together, others on their own. "Tyler, I have to ask you: Why is Custer on probation?"

"I think you should ask him."

"Honestly? I don't want to humiliate him. But he's my employee. And now he's seeing Annie. Every day, I should add. Did he do something violent?"

Tyler squinted up at the sky for a moment, deep in thought. The sun was hidden by puffs of cumulus clouds, and the temperature had dropped markedly from earlier in the day. A slight breeze ruffled the chickens' feathers. "I would like to see Custer be able to put it behind him. And, well, let's just say it wasn't an act of aggression." He frowned. "It was more that he was provoked. You see, Custer is a Wells, and he's a lot like Mick Jagger over there. If anyone tries to hurt someone he loves, he will do whatever it takes to protect them."

"Did he hurt someone?"

"No."

"But what about Annie? Tyler, I worry."

He looked over at me. "You? *Worry*?"

"Butch is after something from Custer. Do you know what that might be?"

"I don't know anything about that." Tyler thought for a moment. "Maybe tell Annie she should stay away from Butch." He looked at me. "You, too, for that matter. Keep out of his way. Okay? Like I said, he can be quite charming when he wants to be."

"Mmm. Sounds like you have that in common."

"Me? Blunt, maybe. Stubborn. Rough around the edges. But this is a first for charming." He looked down at the grass for a moment, then stood abruptly. He held out a hand to pull me up. "I need to get back to work. You done being a chicken?"

I giggled. "Yes." We faced one another. "It was nice spending time with you."

"Yeah, partner. It's good to hang out." He brushed off his jeans. "I really don't enjoy talking about Butch, though."

"Message received."

TWENTY-SEVEN

A basket filled with day-old apple-cinnamon muffins hung from the crook of my arm. I was wearing a pair of shorts and a tank top but had accented the simple outfit with some of my favorite turquoise jewelry. The construction site was bustling. Hammers pounded. Nail guns popped like the Fourth of July. A cement truck beeped as it backed up onto the road.

I decided to keep some distance from the site in order to avoid getting sent away for the lack of a hard hat. I noticed a man under a tree filling a cup from a thermos of coffee. I greeted him when he looked up. "It's a lovely day." I smiled.

"That it is."

"I'm sorry to interrupt your respite, but do you know a man named Cal?"

"Big guy?"

"Yes," I said. "That's the one."

He slugged back some coffee and pointed toward a group of men huddled over a table draped with blueprints.

As I made my way to the cluster of men I tried to decide what to say. But before I could muster up an idea, Cal broke away from the crowd and came over to me. "What's in the basket?"

"Apple-cinnamon."

He put his hands in his pockets and cocked his head. "You didn't come here to bring me more muffins."

I avoided his eyes. "That's one of the reasons I'm here."

"I knew it. What's the other reason? You some kind of investigator?"

I lifted my head. "I told you. I own a café."

"And?"

My shoulders fell. "The woman who has been accused of CJ

Fiddler's murder is the sister of a friend of mine. The sheriff is hell-bent on sending her to prison."

"Did she do it?"

"I don't believe so. But, Cal? I think it has to do with the stolen money."

He shifted his weight. "I can't tell you any more than I already have."

"But if I can find out who killed CJ, you may very well get your money back. Or at least know who took it. Can I ask who is investigating this? Is it the FBI?"

"The college is keeping it private for now. They don't want the publicity. They have a top-notch team interviewing everyone."

"Let me ask you this. Have any of the contractors left town?"

"They were told not to."

"If you'd stolen that much money, wouldn't you take off with it?"

"What are you saying?"

"If no one has skipped town, then the only other person who would want to can't because he's dead. See? I believe finding out who killed CJ will lead us directly to the stolen money."

"So what, we dig up his grave?"

"No need. Someone killed him. That's who has the money." I looked up at him. "Have the investigators come up with anything?"

"Why would I tell you that?"

I opened the paper sack and removed a muffin. "I'm just helping a friend." I held it out to him.

Cal grabbed the muffin and smiled over at me. "You keep bringing me your leftovers, and I'll tell you what you want to know."

"So?"

"So far everyone is coming up clean. Investigators are hitting dead end after dead end."

"And no one has left town?"

"Not a one."

I removed the paper bag from my basket, cinched the top, and handed it to Cal. I smiled. "Cal, I think this is the beginning of a beautiful friendship."

TWENTY-EIGHT

It was after six by the time I got home. A slight breeze rustled the leaves as I stepped onto the stoop. I found Annie in the family room watching reruns. "Hey, Mom," she said brightly. "You know, we never see each other with your hours being completely opposite from mine." Her legs were tucked underneath her. A pillow sat in her lap, and she was eating a bowl of cottage cheese.

"I know," I said. "I miss you."

I dropped my purse in a chair and sat down next to her. "How did it go with Custer last night?"

"Oh." She wiped her mouth. "He had no intention of not seeing me anymore. He was upset about something else."

"Did he tell you what?"

"Did you know his parents are divorced?" She rolled her eyes. "It's like an epidemic."

I swallowed hard, not wanting to be grouped in a category with Butch Wells. "Yes," I said, "I know."

"Apparently he doesn't get along with his dad, so he was upset about him being back in town."

"Annie. I just have to blurt this out. I know he slept here last night."

"You do?" Her eyes widened. "Did you come in my room?"

"Always."

"But my door was shut."

"Annie. That's not the point. It's not okay. I don't want you having sleepovers with men in our house."

She set the bowl down and uncrossed her legs. "But nothing happened. We didn't have sex, if that's what you think. We've only been hanging out a couple of weeks."

I fell back into the sofa cushion. "Do you really expect me to believe that?"

"Yes," she said, her voice harsh. "FYI, I don't lie. Got that?" She stood in a huff. Tears welled in her eyes. "If you had snooped around a little more you would have seen that we were fully clothed." She crossed her arms tight against her chest. "Custer was really upset. He didn't want to go home in case his dad showed up. He didn't have anywhere else to go." She wiped a tear away from her cheek. "I comforted him, okay? I swear—" Annie picked up the remote, switched off the show she had been watching, and threw it on the sofa. "Sometimes you're as bad as Dad."

"Oh, Annie." I stood and walked over to her. "I'm sorry. I didn't realize." I brushed her cheek. "I guess I jumped to conclusions."

"Why did you?"

"I don't think it's all that hard to understand. I mean, I was rather surprised to see him in your bed."

She gazed down at her feet and tucked her hair behind an ear. "Okay. I'll give you that." She looked up. "But what's with you? It seems like something is bugging you."

"I met Custer's dad, and I don't like him. He seems mean. I worried all evening that you two might run into him."

Annie's eyebrows furrowed. "What's he like?"

"Can we sit again?"

Annie nodded, and we sat in unison on the sofa.

"I don't trust him. He's sneaky and sarcastic. And he treated Custer badly."

"Custer is trying to avoid him. He's hoping he'll leave town soon."

"Tyler told me to tell you to stay out of his way. He said Butch can be disarmingly charming."

"Really?" Annie shook her head. Her soft brown hair swayed. "It's hard to believe they're brothers."

"Does Custer talk to you about his family much?'

"Not really. When he mentions his dad he tries to go all Lao Tzu on me and focuses on the moment, that kind of thing. It's nice for me when he does that." She smiled. "It's so lovely when someone is fully present, you know?"

"Yes. It's rare, but it sure is nice."

"He also tells me how lucky I am to have my family."

"He does?"

"Of course. Because it's true."

"I'm really sorry I jumped to conclusions. And I know you don't lie. But just for the record, I would like him to find somewhere else to stay while he's avoiding his father."

"He already has." She reached over and hugged me. "I am lucky."

I hugged her back and took in the sweet herbal scent of her hair. "I'm pretty lucky, too."

She ended the hug. "So, what about this weekend?"

"What about it?"

"Didn't Dad tell you? He's forcing me to go to Chevy Chase. He's threatening to cut off my college tuition if I don't."

"*What?*"

"Oh yeah. He is. Isn't that a lovely thing for a father to do?" Her voice was brimming with sarcasm. "But I don't want to go. I need to be here with Custer to support him." She flipped the remote end over end on her thigh. She eyed me warily. "Maybe you could talk to Dad?"

I sat back and stared at the blank television screen. "He already believes I'm keeping you here intentionally. I don't think he would listen to me."

"But I *can't* go. I can't abandon Custer."

I bit my lower lip. "Annie, I'm not sure you realize how important it is at this point in your life to figure things out with your dad. I don't mean to sound condescending. I think I'm actually speaking from experience."

"What do you mean? Your parents never got divorced."

"No, but my relationship with your grandfather was awkward. And after I moved out of the house, we didn't really have anything to talk about anymore. Your grandmother managed our relationship. So I moved to Maryland and rarely visited. Except once you were born, things changed. I wanted you to know him, so I started going back to Virginia. He adored you. Your grandmother used to complain that he hogged you. Do you remember?"

"Not really."

"Anyway, I regret not knowing him better. And when I finally realized there was a rift between us it was too late. He died in his sleep. And that was it. I know he may have not known what to do with me, but he was a good man. A principled man. I could have learned more from him if I had listened better."

"I can see what you're saying." Annie crossed her arms. "I don't feel like I even know Dad anymore. But maybe . . ." She gazed out the window.

I waited a moment. We were both thinkers, and we took our time understanding our emotions. "Maybe what?" I said after a bit.

She looked back at me and took a deep breath. "I think I'm still angry with him for having an affair. Does that sound plausible?"

"Oh yeah." I nodded my head. "Bull's-eye."

Annie let out a laugh. "That's not going to go away so easy."

"You just took the first step."

"That's true. Forward progress, right? That's what Dad used to say when he was trying to teach me to play golf. When I duffed the ball he would say, *At least you're closer to the pin.*"

"Really? I never knew that." Nice one, Ed, I thought. "So what are you going to do?"

"I haven't quite figured it out. But I have an idea."

I reached out and hugged her. "I love you, pumpkin."

Annie and I agreed popcorn was in order. I pulled out my old dented saucepan that I kept just for that purpose and went to work. Once the kernels had all exploded, I tossed it with butter and sprinkled it with a generous dusting of salt.

As we parked ourselves in front of the television to watch a movie, a roll of thunder vibrated the house. "Want to open the French doors?" I said.

"Okay. But can we close them if the storm gets too close?"

"Absolutely." A gust of wind blew through the room as I pulled open the doors, billowing the drapes and ruffling the newspaper. "Maybe a good storm will cool things off."

I sat back down, and Annie passed me the popcorn. She had chosen *Zombieland* for us to watch on demand. During the first ten minutes she cautioned me to cover my eyes, and I willingly complied. I could hear a lot of disgusting noises, but when the introduction was finished she said it was okay to watch. "It will still be a little gross," she said, "but it's worth it." She popped a piece of popcorn in her mouth. "Besides, you've got to expand your repertoire. You don't even know what a zombie is."

Although Annie spent much of the movie texting with Custer, it was therapeutic for me to have her by my side for a couple of hours. And I found myself laughing pretty hard at the movie, which Annie appreciated. It felt good to laugh. I was sure helping Doris was the right thing to do, but investigating a murder can put a damper on your mood. So I focused on the now: my Annie, a good laugh, and a delicious dose of butter and salt.

After she went up to bed, phone in hand, I opened my laptop and logged on to Facebook. The night sky had been performing quite a production, with continuous flashes of lightning that illuminated the towering thunderclouds, an occasional bolt zigzagging to earth.

I decided it was time to amp up the sleuthing on Facebook. I found Jamie Fiddler on Lori's Family and Relationships page. I clicked on his picture, and his timeline appeared on the screen. His posts were private, but I could see he had 467 friends. In his profile picture he was wearing aviator sunglasses, shirtless, with his hands stretched out and a sparkling ocean behind him. He was single, and his interests included *Call of Duty,* hunting, women, and zombies. Well, that was something we had in common. Trust my Annie to keep me current. I sent him a friend request, unsure if he would accept it.

I hadn't spent much time on Facebook, with everything else going on in my life. But I'd met a lot of people lately. Who knew what I might find out? So I sent friend requests to Kevin, Jake, Jackson, and Gretchen. I liked the pages of the Cardigan Tavern, the Yellow Labrador Winery, and Gretchen's place, the Inn at Sommerville Farm. The photo gallery of the inn was stunning. If Glenn didn't take Gretchen up on her offer for tea, I certainly would.

I jumped when a loud crack sounded from just across the river. A long, low, roll of thunder followed. Instantly, the trees began swaying in the wind, their leaves rustling violently. The metallic scent of air thick with rain met my nose.

I noticed a Facebook message from Annie at the bottom of the screen.

---

can i sleep w/ you tonite? ; /

Yes! Be right up!!!

TWENTY-NINE

The next morning I busied myself in the kitchen experimenting with a Thousand Island dressing for my version of the New Orleans muffuletta sandwich. The oversized rolls baking in the oven filled my work space with a mouthwatering aroma. Just before I set them to bake I had formed them into oversized mounds and embellished the tops with melted butter and sea salt. Once I had perfected the recipe, I would e-mail the instructions to a bakery in town. We had an arrangement: I came up with the recipes and they prepared the bread and muffins for the week. This sandwich would include deli meats, olive tapenade, sliced Gruyere cheese, lettuce, fresh tomato, and my homemade dressing. So far my version wasn't spicy enough. I wanted it to have a nice, subtle kick. I was mincing a serrano pepper when my phone pinged. I looked over to see a text message from Doris.

Lori's upset. A private investigator was at the house. Can you pick me up?

I glanced over at Doris while the dogs encircled the car. "I should have brought you a scarf." I reached out and tried to flatten her curls with my palm.

"What do I care if my hair is a mess? Besides, I had fun." She got out of the car, clutched her purse, and headed for the house. "You know, Miss Rosalie, you could put a little more pressure on that gas pedal, if you ask me. You drive like you're my age."

Lori stood in the foyer and immediately ushered us into the kitchen. There were no cookies or steaming teapots on the table, only a few piles of mail and a littering of toast crumbs. "I just got off the phone with my lawyer. The sheriff has the murder weapon now, and I don't have an alibi. He says now all he needs is a motive and then he's gonna charge me with first-degree murder." Her eyes were wide. "First-degree murder, Doris. I could get the death penalty."

"At least you're not jumping to conclusions." Doris leveled her eyes with Lori's. "What happened with the investigator?"

"Nothing." Lori looked away. "I'm just upset, is all."

"Did he say he's looking for the money?" I said.

Lori's shoulder fell. "He thinks I know something."

"Everyone thinks you know something about that blasted money." Doris plopped down onto a chair. "You got any coffee or something, Lori?" She eyed the state of Lori's kitchen. "This place is a mess."

"I ran out of coffee. I don't like to go to the store." She twisted her fingers together. "Everyone stares at me."

"Well then," Doris said impatiently. "Clear your name and you can go to the moon to grocery shop if you want."

"Lori," I said, "is there any chance CJ stole that money?"

"Why does everyone keep asking me that? Do I look like I'm spending a bunch of money?"

"What about Jamie?" I said.

"What about Jamie?" Doris repeated, sitting straighter.

"Well . . ." I hesitated. "If CJ took the money, maybe Jamie knew about it."

"Now listen here, Miss Rosalie," Doris said, "I appreciate you trying to help, but if you go—"

"The investigator asked me the same question," Lori said, interrupting her.

Doris fell back into her chair. "Leave Jamie out of this."

"Doris, remember what I told you? We have to know the whole story in order to clear both of their names." I turned to face Lori. "Would CJ have confided in Jamie if he stole that money?"

"Why is everyone so certain CJ took the money?" Lori's voice was shrill.

We all turned to look toward the foyer when we heard the front door open.

"Hello?" Lori called.

Butch Wells ducked into the kitchen, an impish grin on his face. "Hey, Lori," he said, his eyes taking in the scene.

"Hey, Butch," Lori said. She smiled, then quickly checked our reaction.

"What do *you* want?" Doris asked.

"Just paying a call, is all." Butch smoothed his hand over his slicked-back hair. "And look who's here. It's Rosalie. Are you following me around, darlin'?"

My stomach tensed at the sight of him. He towered over us, his sheer presence emitting an ominous charge in the room. I slapped my hands on the table and pushed myself up to a stand. "Doris and I were just leaving."

"So soon?" His eyes danced with mischief as he set a bottle of Maker's Mark whiskey on the counter. "I was just about to break out the good stuff."

"Don't you have a job, Butch?" Doris said. "You know, like most people?"

"Sure I do. But I only work between vacations." He grinned. "Now, Lori, you going to have a drink with a thirsty man? I haven't seen you at the tavern, so I thought I'd bring the tavern to you."

"I'm tired, Butch. It's been a bad day."

He stood behind Lori's chair and massaged her shoulders. "That's why I'm here. You were my best friend's wife. You think I'd abandon you in your time of grief?"

Doris scowled at him. "You abandon everyone eventually." Her eyes darted over to me and back to her sister. "Good lord, Lori. Don't you see? You spending time with him? It's all the sheriff needs."

"What are you talking about now?" Lori said.

"Motive! Isn't that what he's wants?" She pointed at Butch. "And there he is, right in your kitchen."

Lori looked up at Butch. "But we're not doing anything."

Doris rolled her eyes and started toward the door. "How are we supposed to help you when you won't help yourself?" She yanked the door open and stepped outside.

Lori's eyes pleaded with me.

Butch stopped the massage but his hands remained on Lori possessively. "Ain't you going with her?"

THIRTY

Earlier in the week I had extended invitations to Janice, Glenn, Crystal, and Kevin to a wine tasting with Alessandra, an Italian-born woman who had married an Eastern Shore farmer named Bradley Cummings. Over many years they had worked together to convert his acreage into what was now the Yellow Labrador Winery.

On Wednesday evening, Alessa, as she preferred to be called, arrived at the café toting a case of wine while in three-inch pumps. I hurried to the door to let her in. She stepped inside as if she were in sneakers. Her perfume was divine. Her auburn hair had been piled onto her head in a haphazard yet elegant way and large gold hoops dangled from her ears. She set the wine on the bar and removed her Prada sunglasses, revealing eyes rich with liner and mascara. "Hello, Rosalie," she said, shaking my hand. "It's so wonderful to meet you in person." The trace of an Italian accent made her everyday words sound exotic and more compelling.

She set the box on the bar and dusted her hands together. I peered inside. "I'm so excited, Alessa."

"As am I. Now why don't you put the sparkling wine in the fridge to chill. It's already cold, but sparklings should be icy. Oh, and here, take a rosé and a chard." She lifted two more bottles from the carton.

"Good idea," I said, unable to contain my enthusiasm. As I headed into the kitchen I almost bumped into Glenn.

"Oh, will you look at that," he said, equally excited. "We're really doing this."

"I know. I hope it's all as good as that bottle of rosé we had."

"How can I help?"

"I've been working on my own version of a muffuletta sandwich. I sliced it into bite-sized pieces. If you carry that platter out, we can taste those as well."

"As in New Orleans? What a fantastic idea."

"Taste them first. But I think they're pretty delicious."

After refrigerating the wines, I returned to the dining room. Crystal had arrived and was showing something to Alessa. Janice charged in the front door next. She had put some effort into her appearance, wearing a pretty cotton dress with Jack Rogers sandals. "Hey, Snow White," I said, and brushed her cheek with a kiss. "You look cute."

"I'm in perimenopause. There is nothing cute about that."

"Rosalie," Glenn said as he set out a stack of turquoise napkins. "Did you know Janice was going through the change?"

"Why, no, Glenn. She hadn't mentioned it."

"Ha-ha," Janice said. "Very funny. But I can't help myself. Sorry if I'm tedious."

"You?" I said. "When you're here the fun factor shoots up a couple of notches. I'm just sorry you're suffering."

"Well, I am. But it seems we are all aware of that." She clapped her hands together. "So, what are we drinking? And more important, when do we start?"

"Oh, hey, Miss Janice," Crystal said over her shoulder. "I made your tincture."

"I highly recommend it," Alessa said. "I've been using Crystal's tinctures for over a year now, and I wouldn't do without them."

Janice's eyes widened. "*You* take them?" She looked at Crystal. "Well—what are you waiting for? I'll have three."

Crystal rolled her eyes. "Just put two drops under your tongue twice a day. It's in the refrigerator so it stays cold. And I put it in a brown bottle, so the light won't break down the essences."

"Crystal," I said, "you really know what you're doing."

"Don't forget I make teas, too, Miss Janice." Crystal slid her hands in the back pockets of her denim shorts. Her hair was free from its traditional braid, and thick wavy tresses flowed to her waist.

"I drink a cup of chamomile every night before I go to sleep," Alessa said.

I studied Crystal and Alessa who seemed completely comfortable together. "May I ask how you two know each other?"

Crystal frowned. "'Lessa?"

Alessa sat down in one of the bar chairs and propped her chin on her hand. "Hmm. Did we meet at the farmers' market?"

"Yes," Crystal said. "That's where. A couple of years ago. It's funny," she said as she sat down next to her. "I feel as if I've known you my whole life."

"And maybe even before that," Alessa said, and winked.

"Excited!" Kevin rushed in the front door. "Hello, I'm Kevin," he said to Alessa.

"Pleased to meet you." She stood and held out her hand. Instead of shaking it, Kevin leaned down and kissed it. Her hands were lovely, with incredibly long, slender fingers. Although she looked to be at least fifty, there wasn't an age spot to be seen. Crystal and I needed to talk.

"Everyone have a seat," I said. "Oh, wait." I went into the kitchen and took a wedge of Brie out of the oven. The cheese had begun to melt out of the rind in a creamy lava flow. I brought it out, along with some light crackers. "This will cleanse our palates."

"Excellent idea," Alessa said. "Let's start with the sparkling, Rosalie."

When I handed her the bottle, she peeled off the foil, and Crystal immediately put her fingers in her ears. Alessa stopped. "It won't be noisy. Not when it's done properly."

"You can never be sure," Crystal said, her shoulders hunched. "I just don't like being surprised."

"Here," Alessa said. "You do the honors." She held the bottle out to Crystal.

"Oh no, I couldn't." Crystal backed away from her.

"You can do it, my dear. It's always best to confront your fears." Alessa smiled warmly at Crystal, her lipstick a rich red. "Otherwise the fear can take over your life."

Crystal's arms dropped to her sides. "I knew you'd say something like that." She accepted the bottle, her face scrunched up in worry.

"First, let the cork out of its cage. And don't worry—it won't go anywhere until you want it to."

Crystal unwound the wire while holding the bottle at arm's length.

"See?" Alessa set the wire on the bar. "That's not so bad." She stood behind Crystal and wrapped her arms around her. "Champagne is one of God's gifts. It should be honored as such." Alessa placed Crystal's right hand on the cork. "Now you're going to remove the cork, see? But we aren't going to pop it out. We're going to massage it slowly."

Kevin leaned in. "I never knew opening champagne could be so sexy."

"I'm sorry, Kevin," Janice said flatly, "but what's more phallic than uncorking champagne?"

Crystal spat out a laugh.

"Hmm, you have a point, JJ," Kevin said.

"Rosalie, do you have a towel?" Alessa said.

I handed her the cloth I kept by the Mieles.

She put the towel over the bottle. "Now, you are in control, princess. Hold the neck of the bottle with this hand, and twist the cork with your right hand, ever so slowly."

Crystal's eyes were squeezed shut. "Am I doing it right?"

"You're doing just fine. Come on, my dear. Keep twisting. You get to decide when you are ready for it to release."

"Holy crap," Kevin said, and shifted in his seat.

"She's very good at this," Glenn said.

Crystal's forehead was furrowed, her cheeks a bright pink. She wiggled and twisted the cork until it at last emerged with a muffled pop. "Oh my gosh," Crystal said, a wide grin on her face. "I did it."

Alessa smiled and patted Crystal's back. "Now you can cross that off your bucket list."

"Yes." Crystal nodded enthusiastically. "Yes, I will."

"Rosalie, glasses, please. I believe Crystal has earned the honor of pouring," Alessa said. "Now let's see how you fill them. I'll bet you will know exactly when to stop and wait for the bubbles to die back without spilling a drop."

Crystal filled the glasses flawlessly, topping off one and then another. When she had finished, Alessa raised her glass. "To our brave beauty, Crystal Sterling."

We toasted, and Janice took a long sip. "Oh, this is yummers. And you're going to start serving Sunday brunches?"

"As soon as I can come up with the menu," I said.

"Are you going to have banana bread French toast?" Janice asked after finishing off her glass.

"I'm sorry," I said, almost choking on my wine. "What did you say?"

"Banana bread French toast. You mean you've never had it?"

"It sounds incredible," Kevin said.

"How have I never had that?" Glenn said, and frowned.

"It's an old family recipe. My kids love it." She held her glass out for Crystal to refill.

"I'll bet it would be good with my lavender honey," Crystal said.

"Lavender *honey*?" I said. "Crystal, sweetie, what else do you make?" I offered the Brie to Glenn. "And I am so putting banana bread French toast on the menu."

"With lavender honey," Kevin said, and dipped a cracker into the Brie.

THIRTY-ONE

As everyone gathered their belongings, I noticed Kevin stacking the dirty plates, and wondered if he would be willing to talk with me more about his and Jake's encounter with CJ. Although I knew the basics of the story, I wanted to know how it had impacted them. I walked over and began filling a tray with dirty glasses. "Kevin, I don't know about you, but I hate to leave so many unfinished bottles of wine just sitting around."

"What are you suggesting, girlfriend?"

"I'll be right back." I walked Alessa to the door, exchanged two quick cheek kisses with her, and waved goodbye to Glenn, Janice, and Crystal. I closed and locked the door and returned to Kevin. "Shall we?"

"I certainly wouldn't want the wine to go bad." Kevin sat at the bar. "Besides, we were only having little tastes. And what about the Brie?"

"Exactly," I said. "What will it be? We have a cab, a pinot grigio, and a rosé. I think Janice finished off the sparkling."

"How about the cab." Kevin dabbed at the Brie and licked his finger. "Poor JJ. I hope Crystal can help her."

"I know Italian women have great genes, but if she can help Janice the way she helps Alessa, Janice may be on the mend soon." I filled Kevin's glass and slid it over to him. I studied the bottles lined up on the bar. "I think I'll start with the pinot."

"Alessa is fabulous," Kevin said. "Jake and I will have to go out to her winery. He already ordered that case of rosé."

"And what a surprise she's good friends with Crystal." I took a small sip. "That's what I love about this town. A fifty-year-old Italian bombshell is good friends with a twenty-five-year-old hippie who makes teas and tinctures. People seem so much more accepting of uniqueness here."

Kevin glanced at me sidelong. "I love you, darlin', but now you're in la-la land."

"Sorry." I sat next to him. "I hope that wasn't insensitive. Especially after your encounter with CJ." I gripped the stem of my glass and gazed over at him. "How awful was it, Kevin?"

"Beyond awful." Kevin took a long sip of wine. "Thing is, it didn't end there."

"What do you mean?"

"CJ didn't just walk away from Jake. I mean, he did that night, but then he started to harass us."

"Oh no," I said. "What did he do?"

"First he spray-painted nasty words on our mailbox. And two days after that incident, someone—well, it had to be CJ—slashed Jake's tires."

"Did you tell the sheriff?"

"No." He shook his head. "We talked about it, but we decided it would only make matters worse. We were hoping it would blow over and CJ would find someone else to pick on. But then he showed up at the college."

I swallowed hard. "And?"

"He went to President Carmichael's office and asked if he knew Jake was a—well, I won't repeat the word. Apparently he caused quite a ruckus."

"I've met President Carmichael. The man doesn't like controversy."

"I know he's not the most popular guy around here, but he's very good at his job."

"So you like him?"

"The guy's smart. Enrollment is way up. They're turning

more and more students away. And their rating has skyrocketed in that *U.S. News & World Report* list. One of the ways he's accomplished it is to attract good professors. And he knows how to keep them. Jake is a popular teacher. The lacrosse team has won their division four out of the five years since he's been there."

"So Carmichael ignored CJ?"

"Well, as much as a person can ignore that man. I think his secretary called security, and they barred him from campus."

"What was Jake's reaction?"

"It was bad. You see, Rosalie, I'm Jake's first openly gay relationship. He came out because of me. For most of his life he was the macho guy, trying to compensate for how he felt inside. This was as public as it had ever gotten for him."

"Top off?" I picked up the cab. Kevin nodded, and I filled his glass. "So how did you two meet?"

"At a bar in Philly. Jake would go out, but only if it was far enough away from Cardigan no one would recognize him. He finally told his family when we decided to move in together and—" He shook his head. "Anyway, Jake's father was not happy, to put it mildly."

"Sounds hard for Jake."

"It is, although once he made the decision it was like a weight had been lifted from his shoulders. We've been happy here."

"And CJ changed that?"

"Jake was beside himself with rage. I was worried about him. Frantic, actually. I begged him to tell the sheriff, but he said he would handle it his own way."

I pushed the small of my back into the chair. "And?"

"He never did anything. He didn't have to. The next day, CJ was dead." Kevin took another long sip of wine. "We couldn't believe it. We even had a little party out on the deck. I grilled salmon, and Jake broke into the good stuff. I'm sort of embarrassed to tell you that. But we did."

"Jake must be so relieved."

"You would think." Kevin's shoulders slumped forward. "But something isn't right with him. Not anymore." He peered over at me, his eyelids at half-mast. "Rosalie, I think I'm losing him."

That night I gave Annie a quick peck on the cheek and carried my laptop into bed. I logged on to Facebook and discovered all my friend requests had been answered. I felt instantly more popular. I clicked on a message notification.

C. James Fiddler

Hi Mrs. Hart. Thanks for the offer of friendship. Any news on my mom? I've been meaning to ask you, what did she tell you the night you were looking at her yearbooks? I've heard from Aunt Doris that you are a very good investigator. I'm curious why those yearbooks were of significance to you. I'll be in town in a few days. Maybe we could talk. I believe you know something I would want to know as well. Thanks, Jamie.

THIRTY-TWO

On Saturday, the Day Lily offered its first glasses of alcohol to the lunch crowd. In addition to Alessa's wine, I ordered two craft beers from a brewery in Delaware. Baby steps, I told my staff.

Jackson had eaten breakfast at the café and stayed straight through lunch. He was on his third pale ale when the sheriff arrived. "Good afternoon," I said. I picked up my tongs, but he waved me off.

"I'm done with those things. I'll have two coffees, black."

"Dieting?" I said. "Love interest, perhaps?"

He said nothing and hitched up his belt.

"Would you like some sweetener?"

"Did you know fake sugar makes you gain weight? And it gives you cancer."

I smiled to myself as I filled the second cup.

Jackson looked over at him. "Been on TV today, Joe?"

"Huh?" the sheriff said.

"Seems you do everything but your job these days." Jackson took a long slug of beer.

"Say what?" The sheriff faced him full on. "You got a bone you want to pick with me?"

"Why don't you figure out who the hell stole that money from the college," Jackson said. "Then half this town can get back to work."

"They hired a private investigator. It's not my business. And if they're taking their time, maybe it's because they don't want you all to go back to work. Maybe they found better workers. Ever think of that?"

Jackson stood. The legs of the chair squeaked against the hardwood as he shoved it back.

"What did you just say?"

I snapped the lids on the coffees. "You can run a tab, sheriff." I watched them closely as I wiped down the counter. "I'm sure you want to get back to work."

"What are you serving here?" The sheriff eyed Jackson's beer. "You got a license, Hart?"

"Yes, of course. Now, do you need anything else?"

"You haven't answered my question." Jackson stepped closer, his fists perched on his hips.

Butch Wells strolled in the front door, the familiar impish grin on his face. "You locking your back door now, Miss Rosalie?"

The sheriff and Jackson were staring each other down. Glenn had noticed and stood close by, punching in an order on the computer.

"Could you two please keep your voices down," I said.

Butch strode right toward the kitchen door. Glenn blocked his way. "I thought we told you you're not permitted back there."

"I'll just be a minute."

"Sheriff?" Glenn said. "We may need your assistance."

"Cool it, Wells," the sheriff said, and I exhaled a sigh of relief.

"Thank you, sheriff."

Butch stopped and took in the scene. He smiled widely. "Hey, Jackson, you ever figure out why that wife of yours keeps calling you a dog? She stopped me just the other day and said, *You know, Butch, my husband is a dog. Why is he such a dog?*"

"What?" Jackson cocked his head, taking in Butch's words. "Why, you—" He took off after him, sloshing his beer and knocking over a chair.

Butch shoved Glenn out of the way and hightailed it into the kitchen with Jackson, the sheriff, and a disheveled Glenn in pursuit.

The café fell silent. I hurried around the bar, righted the chair, and sopped up the beer. "I'm so sorry," I said. "Please, enjoy your lunch. Coffee is on the house." I caught Crystal's eye, and she nodded.

I could hear raised voices and scuffling in the kitchen. Most of me wanted to plug my ears and pretend this wasn't happening. But the rest of me started to move.

I rushed into the kitchen and took in the scene. Glenn's arm was braced against Jackson's chest, blocking him from Butch. Jackson's face was so red I worried he might have a coronary. The sheriff had Butch pinned against the wall. Custer stood in the middle, his arms outstretched, as if ready to tackle the first man to move.

I straightened my skirt and marched to the back door. "Excuse me, sheriff." Once he and Butch got out of the way, I opened the door. "Mr. Wells. You are not welcome here. If you return, I will file a restraining order against you."

The sheriff grabbed Butch's collar and shoved him into the alley. Butch stumbled, righted himself, and straightened his shirt. The sheriff slammed the door in his face.

I faced Jackson. "I know you are a very important customer, but I'm afraid I need you to leave, too."

"I haven't paid my bill," he said, his head hanging low.

"Next time," I said. "No worries."

"That Butch is nothing but trouble," Glenn said. He looked over at Custer. "How long does he usually stay in town?"

"Until he gets what he wants."

"And what exactly does he want?" the sheriff growled.

"How should I know?"

The sheriff stepped closer to Custer. "I think you do know."

Custer lifted his chin but said nothing.

"He came in here looking for you," the sheriff said. "Since when does he want to be around you?"

"Sheriff Wilgus," I said, stepping closer to Custer. "That's an awful thing to say."

Custer's eyes darted from face to face. They landed on mine. "I need to take a walk."

"Yes, of course. Now, will the rest of you please get out of my kitchen? I have a business to run."

Glenn and I stood side by side and watched the men shuffle out the door. Jackson stopped and half turned. His head was still hanging as low as a basset hound's. "I'm truly sorry, Miss Rosalie."

"It seems Butch Wells gets under everyone's skin. I don't blame you. I hope to see you tomorrow for our first champagne brunch. Do you like French toast?"

"Don't forget the oysters," Glenn said.

"Thank you both. You're too kind. And I may very well take you up on it, as long as I am still welcome." He shook his head and started out the door. "Got nothing better to do."

My shoulders fell when the door finally closed. "Oh my."

"Maybe rethink the beer?"

"Our first day serving alcohol, and we have a brawl." I faced Glenn. "You okay?"

He combed his hair back off his forehead. "I was a little worried there for a moment, but yes, I'm fine."

"Do you think Custer knows where that money is?"

"I do, indeed."

I crossed my arms and sank my teeth into my lower lip. "Glenn—"

"Do I think he stole the money?"

I nodded and peered up at him.

"I honestly don't know, Rosalie. I like the boy. I think he has some very good qualities. But what I don't know is how having Butch Wells for a father has impacted him. A hurt like that can run deep."

"Would you excuse me for a minute?" I went through the back door and found Custer leaning against the wall, a cigarette pinched between his fingers. "Did your father leave?"

"Yeah."

"Did you see which direction he went?"

Custer pointed.

"I'll be right back. Hold down the fort." I hurried down the alley and came to a crossroads. The small liquor store on the corner caught my eye. I walked to the window and peered in the cloudy window. Sure enough, Butch was inside scratching off a lottery ticket. After going through an entire stack, he tossed them back on the counter and pushed through the door. He squinted in the sunlight and pulled a pair of aviator sunglasses from the back pocket of his jeans. "Butch?" I said.

He looked startled. "What?"

"Can I ask you something?"

He half smirked. "I knew I would win you over. Women find it hard to resist me." He stepped closer.

"Yes, I've heard that about you." I crossed my arms. "You and CJ were best friends, right?"

"That's right. Thick as thieves. Always were."

"That's an interesting term," I said.

He placed his palm on the brick wall. "Yes, it is."

"He told you about the money. But why?"

"I didn't steal it."

"I know." I nodded my head. "I just don't understand why he told you."

Butch cleared his throat. "You want to know so bad? I'll tell you. You see, CJ called me a few days before he got shot. He said someone was going to kill him. And he was carrying his shotgun in his pickup to defend himself."

My eyes widened. "Did he say who?"

Butch took a deep breath and straightened his posture. "Nope. But he did tell me about the money. He knew I was down on my luck and wanted me to have it if he died. That's how good a friend he was."

"What about Lori? Why wouldn't he want her to have it?"

"She didn't want it. She told him to give it back. He didn't want all his hard work to go to waste, so he told me to come get it."

I stared at the ground. So Lori has known all along that CJ stole the money. I looked up at Butch. "That's why you're spending time with Lori. Why didn't you just take the money and go away?"

"Well, you see, little lady, the problem is CJ didn't tell me where he hid it. And Lori claims she doesn't know."

"But she must."

"Of course she does."

"Why didn't CJ want Jamie to have it?"

"Ha!" he said. "You forget Jamie's a damn cop?"

I looked at my watch. "One more question. Why do you think Custer knows?"

"I don't think, I know. That's why CJ fired him. And he told my boy if he tattled, he'd pin it on him. And my boy's in enough trouble as it is."

"Well, if he hasn't told you by now, he isn't going to. Can't you just leave him alone?"

"Ah, you're sweet, aren't ya? But you just toddle on back to your little café. And don't go telling the sheriff any of this. If he knows Lori has the money, he'll lock her up and throw away the key, and then what will you tell old Doris Bird?"

THIRTY-THREE

The four Day Lily employees were so spent by the time I flipped the sign, we barely spoke to one another. We went about our closing duties like automatons. Glenn and Crystal both admitted that despite the tussle, their tips had doubled as a result of the beer and wine, just as Crystal predicted.

"Thank you both so much," I said and ushered them out the door. "I'll finish up."

Before Custer left, I asked if he had somewhere to stay.

"I'm hanging with a buddy tonight. Annie has other plans."

"Good." I smiled. "Wait. Annie has other plans?"

He shrugged. "I don't control her. She can do whatever she wants."

I wondered if I had scared her with my warnings about Butch. "If your plans fall through, my sofa isn't too bad."

He hesitated. "No need." He dropped his chef's jacket on the counter and walked out the door. I watched as he lit a cigarette, mounted his motorcycle minus a helmet, and drove away.

After a day like today, I relished being alone in the café. Once it was clean and ready for tomorrow, I dimmed the lights and found a Puccini opera on Sirius. The speakers were strategically placed around the room, giving it the acoustics of a grand theater.

I prayed the brunch tomorrow would be a success, but after today, worry of a repeat performance of this afternoon gave me a pulsating headache. At least Annie wasn't going to be with Custer tonight. That was a relief. Butch wasn't going to give up. And he was certain Custer knew the whereabouts of the money.

I slid several loaves of banana bread into the oven and propped the kitchen door open with a wedge. I was still experimenting with the recipe and ran out of time to send one to the bakery. But I didn't mind making them myself. For this batch I added a tablespoon or two of cinnamon. The aroma saturating the air filled me with nostalgia for wintry mornings as a child when my mother would make me cinnamon toast slathered with butter.

I decided to polish the marble counter while I waited for the bread to finish. Next I attacked the floor with some good oil. It had undergone its first beer spill, and I wanted to protect it.

I startled when I noticed a face peering in the window. It was a man who looked to be at least six feet tall. I tried to make out his face but it was backlit by the setting sun. I jumped when he rapped on the glass with his knuckles.

Whoever it was could certainly see me, so I flipped the dead bolt and opened the door. "Ed?"

"Hello, Rose. I thought you'd never let me in."

I swallowed hard. He was wearing the cologne I'd selected for him long ago, a clean, crisp scent that made me think of sailing and fresh ocean spray. I looked up into his bright blue eyes; his handsome, tanned face; the graying sideburns that gave him dignity. "What on earth are you doing here?"

"Annie invited me out for dinner. Didn't she tell you?" He looked around the room and stepped inside. "Rose, this place is stunning."

I closed the door behind him. "Thank you. It isn't very big."

"But it feels big. How did you pick this color?"

"Honestly?" I stuffed my hands into my apron pockets. "I studied photos of Tuscan hillsides."

He turned around. "How clever." He smiled playfully with only one side of his mouth curling upward. I knew that smile. It always reminded me of Harrison Ford.

The music reached a crescendo. Ed walked over to the bar and ran his fingers over the polished marble. "You did it, Rose. You followed your dream."

It felt oddly familiar to share such a moment with him. "Thank you, Ed."

He walked toward the chalkboard and read the special Crystal had already posted. "Banana bread French toast? Is that what I smell?"

"Yes," I said. "Oh, that reminds me, I need to take the loaves out of the oven."

When I returned from the kitchen, Ed was seated at the bar staring at the Mieles, chin in hand. "I would come here," he said. "Even in DC with all the choices, I would come here."

"What time are you meeting Annie?"

"Not until seven. I wanted to get here in time. You never know with the Bay Bridge."

"Would you like a beer? Oh, and I have sparkling wine."

"I would love a wine. Rose, I just can't believe this place. I really can't."

I retrieved a bottle from the refrigerator and stood on my tiptoes to reach two glasses. I took off my apron, rounded the counter, and sat at the bar. "The view is different from here," I said as I eased the cork out of the bottle.

"You open champagne now? What else don't I know about you?"

I looked over at him, feeling confused. "That's an odd question. And I have no idea how to answer it. How about you go first?"

He shook his head. "Okay, got it. We won't go there."

I filled his glass and held it out for him. "I thought you were angry with me."

"Once you told me about the infatuation, I realized what I was up against. I was about to let it go, until Annie invited me over." He accepted the glass and sipped, his face relaxed immediately. "Did you tell her to do that?"

"No. It was her idea."

"And?"

"And what?"

"You said something helpful to her. I know that. And after I read your e-mail, I realized you would never encourage Annie to stay away from me. Even after everything I've done. You don't have it in you."

"Thank you for realizing that." I lifted my glass. "Cheers. To Annie—our wonderful, sweet, precious girl."

"I'll drink to that." After a healthy swallow, Ed set the glass down. "I've really missed her."

I thought for a moment. I didn't want to tell him what to do. He and Annie were making progress. But I still felt he was going to miss out on an opportunity. "Can I tell you a story?"

He cocked his head. "A story?"

"It's about my parents. I think it might be helpful. Or maybe not."

"I always liked your parents, so . . . of course." His face was peaceful, the worry lines less pronounced, as if he too was feeling a little nostalgic.

"You know how much I loved my father, but I'm not sure you knew that he always seemed just out of reach when I was growing up. It made him seem a little on the cold side to me."

"Are you saying I'm cold?" Ed's posture stiffened.

"Just listen for a minute. One evening when my family was sitting down to dinner, I could sense some tension between my parents. I always picked up on their disagreements, even though they tried to keep them private. My mother would pick at her food or stare across the table at my father, her eyes betraying hurt or sometimes anger. Eventually, she would excuse herself and take a walk, or say she had a headache and go lie down."

Ed rubbed his chin. "That's better than my parents. They said whatever they felt like anytime and anyplace. And often at a very loud volume."

I gazed over at him. "So there's some insight into why you remain so measured, even when you're upset."

"It is much more civilized. I think that's one of the reasons I was attracted to you. You rarely raised your voice." He cleared his throat. "Anyway."

"Right." I sipped some wine. "So, on the evening in question, my mother was doing the 'stare across the table' thing and my father was methodically chewing his food and avoiding her eyes. When my mom stood, we all tensed, knowing it was time for her pronouncement. But that night she stayed in place for a moment, then walked over to my father, stood behind him, and gripped the back of his chair. My brother and I worried what she might do. But instead of making a scene, she leaned down and whispered in his ear, loud enough that we could hear. *I'll let you in on a little secret, Charles. When a woman says she's leaving the room, most times she wants her man to come after her.* I swear, the way she sashayed out of that room was incredible. Grace Kelly couldn't have made a better exit."

Ed's brows dipped. "So, what did your father do?"

"What would you have done?"

"I'm not really sure. I think I wouldn't have wanted to indulge the game-playing."

"But you see, that's the thing. I don't think it was a game. I think she was communicating with him better than she ever did with her headaches and long walks."

Ed fell back in his chair. "He followed her, didn't he?"

"Oh yeah."

"Really?" Ed laughed. "That's a good story. So what are you trying to tell me?"

"I'm telling you to go after Annie. Help her to feel you want her company. And don't make her do all the work."

Ed stared off as if considering my words. Eventually he sat forward and picked up his glass. "Tell me about this friend of hers. Where does he go to school?"

I hesitated. I wasn't prepared to describe Custer to Ed. I wanted Annie to do that. "He's taking a break from school."

Ed set his glass down. "Wait, he doesn't go to Duke?" He scowled. "Is he from *Cardigan*?"

"He's my cook," I said quietly.

"Are you serious? Rose, what are you doing? Our daughter goes to Duke University. She went to the Maret School in Washington, DC. If I have my way, her engagement will be featured in the *New York Times*. What do you mean she's dating your cook?" He emphasized the word *cook*, spitting out the consonants.

"It's not like I set them up on a blind date. Annie came to the café the other day, and they met. The next thing I knew, they were hanging out." I started to defend Custer but stopped. Even I was worried about the relationship, but for different reasons than Ed.

"So this is what happens when she lives out here in the boonies with you?"

I slugged back the rest of my wine. "Honestly, Ed? It could have happened anywhere, and with either of us. In case you haven't noticed, she isn't quite as interested in pleasing us since the divorce."

"What are you talking about? And can you please refill my glass?"

There were two empty seats between us, and I was glad of it. After shoving the bottle over to Ed, I clasped both hands around the stem of my glass. "It's not about who is to blame for our divorce. But it happened, and Annie took it hard. As any child would, no matter what her age. She's disappointed in us. And she sees us as having failed at something very important. And maybe, for the time being, she's lost a little respect for us."

"I never thought about it that way." Ed's head dropped forward. After a time he looked up. "So what's this guy like?" His voice had softened.

"Way too good-looking."

"Oh, not good. Family?"

"He's Tyler's nephew—the man who leases my land, whom I admire and respect. But . . ."

Ed's shoulders slumped. "But what?"

"I don't know much about the rest. But Custer—"

"Wait, his name is *Custer*?"

"It's Cardigan, Ed."

"Exactly."

"Look, I'm not going to defend him. He's a good worker. That's all I know. And Annie seems smitten. We have to let her choose who she sees, whether we like it or not."

"I don't agree," Ed said flatly.

"Please judge for yourself. Why don't you include him tonight?"

"I haven't seen Annie in a month. I'm not going to share her with some native Cardiganite."

"Ed?" I took a yoga deep breath. "The situation is what it is. But maybe having you around will help her make smarter decision. Remember my story?"

"Go after her." Ed passed his hands through his hair. He picked up his phone from the bar and glanced at it. "I need to go."

"Of course," I said. "I hope you have a nice dinner with Annie."

Ed stood and faced me, his head dipped a little. "I hope I do, too."

"I appreciate you stopping by. The café is a humble little place but it means a lot that you like it."

"I do. I like it a lot." Ed huffed out a sigh. "You look good, Rose. Really good."

"Thank you." I let go of my glass and placed my hands in my lap. "I guess I've finally found a new normal."

"Oh. Well, good for you." Ed eyed the room again. "I would

definitely come here." I watched as he walked to the door. "Say, how the heck do I get to the Crab Shack?"

"Take a right and keep going until you reach the river. Oh, and don't order the crab cake. All filler. But the fish and chips are to die for."

He studied me. "Take care, Rose." He lingered a moment, as if memorizing my face, then turned and made his exit. The CLOSED sign bounced on the glass as he shut the door.

THIRTY-FOUR

On Monday I spent most of the morning at the house, getting organized, paying bills, and placing orders for the café. Sunday's brunch had been sublime. Something about serving sparkling wine brightened the mood of the day, as if it had instantly become a special occasion. Instead of the raised voices and angry retorts of the previous afternoon, the patrons spoke in hushed tones. Napkins were placed neatly in laps; parents smiled at their children; coffee was sipped delicately, a raised pinky or two in the air. It was as if Miss Manners were overseeing the room. There is something to be said for civility. I had always thought Judith Martin should have run for president.

My stomach growled, reminding me I hadn't eaten anything more than a cup of yogurt four hours earlier. I stood from my desk, stretched my back, and headed for the kitchen. I found Bini seated at the table in her Barclay Meadow T-shirt. She stared out the window, chin propped in her hand. I'd never seen her idle before.

"Hey," I said as I headed for the refrigerator. "You okay?"

She looked over at me, her forehead deeply furrowed.

I started to open the refrigerator but stopped. "Is everything okay, Bini?"

She shook her head. "Tyler is mad at me."

"That doesn't sound like Tyler. Are you sure you didn't misunderstand him?"

"I'm sure. He's mad."

"How do you know?"

"We were fertilizing the tomatoes, and he told me to take a break."

"Maybe he was just being kind." I smiled. "You do work awfully hard."

"No," she said, still looking puzzled. "He's never said that before."

"I wonder what happened." I crossed my arms and thought for a moment. "Bini, would you like to take a walk with me?"

"Why?"

"It's such a pretty day. I think it's finally cooled off a little. And walking has a way of bringing things into focus. Don't you think?"

"We're just going to walk? We aren't going anywhere?"

"Maybe we could stroll around the fields. You could show me what's been planted."

Bini finally stood, and we walked outside together. We rounded the house and followed the tractor path toward the vegetable gardens. Although Tyler still grew the major crops—wheat, soybeans, and corn—he now reserved several acres for produce including fruit trees, vegetables, and herbs.

Bini walked with purpose, and I had trouble keeping up. In an attempt to slow the pace, I broke off a wheat tuft and popped it in my mouth. "Want one?"

She stopped and looked at me. "I guess." She watched as I snapped another one off for her.

I chewed on the stalk while we walked. Eventually Bini slowed. "So, what on earth makes you think Tyler is angry, Bini?"

"Simple. He told me to go away." Bini's tone was without affect, but her face looked pinched, her eyes tensed.

"Did he say take a break or go away?"

"Same difference."

"And he never said that before?" I said, trying to match her demeanor. "That must be perplexing."

Bini walked on, chewing on the stalk of wheat as if it were her last meal. "He was doing it wrong."

"I'm sorry?"

"Fertilizing the tomatoes. He had the chicken compost too far away from the plants."

"And you told Tyler this?"

"Of course. That's why he hired me. Because of what I know."

My mind raced with possible responses. But Bini and I hadn't really figured out our common ground. "You are very smart," I said.

She eyed me, as if checking to see if I was being sarcastic. "Most people don't care."

"And yet, when you know something that someone else doesn't, it must feel like a duty to tell them they're wrong."

"I guess that's right."

"As a woman, you certainly don't want to fall into the trap of taking care of a man's ego."

"I've never done that in my life."

"Good for you."

We were walking along the river, where trees and shrubs lined the banks in order to prevent runoff. I heard the high-pitched cry of an osprey. I watched as it dived out of sight, emerging soon after with a wiggling fish in its talons. It flew away with labored flaps, the fish heavy and struggling in its grasp.

"You know, Bini, I hope you don't mind, but I want to share something with you. I mean, we're walking, right?"

"I don't really have a choice if you do or don't."

I took and deep breath, trying not to react, and decided to continue. "I've been thinking a lot about my father lately. He died almost twenty years ago, and I can't stop wondering if our relationship could have been closer." We had fallen in sync, left foot then right. "And I wonder how it affects my relationships now. For instance, I wonder if I am always trying to please people because I never seemed to be able to please him."

"My daddy and I get along just fine."

"Lucky you." I smiled over at her. "Do you have siblings?"

"Older sister. She's married. Too many rug rats."

"Is she close with your dad?"

"More my mom. She's over there all the time with the kids. The mess drives my daddy crazy."

We rounded a corner, and I admired the neat rows of small apple trees, their foliage a deep forest green. "Is he as smart as you?"

"Smarter."

"So what do you do when you think he's wrong about something?"

Bini tossed the wheat stalk and sank her hands into her front pockets. "I tell him."

"And how does he take it? Because I know my father wasn't terribly interested in my opinions."

"He explains. Sometimes he gets a tone. But then I realize he's right. I just didn't see it his way."

"And then you're back on track?"

"We're never off track. We don't talk all that much. But we do stuff. Now that he stopped farming, he's building purple martin houses. We sell 'em at the farmers' market."

"Those birdhouses on the tall poles?"

"Right. Purple martins eat mosquitoes. They need to be in open spaces."

"I'd like to get one for the farm. If you pick one out, I'll pay you for it."

We walked in silence for a bit. Then Bini said, "Maybe you should think about what was good with your dad, not bad. Like, maybe you should think about your similarities with him."

"Oh." My eyes widened as I allowed the wisdom of her words to sink in. "You know, Bini, that's actually a good idea."

When we reached the end of the apple tree orchard, I spotted Tyler in the tomato plants.

Bini stopped walking. "I'm supposed to stay away from him. And I need this job."

"I haven't seen Tyler since our shared cup of coffee this morning. Let's go and say hi."

Bini looked at me, eyes wary. "You first."

"Good afternoon, ladies." Tyler sank his pitchfork into the ground and held the top with both hands. "Out for a stroll?"

"Yes, actually," I said. "We've been talking. Isn't that right, Bini?"

She nodded.

I cocked my head and smiled. Tyler tugged on the bill of his cap. "You two are making me nervous."

"I'm sorry," Bini blurted out. "I'm sorry for telling you how to do your job."

Tyler's head reared back a little. "You can say what's on your mind, Bini. That's why I hired you."

"You sure didn't like it an hour ago."

"It sounds like there's more than one way to fertilize a tomato," I said.

Tyler grinned. "Is that a fact?"

I shrugged. "And I don't know any of them. I used to buy the stuff at the hardware store. All you had to do was pop off the top and shake out the little pellets."

"Okay, Bini, here's what I was trying to tell you," Tyler said. "The thing about chicken-manure compost is it's full of nitrogen. If you get it too close to the stalk, it can kill the plant. Even if it's not directly touching the plant, the tomatoes will still benefit."

"But I wasn't—" Bini stopped. "Maybe I was."

Tyler walked over to the small trailer behind the tractor and grabbed a large plastic jug of water. His Adam's apple bobbed as he drank. His Barclay Meadow T-shirt was dirty, his jeans hanging low on his narrow frame. I wondered what he was thinking. Had I meddled?

He set down the jug and wiped his mouth with the back of his hand. "You ready to get back to work? I'd like to get these tomatoes knocked out in another hour or so."

Bini walked over to the trailer and picked up a shovel.

"Why don't I go back to the house and make some iced lattes? I'm working on a black bean soup, too, if you get hungry when you've finished here." I started to go but stopped. "Thank you, Bini. I really enjoyed our talk. Your insights were very helpful."

Bini gave me a small wave, placed her foot on the shovel, and plunged it deep into the soil.

I jumped when I realized Tyler was behind me. I turned around. He was staring at me hard, his hands on his hips. "Just when I thought I had you all figured out."

The close proximity caused my heart to thud in my chest. "A lot of people make black bean soup."

He stepped closer. I could feel the heat radiating from his body. "There's a lot to you, Rosalie Hart. You can still surprise me when not many folks can."

THIRTY-FIVE

The sun was dipping low in the sky as I drove into town to get my paper. I buzzed the convertible top down and detected the scent of pine trees mixed with a hint of woodsmoke in the air. I tried not to think about Tyler, how it felt to be so close to him, the way he looked at me with those green eyes. No, I scolded, and eased the car around a curve in the road that mimicked the river's path. Think about black bean soup. A little cumin added a nice touch of warmth, but it needed something else. Maybe Tyler could find me some fresh sweet corn. *Tyler.* No. A side of corn bread would be delicious.

Doris was perched behind the counter of Birdie's Shoe Store, her arms folded. The chairs were vacant, and I guessed she would be closing soon. Lately the once-reliable hours of operation at the shop had become erratic. Some days the doors were locked as early as three in the afternoon.

"I miss bringing you bread," I said. "Maybe I should start that up again."

She rolled her eyes. "That's all I need, to feel even more like I should be giving you money." She bent over and picked up my *Post*. "Anything new?"

"Yes. But I don't really know how to tell you this."

"Tell me what?"

"I'm pretty sure CJ stole the money from the construction site."

Doris's jaw dropped. "How sure?"

I peered up at her. "Ninety-nine point nine percent?"

"Does Lori know?"

"I think so. Doris, let's be careful how we play this, okay?"

Doris frowned. "Why can't we go over there right now and

confront her? What if the sheriff finds out?" She sat hard on her stool. "This is horrible news, Miss Rosalie."

"But at least we have the motive. Well, I think we do. I have one other theory, but I need to explore that a little more." My shoulders fell. "I don't want it to be true. But it could be."

"So where is the money?" Doris's voice cracked.

"I don't know. But Butch Wells knows about it, and he's trying to find it."

"So that's why he's hanging around Lori. I'm surprised he hasn't tried to force her to tell him."

"I thought about that, too. But if he can sweet-talk her into telling him, then no one will know he's run off with it. He could persuade her, I think. If he takes it, she doesn't have to deal with it."

"But that doesn't tell us who killed CJ—and if we can't find out who did, she's no better off."

"Agreed."

"So what do we do?"

"I haven't quite figured that out yet. I need to have a powwow with Glenn. But if Lori has the money, it could lure out the killer."

"Maybe Butch killed him. Did you ever think about that? If he knew CJ had the money, he'd probably do it in a heartbeat. CJ always said Butch was his best friend, but Butch Wells doesn't have any friends. He doesn't care about anyone but himself."

"Yes, I think there is a strong possibility Butch killed CJ."

Doris looked out the window and nudged her glasses up her nose. "Speaking of Mr. Glenn, he's out there in the park. You just missed him."

"Really? Maybe I'll go sit with him."

"Three may be a crowd," Doris said.

"Three?"

"He's talking with that English woman who runs the inn. What's that place called? The Inn at somewhere?"

"Gretchen?" I said. "*Really*?" I walked over to the smudged glass door and peered out. They were seated on an ornate wrought-iron bench facing the fountain in the park across the street. I could just make out the backs of their gray heads, dipped together as if in a serious discussion. "Oh, Doris." I looked back at her. "This is exciting."

"Don't go playing matchmaker. Nothing good ever comes from that."

"I won't. Glenn says he isn't ready, that he already had the love of his life. But Gretchen has been persistent. She comes to the café almost every day we're open. You should see the way she looks at him. I think *moony* is an understatement."

"Well, if it happens on its own, I'm happy for Glenn. He's a good man. But I agree with him about feeling lucky you got it right the first time. Sometimes one is all you need."

THIRTY-SIX

As I walked to my car, I wondered if I was on the right track. Was I deliberately ignoring Kevin and Jake as suspects? I slid into my seat and fished my phone out of my purse. I texted Kevin.

How is Jake?

I waited for a response. I had another day off tomorrow. Maybe he would be up for a talk. My phone chimed.

Not good. He left an hour ago. Said he needed to be alone. My guess is he's at the tavern. I'm really worried.

I typed quickly.

Would you like me to go and talk with him?

The talk bubble appeared immediately.

Yes! I love you!!!

The bar was quiet, with just a handful of people occupying the stools. Chuck approached immediately. "I sure am glad to see you," he said. "I was worried you didn't like the place."

"Are you kidding? I love it here. Glenn and I are excited to have discovered it. I've just been very busy."

"Blue Point?"

"Oh my goodness, yes."

"Coming right up," he said as he filled my pint glass.

"So, Chuck, when you get a moment, I need some advice."

"It's a Monday. Everyone spent their money over the weekend. I've got all night."

I took my first sip. "Oh, that is even better than I remembered. I would serve this at the café, except I would never compete with you."

"You serving spirits now?"

"Just some local beer and wine. But that's my problem. One of my customers drank three beers in less than an hour on Saturday, and I had myself a skirmish."

"You tussled with a customer?"

"Everyone but me. Let's see, we had the sheriff, Butch, Jackson, and then Glenn and Custer tried to break it up."

"You don't say? In a café?"

"In the kitchen, no less. So what do you do when someone is drinking too much? Cut them off? Maybe I shouldn't have served Jackson that third beer."

"Jackson?"

"Yes. He's a regular. And he's always been very affable."

"He's a regular here, too, and he almost got into it with a tourist this weekend. I'm telling you, it's like everyone in town is on edge these days. Ever since CJ was killed. I get arguments breaking out in here all the time. You know, you just can't have people shooting each other in a small town. And whoever did it hasn't been caught." He leaned in. "Do you think it's the zombies?"

"Maybe. Perhaps they dug up a burial ground or something over at the college. You know with zombies it's a virus."

"Now how do you know that?"

"I have a twenty-one-year-old daughter." I smiled and took a sip.

"So you must be savvy with the social media, too. Selfies on Instagram?"

"No. I have short arms."

Chuck picked up a rag. "Well, as I was saying, I wish the sheriff would just figure this out so we can all go back to normal. Whatever *that* is, anyway. Speaking of zombies, your friend is at the other end of the bar nursing a bourbon."

"Jake?"

"Yeah, Jake. How did you know?"

I narrowed my eyes. Then I spotted him slumped over a glass.

"Kevin is worried, so I offered to talk to him."

"He's been here every night this week."

"Was he ever with Kevin?"

"Alone."

I straightened my spine. "I hope he'll talk with me."

"Good luck. He's been monosyllabic with me. I don't know what's eating him, but something is."

"Wish me luck," I said as I picked up my beer with the napkin still underneath and approached Jake. I sat down and rested my elbows on the bar before he even noticed me.

"Hi, Jake," I said, keeping my voice soft.

He looked up. His dark eyes drooped at the corners; his usually bright, cheery face was drawn, as if the heaviness of his heart exerted a gravitational pull on his skin.

"Hey, Rosalie." He sat up a little and placed his palm over his glass. "Jim Beam. My new best friend."

"I have a good friend who drinks bourbon with coffee. He calls it *grounds for divorce.*"

Jake nodded in appreciation. "Clever guy?"

"Very." I paused. "Um, Jake? Not to state the obvious, but you seem blue."

"I'm just trying to figure some things out, is all." He sipped his drink. "Not making much progress, though."

"I'm a good listener."

"That doesn't surprise me." Jake leaned forward, his elbow on the bar, his hand tangled in his dark curls. "Kevin said he told you about the crap CJ pulled on us."

"Yes. Including his visit to President Carmichael's office."

"He outed me."

"Didn't the president already know? I mean, you and Kevin are a couple. An adorable couple, I might add."

"Carmichael and I never acknowledged it openly. We had an unspoken agreement to keep my life private, especially in front of the lacrosse team. Carmichael knows how to keep John Adams in the limelight. He's a public relations genius. So I went along with him. Preferred it, actually."

"And you feel you can't do that anymore?"

"It's more than that." Jake flopped back in his chair and drained his drink. He caught Chuck's eye and nodded. "You sure you want to hear this?"

"Let me go first." I gripped my glass. "I know a little of what you've experienced. I mean, when it comes to living with a stigma. When my husband asked for a divorce very suddenly two years ago, it seems I had been branded with a new label. I could practically hear the whispers: '*Ed* is divorcing *her*.' And because he was the one who wanted out, everyone wondered what was wrong with me. Did you know a friend of mine asked me if I hated sex?"

"No way." Jake let out a laugh. "Someone really said that?"

"She did. People jumped to conclusions trying to figure out what was so wrong with me that Ed ended the marriage. I think they do that to feel better, maybe explain why it won't happen to them. So not only did I feel unlovable, I felt like a pariah. Labels can be devastating. To all of a sudden be lumped into a group and pushed into that box . . . it was hard to just be myself. I always wondered what people were thinking but not saying."

"I never thought about how it must feel to be divorced. So this was your husband's idea and not yours?"

"I loved being married. And I loved my family. I'm not saying my marriage was perfect, but I never would have considered divorcing Ed. It wasn't an option I'd ever entertained."

Jake slapped his thighs. "Now I feel worse."

Chuck delivered another glass. "You walking?" he said to Jake.

"I am," he replied.

Chuck winked at me and disappeared.

I studied Jake. "Are you considering leaving Kevin?"

"It's not because I don't love the guy. I'm crazy about him. I mean, who isn't?" Jake looked over at me, eyebrows raised. "But I don't know if I'm cut out for this lifestyle. I've been in the closet my whole life, and I've been okay with it. I've had relationships, but they were always discreet. I mean, I'm an athlete and a teacher. I love what I do. And I love the esteem I have earned from others. To think some SOB can try to yank that all away from me is too much to take."

"But you and Kevin have a home together."

"Which is exactly what I don't think I can do anymore. God knows it would make my father happy. He hasn't spoken to me in three years. My baby sister won't bring her kids around me anymore. The only family member I hear from is my mom. She sneaks out here when she can. Or we meet in DC for dinner. But, Rosalie, I can see the pain in her eyes. My being openly gay is tearing my family apart."

My heart ached for Jake. I wanted to offer him advice, but I had none to give.

"It doesn't help that the bastard is dead. You'd think it would, but it doesn't. The damage was already done."

"Except maybe he wouldn't have stopped," I said. "Who knows what he might have come up with?"

"Well, he was stopped. Once and for all." Jake slugged back half his drink.

"Yes, he certainly was." I sipped my beer. "Have you talked with Kevin about this?"

"It's going to kill him."

"So you've made a decision, then?"

"Depends on when you ask me."

"Do you think the torment will go away if you go back to hiding an important part of who you are?"

"It's a different kind of torment, isn't it? And it does feel good to be with a guy I love and see him every night and make him coffee every morning."

"I get that," I said, and took a sip of my beer.

"We share so much—it's nothing like just hooking up at clubs.

And he needs me; I know that. I like being needed." He exhaled a rough laugh and looked over at me. "Freakin' mess, right?"

I placed my hand over his. "I hope you won't let one man change the course of your life. It seems to me you and Kevin have settled here in Cardigan. You are both very well liked. Maybe your family will eventually come around. It takes time."

"I appreciate that, Rosalie. I really do. But I'm afraid it's too late for all that." He signaled Chuck for another drink. When Chuck arrived, Jake asked him to turn on the Orioles game. That was it. End of discussion.

"Jake?"

He looked over at me but said nothing.

"Take care of yourself. And I'm here if you ever need to talk." I left a ten-dollar bill on the bar, slid off the stool, and waved goodbye to Chuck. I climbed into my car and rested my forehead on the steering wheel. An overwhelming feeling of dread washed through me as I realized Jake could very well be the murderer.

THIRTY-SEVEN

On Thursday morning, the Day Lily was geared up for another four-day run. Previous weekends, we'd all just started where we left off, going about our routines, checking in with one another about our time away from the café—but this morning was different. All three of my employees seemed distracted, as if a lot had happened to them since that dazzling Sunday brunch. I wondered briefly if there was a full moon.

Custer leaned against the building brooding over a cigarette when I parked my car in the alley. I got a grunt instead of a greeting as he stubbed out the butt with his sneaker. Glenn had forgotten the coffee mugs, and no one had put in the menu inserts I'd printed up for that day's special.

Crystal nursed a steaming cup of tea while intermittently filling the flower vases at the bar. I poured the first batch of coffee into a carafe. "Everything all right?"

"Mm-hmm," she said, and swallowed her tea. "Except I've been having the weirdest dreams lately." She snipped off the stem of a lemon yellow day lily. "They're crazy powerful."

I started the next batch. "What kind of dreams?"

She pushed a vase down the bar and snipped another flower. "You know that Edgar Allan Poe story—'The Tell-Tale Heart'?"

"That story is terrifying."

"Exactly. At about two this morning I woke up, and I was convinced someone was buried under my floorboards. You know I have that first-floor flat? The wood is really old and creaky. My heart was pounding so hard my ears were throbbing." She dropped the lily into a vase. "I couldn't shake it. I still can't."

I started adding the inserts to the menus while the next batch of coffee filled the air with a rich, nutty aroma. "Do you ever analyze your dreams, Crystal?"

"No, not so much. But I do think they're telling me something. Like when my older sister was pregnant I had this dream where everything was pink—the sky, the grass, this striped cat."

I smiled. "And she had a baby girl?"

"Two," Crystal said.

"Okay, so maybe you need new floors?"

She shook her head. "I don't want to know if something's under them."

I set the last menu on the counter and thought for a moment. "I wonder . . ."

Crystal studied me. "What are you wondering?"

"It's nothing. Just an idea. Anyway, the breakfast special is an open-faced crab melt bagel. Can you write it on the board?"

"Open-faced bagel and some mini doughnuts." Kevin had arrived and was heading toward us. "What do you think? I have glazed and cream filled. And some espresso bars for poor Janice."

"I think I need a cream filled," Crystal said. "A little sugar should wake me up."

Kevin opened the box, allowing her to select a doughnut. He looked up at me while she pondered her choices, his eyes tense with pain. "And then things fell apart."

"Coffee?"

"Please, darling."

"Sit," I said.

Glenn sidled up next to Crystal and gazed into the box. "Those look too good to eat."

Crystal was chewing. "They are. So save the rest for me."

Glenn straightened his bow tie. His fingers hovered over the box like a helicopter waiting to land. I hadn't seen Glenn wear a tie in months.

"Anytime now," Crystal said.

Glenn removed a glazed doughnut. "Good morning, Kevin," he said brightly. He popped the small doughnut into his mouth, spun on his heel, and picked up a tray of coffee mugs.

Kevin toted the box over to the pastry display case. "I should have—" He stopped. His shoulders fell. "I mean, it didn't happen soon enough."

"What didn't happen soon enough?" I said while I poured his coffee.

Kevin plopped into a chair, tongs in hand. "CJ. If he hadn't gone to the college, Jake wouldn't be feeling this way. I should have done more."

"Like what?" I pared a small sliver of lemon peel.

"He thought it would blow over. But he hasn't been out long enough to know the wrath being openly gay can provoke." He looked up at me and blinked a few times. "Or maybe he has all along. Maybe I pushed him too soon."

"Oh, Kevin. I'm so sorry you are going through this. Maybe once CJ's murder is solved, it will blow over."

"I don't know, friend. I think I might have lost him."

During a lull in the morning crush, Glenn dropped some menus onto the hostess stand and walked over to the bar. "What was wrong with Kevin?"

"He and Jake are having problems. It all started when CJ confronted them in the bar. It shook them both up. And I think they would do anything to protect each other."

Glenn peered at me over his glasses. "Anything?"

"Yes. I'm afraid so. CJ did some horrible things after that night."

"I didn't have this feeling with Megan," Glenn said. "This feeling of dread that the killer would be someone I cared about. But I'm having it a lot now."

"Me, too. I talked with Jake the other night. He's in a bad way, Glenn. He's thinking of leaving Kevin. Oh, and I got a Facebook message from Jamie." I looked up. Gretchen was waiting at the hostess stand. Her cheeks were a bright pink, and she wore a light linen dress with pearls. "I have so much to tell you. Let's find some time to talk later."

"I look forward to it." Glenn turned and walked over to Gretchen. Her smile widened. After chatting with her for a bit, he escorted her to the bar. He pulled out her chair, and she perched on it. "Did you know there is a hook under here for your handbag?"

"Oh," she said, "how convenient."

"Good morning, Gretchen," I said.

"Cheerio," she said, and folded her hands in her lap.

"The doughnuts are dangerously good," Glenn said.

"I like the sound of that." Gretchen smiled.

"All right, my dear, you are in good hands." Glenn picked up a tray and headed for a table that needed clearing. He was whistling.

"Tea, Gretchen?"

"I think I'm in the mood for an espresso. Make that a double."

Definitely a full moon, I thought as I started up the Miele.

Within a few minutes, Janice plopped down next to Gretchen. "Hey, Snow White," I said as I unloaded a dish rack of coffee mugs. I looked up at her. Her blond hair was curled into soft waves. She had gone to some effort with her makeup, and her eyes were brighter than I'd seen in a long time. "You look stunning."

She sat with a straight back and placed her palms on the bar. "Why, thank you. I went to New York a few days ago and had my hair done. And I bought a new outfit. What do you think?"

I came around from behind the counter so I could see her full regalia.

"Stand up and twirl," Gretchen said.

Janice spun around. She was wearing a floral flouncy romper with a tie at the neckline ending in royal blue tassels. "It's a Trina Turk. What do you think?"

"You are gorgeous," I said. "But not because it's a cute outfit. You're glowing. From within. And I haven't even given you an espresso bar."

Janice sat down again. "I'll have green tea, please. And do you still have that arugula salad with goat cheese and pomegranate dressing?"

Gretchen and I exchanged glances.

Crystal walked up with a tray of dirty dishes. "Hello, Miss Janice."

Janice stood and curtsied dramatically in front of Crystal. "My savior."

Crystal smiled. "How's your essential oil lamp?"

"I'm using the calming oil at night. But I've started a watercolor class at the college. What's good for creativity?"

"I have the perfect blend. I'll mix it up tonight." Crystal headed into the kitchen.

Janice grinned as she sat down. "That girl is Cardigan's best-kept secret."

"Maybe she should open a woo-woo shop," Gretchen said.

"So no coffee?" I asked Janice. "Or chocolate?"

"I'm avoiding foods that cause inflammation. Did you know inflammation can cause depression? Dropped three pounds in a week. And my hot flashes are history. Trevor has offered to buy Crystal a BMW." Janice sipped her tea. "Well, not really. I just made that part up."

"I'm so happy for you," I said. "I'll go fetch you a salad."

"I'll have one, too," Gretchen chimed in as I pushed through the doors.

THIRTY-EIGHT

The black bean soup was a crowd favorite. I added coconut milk and pureed some of the beans to make it creamy. It came with a thick slice of corn bread and a Cuban salad.

"This needs to be on the permanent menu, my dear," Glenn said.

"Really? Plain old black bean soup?"

"I don't know what you did to it, but if one person ordered

it today, the rest of their party would take one taste and order their own." Glenn began emptying his pockets. Crumpled bills unfurled on the bar. Only a few tables still had customers.

"I've been dying to ask you all day," I said.

"Oh, really? I can't imagine about what."

"Ha-ha. Not what. Who. What happened, Glenn?"

"First of all, I'm a terrible person."

"Well, yes, everyone knows that." I rolled my eyes. "Seriously, Glenn, how could you even think about calling yourself a terrible person?"

Glenn sat down and looked up at me. "I judged her, Rosalie. Without getting to know her. I thought she was frivolous just because she had such a pleasant demeanor."

"Tell me about yesterday."

"You know?"

"I saw you from Birdie's. You looked to be having a serious conversation."

Glenn took a deep breath and exhaled. "She came into Birdie's to get the London *Times*. Doris orders it special for her. She asked me if I wanted to sit in the park, and I couldn't think of a way to say no so I did."

I crossed my arms and leaned back against the counter. "I'm glad you said yes."

"Frankly, so am I. Did you know she is widowed as well?"

"I always wondered why she ran the inn on her own."

"You see, dear, she's lost the love of her life, too. She had a wonderful marriage to a man named Niall. They were married for thirty-six years. She asked me about Molly, and then she listened to what I had to say. We talked for a long time about our spouses and how much we miss them. It was lovely to share my experiences with her. And I think it helped her, too."

"Oh, Glenn. I'm so happy for you. Are you going to start spending time together?"

"She's invited me over to the inn. We are going to show each other pictures of our families. Isn't that a lovely idea?"

"So you are embracing the fact that you both had wonderful loves. I like that, Glenn. And instead of worrying you might accidentally say Molly's name, you can talk about her anytime and Gretchen will understand."

"Exactly. She's been through it herself. Who better to understand?"

Just as the last patrons stood up and dropped their napkins on the table, Doris hurried into the café. She strode over to the bar and waited for the diners to leave. Crystal followed them and looked over at me. She held the sign on the door. "Shall I?"

"Flip it," Glenn and I said simultaneously.

"Have a seat," Glenn said to Doris, and pulled out a bar chair.

She sat down hard. "Butch has ransacked Lori's house."

"Oh my goodness," I said. "When?"

"This afternoon. Lori was in the kitchen, and he barged in and started yelling at her, accusing her of knowing where the money was. When she denied it, he started tearing through the house, tossing furniture, emptying drawers."

"Did she call the sheriff?" Glenn asked.

"No," Doris said. "She can't stop crying."

"Did he hurt her, Doris? Oh my goodness. If he murdered CJ trying to get the money . . ."

"He didn't hurt her," Doris said.

"I wonder if he found the money," Glenn said.

"Lori said no. But he's on a rampage."

"We need to close up," I said. "Then I'll take you out to Lori's."

"I'll join you." Glenn hopped up and began clearing tables.

THIRTY-NINE

Butch had nearly upended the entire contents of Lori's house. The furniture was thrown about and every drawer in the kitchen had been emptied out onto the floor. We found Lori on the screened-in porch hugging her knees and rocking.

Doris knelt down and enveloped Lori in her arms. "There, there," she said. "He's gone now."

Glenn eyed the dogs scrambling for the prime spot by the door. They were more agitated than ever, most likely due to the chaos coupled with their owner's distress. "Are all those dogs yours?" he said. It was his first visit.

Lori sniffled and nodded her head.

"Can I get you anything, Lori?" I said.

"I have some Valium upstairs in the medicine cabinet. I could sure use one."

Doris patted Lori's shoulder.

"I'll be right back." I climbed the stairs and looked around. There were only two bedrooms, both off a center hallway. The bathroom was next to the smaller bedroom. Butch had left the bathroom alone. The cabinet was open but orderly. After reading several prescription bottle labels, I learned that Lori had not only Valium and Xanax, she also had a powerful sleeping aid. I wasn't about to judge her. The cold-blooded murder of one's husband is enough to make anyone renew their refills.

I started down the stairs but decided to take a look around. Jamie's bedroom was small and sparse. His mattress was up against the wall, which was painted navy blue. The closet was open but empty except for a few wire hangers and opened shoe boxes.

Lori's room had been tossed about as thoroughly as the

downstairs. The mattress and box spring were in a pile on the floor. Her clothes were strewn everywhere. Dresser drawers hung open like gaping mouths. A pair of Lori's panties had gotten caught on a knob. I gripped the orange pill bottle. The entire scene was a complete violation. Lori said Butch hadn't found the money. So it had to be here somewhere. I walked around the room, and then it hit me. I tossed the bottle in the air and caught it.

I found Doris in the kitchen returning contents to the drawers. Glenn was righting chairs. "Glenn, Doris?" They both stopped and looked at me. "I know where the money is." I walked out to the porch with them in pursuit, and handed Lori her pill bottle and a glass of water. After she popped two in her mouth, I said, "You know where it is, Lori. I know you do. So can you please show us?"

Lori stared ahead. The dogs were calm now. The air was still and close. Not a leaf rustled in the trees.

"The money is in your bedroom, isn't it?"

"Lori?" Doris said. "Is Rosalie right about this?"

She nodded slowly. "Yes."

"You've had it all along?" Doris said. "And you never said a *word*?"

"Let's go," I said, "and get this over with once and for all."

Lori stood. She moved as if riddled with arthritis. Doris looped her arm through her sister's, and the four of us ascended the stairs.

I led the way into Lori's bedroom. I turned to face her. "Which floorboards are loose?"

"What?" Doris said.

"Under the nightstand."

I walked over to the ivory-painted chest and moved it aside.

It was obvious which boards would pry loose. I slid my fingernails between two, and they came up easily. "This is why he put the new floor in, isn't it, Lori?"

"Yes," she said in a weak voice.

The camouflage duffel was dusty, the zipper sealed shut. I lifted it out of the subfloor and brought it over to Lori.

"Will you look at that," Glenn said.

"Is it all there?" Doris said, a hint of disgust in her voice.

"I never had any intention of spending it, Doris. The sheriff is already convinced I'm guilty. If he knew I had it, he would have locked me up weeks ago."

"And maybe he *should* be locking you up." Doris grabbed the duffel out of my hands and unzipped it with a flourish. She opened it wide and peered inside. "Well? Is there a secret compartment or something?"

Lori paled. "What do you mean?" She walked over to Doris. "Oh, oh my Lord." She placed her hand over her heart. "It's gone."

Glenn slipped his phone out of his pocket. "I believe it's time to call the sheriff." He stepped out of the room. In a moment I heard him say, "Lila? It's Glenn Breckinridge."

"Mom?"

"Who's that?" Doris said. "Is Jamie home?"

Lori's face was ashen. She shook her head as if waking up from a dream. "Wait, what?"

"Mom?" Jamie called in a louder voice. His footsteps were heavy on the stairs.

Doris dropped the duffel on the floor. "Good luck explaining this to him."

"He said he wanted to talk to me about something," Lori said. "He called me this morning."

Jamie stepped in the room. It suddenly felt extremely small. "Explain what to me?" He was still in his uniform, but his shirt was unbuttoned most of the way. His thick, dark hair was damp with perspiration. He held a manila folder in his hand. "What's going on in here? Why is the house such a freakin' mess?"

"It's a long story," Lori said, her eyelids heavy. Maybe she should have only taken one pill, I thought. "What did you need to talk with me about?"

Jamie glanced around the room then back at Lori. "It's pretty serious, Mom."

"I don't have any more secrets from these people."

"Yes, you do," Jamie said in a measured voice. "You have one more, at least."

Lori blinked several times. "I'm sorry?"

Jamie held up the folder. "I had a little blood work done."

"What's wrong?" Doris said, taking a step toward him. "Are you sick?"

"Mom—"

"I need to sit down," Lori said.

"Why don't we go downstairs?" Glenn dropped his phone in his shirt pocket and took Lori's arm. I followed. Doris walked over to Jamie.

"You don't have the cancer, do you?"

"No, Aunt Doris. My health is fine."

We found Sheriff Wilgus in the foyer, eyeing the ransacked house. "Don't you clean houses for a living?" he said to Lori as she descended the stairs. "You must not get paid very much." He chuckled to himself.

Glenn guided Lori into the kitchen and eased her into a chair. We all followed and gathered around the table—everyone except Jamie. He stood in the doorway, staring hard at the sheriff. Lori hugged herself tight, her eyes downcast, her face even paler than before.

"So Butch Wells did this?" the sheriff said.

"Yes," Lori said in a barely audible voice.

"And he was looking for the money because you had it all along?"

"That's right, he was looking for the money."

"How much have you spent of it?"

Lori looked up at him. "Not a cent. It's not my money. It belongs to the college."

The sheriff shifted his weight. "So why didn't you give it back?"

"I wanted to. I begged my husband to return it. I even threatened to do it myself. And then after he died, I decided to wait until Rosalie figured out who murdered Carl James."

He glowered at me. I immediately tensed. "*Rosalie*? You think Hart is going to figure out who murdered your husband?" He shook his head. "Oh, this is rich."

"Sheriff Wilgus," Glenn said, "maybe we should focus on who took the money. That will lead us to the murderer."

"It already has," he said. "And she's sitting right here."

"But the money is gone," Lori pleaded. "Someone took it from the floorboards without my knowing."

Glenn rubbed his chin. "Maybe whoever killed CJ got him to say where the money was hidden. And it was just a matter of time before he came for it."

"When did you last see the money?" Doris said.

Lori looked warily at Doris. Ever since Lori had showed us where she thought the money had been hidden, Doris had been giving her sister the cold shoulder, her eyes sharp with accusation. "The only time I saw it was when Carl James showed it to me. Then he put it in the floor and closed it up."

"Says you," the sheriff said. "For all I know you messed up this house yourself. It's a good cover. The thing is, I'm smarter than you. Always have been."

"It was Butch Wells," Lori said. "I swear to it." She lifted up the sleeve of her top. "Look." Red marks encircled her upper arm. "This is where he grabbed me."

"And how many witnesses saw him here? Hmm, let me guess. None? Zip? Zero?"

Glenn frowned at me. The sheriff was making a good case, and we both knew it.

"Lori," I said, and cleared my throat. "Did anyone else know where the money was hidden?"

She shook her head. "I don't think so."

"CJ was a braggart," Doris said. "He could have told anyone after a couple of whiskeys."

"How many days after he showed you the money did he die?" Glenn said.

Lori brushed a strand of hair from her face. "No more than a week."

"Excuse me," the sheriff said in a thundering voice. "Did I miss something, or am I the one with the badge?"

Lori's shoulders fell.

"Put some shoes on, Mrs. Fiddler. You're coming with me."

"Sheriff, maybe you should tell the college CJ took the money," I said. "Then everyone can get back to work."

"You hard of hearing, Hart?" He looked at Lori. "Move."

"Slow down," Jamie said.

The sheriff looked over at Jamie. "What?"

"There's something I need my mother to say first. I think you need to hear it, too, sheriff."

Joe Wilgus's mouth twitched. I squeezed my hands together. The tension in the room prickled like static electricity.

"Were you ever going to tell me?" Jamie said through gritted teeth.

Lori sat back in her chair. "I never knew for sure."

"Knew what?" Doris said.

"I think you did," Jamie said.

"No, I never found out because I didn't want to destroy our family." She looked over at Jamie. Tears glistened in her eyes. "Your father and I loved you with all our hearts, Carl James Junior."

"My name is Jamie." He tossed the folder on the table and roared, "And Carl James is not my father." He looked at the sheriff and stabbed a finger at him. "He is!"

"Oh no," Doris said. "Lori, for goodness' sake. What is he saying?"

The sheriff's eyes searched the room. His lips trembled with emotion. He stood quickly and gazed down at Lori. "I have to get out of here." His boots thudded on the gleaming hardwood floors. He jostled Jamie as he brushed past him. In seconds his engine roared to life, and his tires squealed as he drove away.

FORTY

Glenn and I offered to help straighten up the house, but it was clear that Lori, Jamie, and Doris had much to discuss. Neither of us spoke for the first half of the ride.

"How did you know where the money was hidden, Rosalie?"

I gripped the steering wheel. "Crystal. She was telling me about her dreams."

"Did Crystal have some sort of vision?"

"No." I glanced over at Glenn and smiled. "I don't think she's clairvoyant. At least not yet. But she was having disturbing dreams about something being buried under her floor and it scared her. You know, like "The Tell-Tale Heart"?"

"Good Lord, that story is certainly frightening. I wouldn't want to be having dreams like that."

"I know, right? But it made me think: floors. Why would CJ install a new floor when he'd lived in that house for so long?"

"And *that's* how you figured it out?" Glenn leaned back against the headrest and adjusted his seat.

"When she told me about her dream, it triggered the idea. So when I went upstairs and stood in Lori's room, I looked at the new floors and thought, that's it. I didn't know for sure, so I called Lori's bluff. I almost choked when she willingly walked up the steps."

"So where is the money, Rosalie?"

"Lori is certain Butch didn't find it. Mainly because he was still furious." I stopped at a red light, my blinker flashing so I could turn into the alley where Glenn's Prius was parked. "Remember, CJ called Butch and told him someone was after him. Maybe CJ took the money out of the floor and put it in his truck for safe-keeping. And so when the murderer confronted CJ, he or she somehow got the gun out of his hands."

"Yes, that scenario is plausible," Glenn said.

I turned down the alley. "Or the money is still in the truck, and Jake killed CJ."

"Yes." Glenn frowned. "That, too."

"I have another thought."

"Please share." Glenn adjusted his seat again.

"Are you uncomfortable?"

"Oh, no. I'm quite comfy. I'm just having a little fun." The small motor buzzed another time. "Oh, that's nice. Did you know you could adjust the firmness of your lower back support? Oh, Rosalie, does this car have a seat warmer?"

I tapped the icon of a chair with vertical wavy lines. It

glowed orange. "Glenn, do you think Custer knows about the money? Butch certainly thinks he does. He said that's why CJ fired him."

"Custer is an enigma to me. I like him very much. And I respect his work ethic. And he's talented, too. I don't know what we would do if he ever called in sick."

"*Kina hora,*" I said. "Say it. Now."

"*Kina hora.*"

"Whew. That was scary. Okay, you were saying?" I stopped in front of Glenn's car but left the motor running.

"I don't think he has the money." Glenn unbuckled his seatbelt.

"But he could have had a confrontation with CJ. Maybe Custer pushed him to give it back. Maybe he threatened to tell, and CJ tried to shoot him but Custer retaliated in self defense."

Glenn frowned. "Oh my. Yes. That's an excellent point."

"His father is an awful man, Glenn. Who knows what Custer had to endure?"

"Yes. And that sort of experience can dig a crevice in your soul."

"Exactly." I sighed and looked over at Glenn. "What's our next move?"

"Can we find out if Jake was at the tavern the night CJ was killed? Would Chuck tell us?"

"Maybe. He said the other day that people have been acting a little crazy ever since CJ was murdered. He's ready for this to be solved."

"I wonder if Gretchen likes martinis," Glenn said.

"You're going to the tavern?"

"You said I needed to go out more. We need Chuck to tell us who was there that night."

"That's so great. I would go, but I am really feeling out of touch with my family. Especially Annie. I've never seen her with Custer, and I need to make sure she's okay."

"How long has it been since you last spent time with Tyler?"

"Without Bini? A while."

"That's a relationship you need to maintain, too, my dear." Glenn gazed over at me, his face serious.

"Glenn? You think . . ."

"Weren't you the one to tell me life is incomplete without love?" Glenn popped open the door. "That Tyler is a keeper. And I think he has feelings for you." Glenn winked. "Just in case you hadn't noticed." He climbed out of the car, shut the door, and gave the roof a tap, signaling it was okay for me to drive away.

FORTY-ONE

I invited Tyler, Annie, and Custer to join me for dinner that Friday. The day had been rainy, with intermittent thunderstorms, and the Day Lily had its first slow day. We closed early, allowing me time to pick up the ingredients for deep-dish pizzas, Caesar salad, and several bottles of Sangiovese chianti from the Yellow Labrador Winery.

Annie set the table while I topped one of the pizzas with mushrooms, tomatoes, fresh mozzarella, and Kalamata olives. She had insisted on eating in the kitchen because she didn't want Custer to feel uncomfortable in the more formal dining room. She was dressed in white short-shorts and a flowing peasant top. Although she usually tamed her hair with a flat iron or a headband, that night it was a mass of loose brown curls. "You look cute," I said. "My little hippie."

"Thanks," she said, and folded a paper napkin—something

else she had insisted on. "I had a good run after work. I need to start getting back in shape for rugby."

"Does Custer work out?"

"*Hello*? Have you noticed his arms? Oh, and he has a very nice set of abs."

"Annie—"

"That I saw while we were swimming. So, Mom, how did you come up with this idea? I mean, getting the four of us together. It's a little strange, don't you think? It's like we're some weird blended family."

"I guess because I don't get to see you or Tyler enough. I also thought it would be nice to spend time with Custer in a different environment. Especially now that you two are hanging out. Just about every day, I might add." The rumble of Custer's motorcycle approached. Annie ran out to meet him.

I checked my watch. Tyler was late. That wasn't like him. Other than Glenn, he was the most punctual person I knew.

Annie was chattering away when she and Custer came through the front door. "And then he just walked out," she said in an animated voice. "He complained I was hurting him, and he was going to tell the manager. But I was just doing the exercises. I swear he almost cried."

They entered the kitchen. "You should lighten up on the guy, Wonder Woman." Custer squeezed her bicep.

Annie laughed. "Hey, what do you call my mom, anyway?"

"Good question. I guess I call her *boss*."

"I think you call me *yes, boss,* actually."

"Really?" Annie grinned. "That's so cute. You never told me that, Mom. Hey, can we have some wine?"

"Hi, Custer," I said.

"Long time no see." He walked with Annie to the counter.

She picked up the crystal wine decanter. "Hey," Custer said, "Smitty's got tickets to that show tonight in Annapolis."

"The one you wanted to see?" She filled two glasses with wine. "You want some, Mom?"

"Sure," I said, feeling a little like the third wheel. Where was Tyler?

Annie and Custer picked up their glasses and headed out to the screened porch. "Why aren't you going with him?"

"'Cuz I was coming here."

"Oh my gosh, Custer. You gave up that ticket to have dinner with us?" She kissed him on the cheek. "You're so awesome." Their voices faded as they settled into Aunt Charlotte's old wicker furniture I had yet to replace.

I sipped my wine and checked my watch again. Maybe some music. What would the kids like? I started toward my computer but stopped when I heard the front door open. I went back into the kitchen and tried to act nonchalant when Tyler entered the room.

"Hey," he said, his voice rough. He was freshly showered and wore a faded denim shirt and dark-wash jeans. The whites of his eyes looked like road maps. Dickens followed him inside and found his bed in the kitchen, flopped down hard, and exhaled a soft moan.

"Are you okay?" I said to Tyler.

"You drinking alone again?"

"Ha-ha. Annie and Custer are on the porch." I filled the fourth glass for him. "Want to sit in the living room? When's the last time we did that?"

He followed me out, and we sat next to each other on the sofa. The evening sky blended in with the blue-gray of the river. An occasional flash of lightning shimmered high in the clouds.

Tyler sipped his wine. "This is good," he said, and sipped again. He fell back into the sofa cushion with an *oof.*

"Are you sure you're okay?"

"I never said I was okay."

I turned sideways to face him. "Has something happened?"

He set his glass down on the end table. "I took Dickens to the vet this afternoon."

"And?" I reached out and squeezed his hand.

"Those lumps you found? Lymphoma." Tyler's voice hitched in his throat. "I knew he wasn't right. He was just sitting there looking at me with those big brown eyes like he was apologizing for something. What has that dog ever had to apologize for?"

"Oh, no." My eyes filled like a flash flood. "Is there anything they can do?"

Tyler nodded stiffly. Pain creased his forehead. "They did blood work." He rubbed an eye with his knuckle. "They're going to call me in the morning. They said something about chemo, but I don't want to put him through anything painful. Especially if it won't help."

"I'm so sorry, Tyler."

"Yeah, me too." He picked his glass up again. "Sorry to ruin your dinner party."

I brushed a loose tuft of hair from his forehead. "It's just a meal shared with friends. But if you're not up to it, I understand."

"I'm just grateful I took him." Our eyes met. "You knew something was wrong with him long before I did. I should have listened to you."

"We're hungry," Annie said, as she and Custer entered the room. "Hey, Tyler." She stopped in her tracks. "What happened?"

"Dickens has been diagnosed with cancer," I said.

"Oh no." Annie slapped her hand over her mouth.

"Sorry to hear that, man," Custer said.

"Thanks."

Once the cheese had melted and started to brown, we filled our wineglasses and sat down to dinner. Tyler was on his third glass. His eyelids were heavy. He wasn't normally a big drinker. In fact, I rarely saw him consume any sort of alcohol other than an occasional beer.

Annie talked as we ate. She mentioned her job, the latest zombie series, anything that popped into her head. Custer chimed in now and then, but he was more subdued in the presence of his uncle.

After the pizzas and salad were consumed, I cleared the table and put on some soft music. "Can we open another bottle of wine, Mom?" Annie said. "I'm having fun. Oh, and let's light some candles." She hopped up and grabbed two candlesticks. "We used to do this when I was growing up," she said to Custer.

"Drink wine?"

"No, silly." She gave him a light swat on the head. "Light candles after dinner and sit around and talk for hours. Right, Mom?"

I smiled and fetched some matches from a drawer.

"Really?" Custer said, trying to take it in. "You lit candles after dinner and sat around the table? And you just talked?"

"Yeah." Annie nodded her head. "About everything."

"We ate in front of the TV for pretty much every meal," Custer said.

I opened another bottle of wine, not sure if it was a good idea, but I wanted to continue the evening. After refilling and distributing our glasses, I lifted mine and said, "To Dickens, for encouraging me to bake. If not for him, I might never have opened the café."

We toasted, and Tyler took a long sip. "He's a damn good

dog." He closed his eyes for a moment and set his glass on the table.

"Tyler," Annie said, "I finally met your brother."

My eyes shot over to Annie. "You did? Where?"

Custer monitored my reaction.

"Last night. We were at Joey's listening to some music. He came over to our table." She said to Tyler, "You two look a lot alike. Only he has more wrinkles."

"Nah. My brother is much better looking than me." He gave Annie a small smile.

"What did he want?" I said.

"Just to say hi," Annie said. "I mean, Custer *is* his son. It doesn't seem so strange to me that he would come over and say hi." She turned to face Custer. "I know you don't get along, and I understand why, but he was sort of nice to me."

I clenched my jaw.

Custer lifted his chin. "You see him yet, Tyler?"

"No," Tyler grunted. "Not if I can help it."

"But he's your brother," Annie said.

"Not really," Tyler said. "Never really was my brother."

Annie searched Custer's face. "You okay with this conversation?"

"None of this is breaking news. I like to pretend I don't have a father. But that doesn't always work out so well."

"No," Tyler said. "In fact, it got you put on probation."

I checked Annie's reaction, but she seemed completely unfazed.

"It wasn't Custer's fault," she said.

"You know he's on probation?"

"Of course." She smiled at Custer. "We don't keep secrets from each other. Aren't you the one who taught me keeping secrets is destructive, Mom?"

"Everyone knows why you're on probation but me." I glanced at Tyler. "Could someone clue me in?"

Custer leaned back in his chair. "My illustrious father had me charged with assault after he sucker-punched me in the gut."

"Oh," I said, "how awful."

"It happened, and I'm trying to put it behind me. But when he shows up in town, he makes that a little hard to do."

"I think it's better if we all just stay out of his way," Tyler said. "Once he gets what he wants, he'll leave town as fast as he can."

"What does he want?" Annie said.

"I hope you don't mind me saying this, Custer," Tyler said. "Butch has many vices, gambling being one of them. When he runs out of money, he usually starts nosing around Cardigan."

"Will he ask you for money, Custer?" Annie said.

"If he thought I had some, hell yes. He would ask his preacher if he thought of it. And maybe snatch some out of the offering plate on his way out the door."

"You let me know if you need some help," Tyler said.

"I can handle him."

"That's what you said last time."

"Thank you for the offer." Custer stared down at the table then looked back at his uncle. "I know you mean it."

"I'm always here for you. Don't forget that."

"I have a question," Annie said. "How did Custer's dad turn out to be such a loser when you two are so great?"

"Simple," Tyler said. "Custer's dad's a narcissist."

"'One who advertises himself too much is ignored,'" Custer said, quoting Lao Tzu again.

"That's exactly right." Tyler looked at Annie. "I'm sure you are aware of the term. But look it up if you really want to understand all it entails. I did when I was ten, and that's when I stopped expecting anything from my older brother."

"I'll do it right now." Annie picked up her phone and typed with her index finger. She waited a moment "Here it is. Okay, narcissism: extreme selfishness, with a grandiose view of one's own abilities and an insatiable thirst for admiration. And a complete lack of ability to feel empathy for others." She looked up. "Has he always been like that?"

Tyler nodded. "Focus on the grandiose view of his own abilities."

Custer shifted in his seat. "Subject change?"

"It's harder for you being his son." Tyler studied his nephew. "A lot more than being his brother. I probably realized that on some level but I see it now. You can't ignore him the way I can." He finished his wine and cleared his throat. "I'm sorry if I haven't done more for you." Tyler's gaze was intense, exuding emotion, his eyes watery.

"It's okay, man."

"You're a good kid, Custer. Don't ever forget that."

Custer scooted back from the table. "Anybody notice the Orioles just swept the Red Sox?"

After more conversation about anything but Butch, Annie walked Custer out to his motorcycle. I made him drink an espresso and conducted my own makeshift sobriety test. No one had consumed as much wine as Tyler, which is why I insisted he stay. Once I heard Annie's bedroom door click shut, I took Dickens outside and brought him back to his bed, giving him a long scratch behind the ears. I found Tyler on the sofa I had already covered with sheets and a blanket and two fluffed-up pillows.

He lay on the blanket fully clothed, his arm draped over his forehead, his shoeless feet crossed at the ankles. "Hey," I said.

"I told you I didn't need any sheets."

I put a glass of water on the end table and perched on the edge of the sofa beside him. "Are the pillows okay?"

He shifted his head to look at me, his arm still on his forehead. "You know I hate this."

"I can't help myself. It's who I am. You should know that by now."

His face softened, and he folded his hands over his stomach. "Yeah. I guess I do."

"I'm sorry about Dickens."

"Me, too." He continued to gaze at me.

"What a conversation with Annie and Custer, right?"

"Butch was like the elephant in the living room," Tyler said. "I'm glad we talked about him."

"Do you think Custer's okay?"

"He'll be better once Butch gets the hell out of Dodge."

"What you said to him? That was incredible. You helped him a lot, I think, by acknowledging how hard it is for him."

"We aren't out of the woods yet, Rosalie. Custer thinks he can handle his father. And he rarely asks for help. The first time he asked me for anything was when he wanted to apply for the job at the café. But he doesn't like feeling indebted to either of us. It's not his thing. He's pretty stubborn that way."

"A family trait, perhaps?"

"Well, yes. There's that. But I'm getting a bad vibe about Butch this time. He's more aggressive than usual."

"There's a lot of money at stake." I straightened the blanket edge. "What do you think about Custer and Annie's relationship?"

"I didn't see any red flags. Other than her being a little besotted."

"Annie loves hard."

"And that's *your* family trait." Tyler patted the sofa next to him. "Come closer." He moved his leg so I could scoot in. He gazed up at me.

"I took the pillows off so you would have more—" Tyler cupped my head in his hand and kissed me deeply.

"Oh," I said, after a luxuriously lovely kiss.

He lay his head back on the pillow and smiled at me provocatively. "I've been wanting to do that since the day I met you."

"Really?"

"Hope that's okay."

"It's not just the wine?"

"Maybe." Tyler was still grinning. "You sleep well, Rosalie."

FORTY-TWO

Tyler was gone when I awoke the next morning. I found the sheets and blankets folded neatly on the ottoman. I couldn't stop thinking about our kiss as I went about my routine. The thought of it sent a surge of warmth through me and lightened my heart. I could still feel his lips on mine. But then I remembered what he'd said about the wine. Maybe he regretted acting impulsively. I had learned long ago that the urges or brilliant insights I had when I was a little tipsy often lost their allure in the morning. Perhaps Tyler had come to the same realization.

The rain had moved on and it was a glorious sunny day with unseasonably cool temperatures. Today would be a fairly easy day for Custer. Glenn had been making a list of the customers' favorite specials so far, and I'd come up with a brand-new fixed menu. The only special today was a grilled quinoa burger with a creamy curry mayo that I'd whipped up yesterday during the lull.

"Omelet," Crystal called. She was on the small step stool, a piece of neon chalk in her hand.

"Margherita," I said.

"How—"

Glenn had already begun to spell it.

I placed a vase filled with lavender stems on the table Glenn was setting. "How was your martini?"

"Very satisfying."

I put my hands on the back of a chair. "Do tell."

"It seems just about everyone in town was at the tavern the night CJ died." Glenn smiled.

"Jake?"

"No, but CJ was mouthing off about Kevin and Jake. According to Chuck, it angered a lot of the patrons." Glenn set the last spoon down and straightened the topper. He peered at me over his glasses. "Jamie was there with him."

"Jamie?" I said, surprised.

"And our regular, Jackson. And are you ready for this?"

My eyes widened. "What?"

"Butch came in late that night. After CJ had supposedly gone home. Chuck said it was almost time to close, but he gave him a drink on the house so he wouldn't stay too long."

"Was there anything unusual about Butch? Did he seem upset?"

"I don't know the answer to that. Chuck didn't say."

"Glenn, did the sheriff ever question Chuck? I mean, shouldn't he be asking these questions?"

"Not that I know of. Speaking of the sheriff, have you seen him?"

"No. I wonder how he's doing after learning Jamie is his son." I checked the door. "I thought Doris would stop by this morning." I looked back at Glenn. "Let's get through today then stop in and see her. Oh, and Glenn, have you heard whether they let the workers back? Did anyone tell the college CJ stole the money?"

"Maybe Jackson will come in today. We can ask him."

Crystal approached with a cardboard box. She lifted a mesh bag tied with a silk ribbon. The label affixed to the ribbon read: *Crystal Sterling Herbal Teas.*

"Oh!" I lifted another from the box. I held it to my nose and breathed in the enticing mixture of scents. "You did it, sweetie."

Glenn gave her a warm hug. "This is terrific, my dear."

"We'll serve them today," I said. "Can you display them somewhere on the bar? I have a wicker basket in the kitchen."

"I have different kinds," Crystal said. "I have a little card that explains what they're good for. The ribbons are color coded."

"I have to buy them from you so we can serve them," I said.

"We can figure that out later." She smiled. "I typed up a menu insert about the teas, too."

"All right, so when someone orders tea, you or Glenn can bring them the basket and they can choose. Oh, this will be so great. I'll get the basket."

"And we're off," Glenn said, and headed for the door.

Janice and Gretchen were admiring each other's outfits. They had both ordered the quinoa burger, no bun. "Hey, Rose Red," Janice said when I returned to the bar. "Where's Jackson? Isn't he usually here for lunch?"

"That's a good question." I refilled their water glasses. "Are the workers back at the college?"

"It's Saturday, girlfriend," Janice said.

"Maybe Jackson finally found another gig," Gretchen offered.

Glenn approached and placed his hand on Gretchen's back. "Pedigree," he said.

Gretchen smiled. "I'm sorry?"

"That's the answer to the crossword clue you were working on. It has to be. It came to me last night while I was falling asleep."

"Oh. I think you're right. I'll give it a go."

Glenn smiled and went back into the kitchen.

I noticed a tall man with dark muttonchops at the hostess stand. He wore a pair of mirrored sunglasses and a Yankees ball cap pulled low on his forehead. I walked over to him. "One?"

"Okay if I just have a cup of joe?"

"Yes, of course. Do you mind sitting at the bar?"

"I prefer it."

He was dressed in black jeans and a snug black T-shirt that muffin-topped over the sides of his belt. His black cowboy boots clicked rhythmically on the wood floors as if someone were playing a timber drum.

The man sat next to Janice and rested his sizable forearms on the counter. They looked like Popeye's after he downed a can of spinach. Crystal was humming while she punched in an order on the computer. "Do you know that guy?" I whispered.

She peered over her shoulder. "No. Definitely not." She looked back at the screen. "But he's got a mustard brown aura. That's never good."

"Maybe you should make a tea recommendation for him."

She looked at him again and chewed on her thumbnail. "That might be a tough sell."

"I think you're right." I went back to the bar. "So what will it be? I can make you any kind of coffee drink you like. Today's grind is Honduran."

"Just a regular coffee. Nothin' fancy."

"I'm Rosalie," I said. "Welcome to the Day Lily Café."

"Name's John." He scanned the room.

"Are you looking for someone?" I said.

Janice and Gretchen had stopped their conversation about neck creams.

"You still got that Wells boy working here?"

"Why do you want to know?" I crossed my arms.

"I could use that coffee."

"Yes, of course." I filled a mug from the carafe. "Cream?"

He shook his head and moved the mug closer with his massive arm.

I waited until he took his first sip. A droplet of coffee lingered on his beard. "Why do you want to know, John?" I hated mirrored sunglasses. I needed to see this man's eyes.

He set his mug down on the saucer with a thud. "I thought he might know where his old man is hiding out."

"Oh," I said, relieved. "Custer won't know. I promise you that. He is doing everything in his power to avoid his father."

"You're not from around here, are you?" Janice said.

"Is it that obvious?"

"Pretty much," Janice said. "You work out?"

"Requirement for the job."

"What do you want with Butch?" Janice said.

"He owes someone some money."

"Butch back to gambling?"

"Mr. Wells is back to gambling badly." John drained his coffee. "So if you were Butch, ma'am, where would you be right about now?"

"Hiding my butt from you," she said, and laughed.

"And if you didn't know I was in town?"

"You could try the Cardigan Tavern up the road." Janice wiped her hands on the napkin in her lap. "If you want to run him out of town, or maybe break a couple of his fingers, I think that would be all right with most of the folks around here. Isn't that right, Rose Red?"

"The sooner the better," I said. "Would you like something to eat, John?"

"The quinoa burger rocks," Janice said.

"I don't know what that is," he replied.

"Grilled cheese?" I said. "Side of fries?"

"Better."

As I walked over to the computer I heard Janice say, "Your name isn't John, is it?"

"It is to you."

Glenn drew close. "That man is after Butch?"

"Yes. He must be some sort of bounty hunter. And he's giving me the creeps."

"The plot thickens," Glenn said, and pushed through the kitchen door.

FORTY-THREE

Not long after we closed, I carried a bin of dirty dishes back to the kitchen. As I loaded them into the dishwasher, a soothing tone emanated from Custer's phone. He picked it up and studied the new message.

"What the—" He ripped off his bandana. His head shot up to me.

"What is it? What's happened?"

"I have to get out of here."

He grabbed his keys and started for the door.

"Custer?"

He looked back at me, an almost feral panic on his face. "My dad has Annie."

"What? Oh my God, where?"

"Your place." Custer flew out the back entrance, the screen door slamming hard. I heard his motorcycle tires patch out as I ran into the dining room. "Glenn, I have to go. Butch has Annie."

Tears streamed down my face. I searched for my purse. I hiccupped a sob and clutched my stomach. "Where's my—"

"Let me get my keys," Glenn said. "I'll get you there in no time."

I looked at Crystal. "Go," she said, and waved us away. "Hurry."

Glenn fired up his car and sped down the alley. "Custer already left," I said.

"That's not necessarily a good thing." Glenn screeched to a halt when two pedestrians leisurely entered the crosswalk.

"Oh, Annie." I pushed my palms against my temples.

"I'll get you there," Glenn said, and hit the gas.

Butch's rusty black pickup idled ominously in my driveway. Tyler's truck was gone. Annie had been alone. Custer's bike lay on its side and he stood planted next to the truck, screaming at his father through the open window. I leapt out of the car before Glenn came to a complete stop.

"Where is she, you son of a bitch?" Custer demanded.

"Hey, looks like we have ourselves a little party," Butch said, a sickening sneer on his face.

"Where's Annie?" I cried when I reached them. "What have you done to her?"

"I'll tell you where your little Annie is," Butch said, "once Custer here tells me where the money is stashed."

Custer reached through the window and grabbed Butch's collar. He squeezed it tight. "You tell me now."

Glenn caught up to us, out of breath. "I've called the sheriff."

Butch fisted his right hand and punched Custer solidly in the nose. Glenn caught him as he stumbled back. Blood spewed from between Custer's fingers as he clutched his nose.

"Stop this!" I said.

"You tell me where that money is, you good for nothin' son or I'll drive away and you'll never know where your girlie is."

I clutched my stomach. "Please, Custer, just tell him."

"I don't have it," Custer said, his voice muted from the hands covering his face.

"Son," Glenn said to Custer as he eased him onto the driveway, "if you know where it is then please, just tell him."

"All right," Custer whipped off his T shirt and held it over his face.

"'Bout time," Butch said.

"It's at CJ's house. Now tell me where she is."

"It ain't there, you lying good for nothin. I already looked."

"Did you look under the floorboards in the bedroom?" Custer pushed himself up, scuffling in the gravel. "I don't care if you take it. I never did. Now where is she?"

"She's sitting under a tree," Butch said. "Having a little picnic. I'll tell you where once I have the money." He shifted the truck into gear.

"You tell me now!" Custer demanded

Panic constricted my throat. "Custer, the money isn't there anymore."

His eyes shot over to me, mirroring my panic. "How do you know?"

"We looked. The duffel is empty."

Glenn frowned. Our eyes met and he took off around the side of the house.

Butch glared at me. "You ever want to see your daughter again?"

A souped-up Mustang with blacked out windows sped down the lane. It squealed to a stop, and out jumped the man from the café. He started toward Butch, handcuffs hitched to his belt.

"You find that money." Butch called to Custer and hit the gas just as John reached the truck.

A loud whistle pierced the air from behind the house. "That's Glenn," I said. "He must have Annie."

Custer tossed his shirt on the ground and took off around the house. All that was left of Butch was a cloud of dust. John pivoted in the gravel and sprinted back to his car, climbed in, and took off in pursuit of Butch. My knees weakened as I ran toward my Annie.

She was sitting on the ground next to an oak tree. Custer knelt behind her, untying a rag that hung around her neck. Glenn held two bungee cords in his hand. "Oh, Annie," I said as I ran faster. I slid onto the grass, landing on my knees, and scooped her up.

Custer sat back on his heels, holding the cloth. A portion of it was darkened from where it must have been in Annie's mouth. He watched us, a pained look on his blood-stained face. Annie sobbed into my shoulder.

"What did he do to you?" I had never been this close to losing her. "Did he hurt you? Are you okay?"

"I'm okay." She nodded into my shoulder. "He tied me up." She sniffled. "But I was so scared he'd do more."

"Annie," Custer said, his voice hoarse, "I'm very sorry my father did this to you." Our eyes met over the top of her head. "I'll be going," he said. His nose was so swollen his eyes were partially closed. "You take care of her, okay?"

I shook my head. *No,* I mouthed. *Don't go.*

"I have to," he said, and stood. "I don't expect you to understand."

"Son," Glenn said, "The sheriff will be here any minute. Don't even think about going after your father."

He gestured to Annie. "I can't let that bastard get away with this."

"He's not about to," Glenn said.

I stroked Annie's hair, rocking her. "Do you need to go to the hospital?"

"No," she said in a muffled voice.

I looked over my shoulder at Glenn and Custer. "Can you two help me get her inside?"

Custer's head hung down. "I can't stay. I have to go." He turned to leave but stopped. "Annie . . . I . . . I love you."

Annie's head shot up, but Custer was already hurrying away. "Come on," I said. "I want to make sure you're not hurt." Glenn and I each took an arm and eased Annie up to her feet.

"How long have you been out here?" Glenn said as we walked.

"I don't know, but it seemed like a lifetime."

"At least you were in the shade," Glenn said.

"Your arm is red," I said.

"That's where he pulled me out here."

We rounded the house. "How are your wrists?" Glenn said.

"Sore, but the cords didn't cut into my skin."

"The bounty hunter showed up," I said to Glenn as we walked up the steps to the house one at a time. "He had handcuffs."

"Good lord. What happened?"

"He took off after Butch in his car."

"Mom," Annie whispered as she waited for Glenn to open the door.

"What is it, sweetie?"

"Did Custer just say he loves me?"

FORTY-FOUR

Once the sheriff arrived and asked Annie everything he needed to know, he allowed me to take her upstairs. I tucked her in my bed and set a glass of water and a couple of Advil PM gel caps on the nightstand. "I'll bring you some hot cocoa once Sheriff Wilgus leaves."

"That sounds good." She propped up her pillow and leaned back against the headboard.

"Let me see your wrists." She held them out. "Just a little red. You're right." I turned them over in my hands. "I don't think the cords broke the skin." I looked up at her. "Where were you when he came in?"

"At the kitchen table on my computer. I heard his footsteps and assumed it was Tyler." She rubbed her wrists. "Can we start locking the door?"

"I don't know why I ever stopped."

Todd trotted into the room and jumped on the bed. She scooped him up. "It's about time, you fickle cat."

"So what happened?" I said. "Did he grab you?"

"He said hello, or hey there, or something creepy. It surprised me so much I spun around. Then he said I had to go with him, so I punched him. Right in the face."

"Annie!"

"I held my own for the most part. Next I socked him in the gut, and then he grabbed my arm, so I bit his hand."

"Really?"

"*Hello*? Rugby."

"So then what happened?" I was so relieved she was ready to talk about it.

Annie picked up a couple of the pills and popped them in her mouth. After a long drink of water, she said, "I would have gotten out of there, Mom. I know I'm short, but sometimes it's an advantage. You should remember that."

" I will. But—"

"When I started to duck under his arm, he pulled out a knife."

"Oh, thank the Lord you didn't try to fight that." A shiver of fear passed through me. My mind raced with possibilities. Careful not to jostle Annie's glass of water, I tucked my arm through hers and scooted closer. I needed to feel her next to me. Alive. Safe.

"Knives are the worst. Once I saw it, I agreed go with him. But I was still thinking of ways to get away. When Glenn found me, I was almost out of the bungee cords. I could hear you screaming at that man. I wanted you to know I was okay. I didn't want him to hurt anyone else."

"The good news is Butch doesn't have a reason to come back. Custer can't help him anymore. Although Custer knew where the stolen money was stashed, it's not there anymore. That's the only reason Butch came here."

"I hope Custer is okay." Tears welled in her eyes. "This is the worst thing that's ever happened to me."

I pulled her closer. "It's the worst thing that's ever happened to me, too." I leaned my head against her soft hair. "We should tell your dad what happened. He has a right to know." I took a deep breath and exhaled. "He's going to be very upset."

She looked down at the covers. "I will. Eventually."

"Why not now? He would want to know."

"He wasn't so into me being with Custer. He might say *I told you so.*"

"Tomorrow, then. You don't need anything else to upset you." I smoothed her hair. "I love you more than I have ever loved anyone or anything."

"Me, too. I'm going to take a few days off from work. I think they'll understand."

"Good idea. Remember, we're closed Monday through Wednesday, so I'll be off for three days after tomorrow."

"I love that you have the café, Mom. Don't ever neglect it on my account. And just for the record, you should stay open all week."

"That's certainly the goal. But I'm overwhelmed as it is. And I can't help but think this wouldn't have happened if I were home."

Annie snuggled under the covers and turned on her side, her arm embracing Todd. I think the pills were kicking in.

"Good. I'll come back upstairs as soon as I finish talking with the sheriff." I pulled the drapes closed and trotted down the stairs.

Sheriff Wilgus was seated at the kitchen table staring out the window. The chair seemed too small for his large girth, although it looked as if he'd shed a few pounds. "All tucked in," I said.

He looked up. "She okay?"

"As okay as she can be. Would you like some coffee?"

He hesitated. "Yeah. I think I would."

I poured us each a mug full and sat across from him. "How are you, sheriff?"

He wrapped his hands around the steaming cup. "I'm real tired."

"Have you spoken with Jamie?"

He shook his head. "Haven't seen him. I think he went back to Delaware."

"It must be so confusing for you."

He huffed out a laugh. "It's a hell of a lot more than that."

"Have you arrested Lori?"

"I haven't done a damn thing."

"Any idea where the stolen money is?"

"If you had asked me that a couple of days ago, I would have said Lori still had it. And she may. It's probably socked away somewhere. It's not like it was marked or anything. It was just payroll cash."

"And the college?"

"I sent them an e-mail. Everyone will be back to work on Monday."

"Are you going to leave Lori alone?" I eyed him over my mug as a I sipped.

He grimaced. "I can't. It ain't right if she killed her husband." He slugged back some coffee. "And it ain't right what she did to me." He looked back out at the river. "That woman sure knows how to bust up a few lives."

FORTY-FIVE

Doris was at the door at six a.m. Glenn ushered her in.

She clutched a large stack of newspapers. "Neither of you has been in for your papers for a couple of days now." She dropped them onto the bar with a loud smack.

"How are you, Doris?" I said. "I've been thinking about you. Can you sit for minute or two?"

Doris situated herself on a bar chair.

"What's been going on?" Glenn said. "How has Jamie taken the news?"

"Jamie got that blood test a long time ago. He's known for quite a while that CJ wasn't his father. Those yearbooks were what tipped him off about Joe Wilgus. He did the math and looked in the mirror." Doris glanced around the room. "I smell coffee. Is it ready yet?"

I poured her a cup and set it in front of her. "What happened after we left Lori's house?"

"Jamie screamed at his mom for a while, then he tore out of there." She stirred a generous portion of sugar into her coffee. "I'm worried sick about him. He took a leave of absence from work." She looked up. "I don't have any idea where he is. My Betsy said he hasn't been on the Facebook or that Insta-telegram thing. And she said ordinarily he'd be posting pictures of his body because he works out so much."

"And Lori?" Glenn said with furrowed brows.

"I'm so mad at her. And yet I feel sorry for her. I don't know what to think. She's botched up just about everything she could in her life. Why did she have to go and lie about it all? The money, Jamie's paternity?" Doris shook her head. "At least we got her house put back together. And I think Butch is going to leave her alone now."

"Should I let the sheriff in?" Crystal was standing close, her hands tucked in her apron pockets. Her shoes were quieter than slippers.

I walked over and unlocked the door. "Hi," I said. "I'll get you some coffee."

Sheriff Wilgus shuffled in the door. He stopped when he saw Doris. They eyed one another warily. Doris looked down at her coffee.

His cheeks flushed. He adjusted his heavy belt and walked up to the bar. "Deputy found Butch Wells's truck by the side of the road out on Route Twenty-seven."

"Any sign of Butch?" Glenn said.

"No. There were tire marks all around the truck. And footprints. He could have made a run for it."

"What about the bounty hunter?" I said. "He could have taken Butch."

"I thought of that, too. I need a description of his vehicle, and I'll put out an APB. It's not that I'm overly concerned about Butch's well-being. But I want him in my jail, not someone else's. I want to talk to your cook, though, before I do anything else. He's gone after his daddy before. No reason he didn't do it again."

"I understand," I said. "Of course you can talk to Custer. I'm sure he wants to know where his father is, anyway."

I filled a cup with coffee and popped on the lid. Kevin hadn't arrived with the pastries yet, but then the sheriff didn't seem to be eating much of anything lately. His pants were so baggy he had to cinch his belt at the last notch to keep them up.

Sheriff Wilgus looked at Doris. "State's attorney says I got enough to haul your sister in."

"What?" Doris's eyes were like saucers behind her bottle-thick glasses.

"We got the motive now with the money. And we got the weapon with her prints and no alibi."

"What's the motive?" Glenn said.

"She wanted the money for herself."

Doris took a long swig of coffee. "Things just keep getting worse."

"Seems to be the case." He lifted his hat and scratched his head. "No need for her to stay in the jail, though. We'll let her out on bail. You just make sure she don't go running off."

Doris's eyes pleaded with me. I was glad it was Sunday and the Day Lily would be closed for the next three days. Glenn and I needed to wrap up this case, and fast.

"I'll be going back into the kitchen. Don't get yourself all worked up, Hart. Got that? Your shenanigans are the last thing I need right now."

We watched him go.

"Doris," Glenn said, "we've narrowed down our list of suspects. Rosalie and I are going to figure this out."

She finished her coffee and pushed herself up. "And what if you figure out it was Lori?"

"That doesn't seem to fit, Doris," I said. "I think she's as confused as the rest of us."

The sheriff reappeared. "What time is he supposed to show up for work?"

Glenn and I exchanged a quizzical look. "An hour ago," I said.

"Well, there ain't no sign of him back there. His cycle ain't in the alley, either."

The sparkling wine was chilling, the coffee brewing, the tables set, and still no Custer. "He's not coming," I said to Glenn. "He's too ashamed."

"He's not responsible for his father's behavior."

"What should we do?" Crystal said.

"Can you two handle up front? I'll have to take over the food." I reached for my purse and pulled out a hair clip. "Play up the French roast so we have fewer special coffee orders."

"Is everything ready?" Glenn said. "We ran out of here yesterday before you had a chance to prepare for today."

"I honestly don't know." I looked over at Glenn. "You predicted this."

"Not predicted, just wondered what we would do if Custer didn't show up for work one day."

"Okay," I said. "Stall, entertain, and pour lots of champagne."

"Now you're a poet," Crystal said.

"That's a first." I twisted my hair up and snapped the clip in place. "I have no idea how this is going to work."

"I'll be in charge of opening the sparkling wine," Crystal said. "I can channel Alessa."

"If anyone can pull that off, it's you, my dear," Glenn said while he filled the vases. "Um, Rosalie?" He peered at me over his glasses. "Perhaps you should head back to the kitchen. I think you have a few things to do."

FORTY-SIX

When I'd first devised a business plan for the café, I met with the Cardigan Bank and Trust and took out a small business loan. One of the most expensive items I needed to purchase, in addition to an eight-burner commercial stove, multiple dishwashers, and an enormous refrigerator, was a POS computer system. The POS, or point of sale, included the computer on which Glenn and Crystal typed their orders and a monitor in the kitchen where the orders were displayed for the cook. Who was now me.

I fired up the monitor and brushed my hands together. Brunch consisted of an à la carte menu with a choice of three items from the following: banana bread French toast, potato cake, florentine omelet, arugula salad, choice of breakfast meat, fruit, and fresh oysters. Every order included a side of buttermilk biscuits and local creamery butter. What was I thinking?

I opened the refrigerator and began removing ingredients. The salad was ready. It just needed to be tossed. The banana bread had been baking all morning. The eggs were whipped. Where to start? Although Custer and I had worked out a prioritization system when I first trained him, I felt like a triage nurse in an overwhelmed ER. One at a time, I thought. Start with the French toast. The monitor flashed. An order already?

I rushed over to read it. Four diners and four completely different orders. I ran back to the refrigerator and looked for the oysters. They weren't opened. Are you kidding me, I thought. I peeked through the door to the dining room. Three tables were already filled. Crystal was opening a bottle of sparkling wine. Glenn had turned on some soothing classical music.

"Psst," I said when Glenn passed by.

"What is it?"

"I didn't open the oysters."

He looked over his shoulder. Crystal was seating a party of three. "Maybe we should cancel them for today."

"Can you try?"

He hesitated. "Let me make sure everyone has their drink orders, and I'll be right there. How are the biscuits coming along? That might tide everyone over."

"Ready to go." I let the door swing shut, lined four baskets with cloth napkins, and piled in the biscuits the bakery had delivered that morning. I folded the napkins over the biscuits and topped each basket with a dish of maple butter. I balanced them on my arms and hurried to the door. Glenn barged through, and we barely avoided toppling into one another.

"I'm not used to someone coming the other way." Glenn righted his glasses. "Are you okay?"

I nodded. "There are two orders for oysters. Each order includes three."

"I just got another one," he said. "Wish me luck."

I passed out the biscuits and greeted the customers. So far everyone seemed relaxed and composed. Except me, of course. "I'm telling people our espresso machine is out of commission," Crystal said as she walked by with two sodas.

"Really?" My shoulders fell. "Okay. I guess we have to."

I went back to the kitchen. Glenn hadn't opened a single oyster. "They're not cooperating," he said as he tried desperately to pry one apart. "Where's the shucker?"

"Cancel the oysters," I said. "Tell them our cook is out for the day."

Glenn picked up the tray and flung it back into the refrigerator.

The French toast was sizzling. I flipped several over and noticed the omelet was starting to brown. I could smell the potato cakes in the oven. I tossed some bacon in a pan and slid the omelet off the stove. Glenn opened the oven. Dark smoke billowed out.

Our eyes met. "Go entertain," I said. Glenn washed his hands and headed for the door. "How are you at soft shoe?"

He pushed through the door. "That's Crystal's department."

By ten o'clock, all the tables were full but only three orders had been delivered. I was beginning to wonder if we would make it until two. I looked at the stovetop. One pan held sausage and local bacon sizzling and popping together and I had another batch of potato cakes in the oven. Crystal came back for more biscuits. "Here," she said, and picked up some tongs. "I can toss this salad for you in a jiff." She whipped it around, set the tongs down, and reached out to turn over several slices of bacon with a fork. She patted my back and hummed *We will rock you* as she exited.

Glenn hurried through the door. "I have a very unhappy gentleman. He came here specifically for the oysters." He opened the refrigerator and removed the tray again. "I can do this." He picked up a knife.

"Whoa," Custer said as he dropped his keys on the counter. Gauze had been taped over his nose and the skin under his eyes was a deep purplish blue. "Take it easy. You're gonna cut yourself, dude." He opened a drawer and removed the missing shucker. He took the oyster from Glenn's hand and pried it open with one twist.

"So that's where that thing was," Glenn said. "How did you do that, anyway?"

"Eastern Shore, born and bred."

Tears escaped down my cheeks. "Custer," I said. "I—"

"Bacon's burning." He slid the pan off the flame. "The organic stuff burns faster. No preservatives." He walked over to the oven and removed the potato cakes. "These puppies start to turn black about a minute after they've cooked just right."

"I've learned the hard way."

He slipped into his chef's coat, tied a black and white bandana around his head, and sized up the kitchen. "This place is a frea-kin' mess."

"I don't appreciate you enough." I pushed my hair from my face.

He stood next to me and stared at his feet. "I'm sorry."

"I'm just happy to see you." I grabbed four plates and spread them out on the counter.

He peered over at me. "How is Annie?"

"She's going to be okay, Custer. You should be proud of her. She fought back."

He nodded slightly.

"Okay," I said. "This one gets a salad, French toast, and fruit."

Custer began to move as if he had just snapped out of a spell. He slid a spatula under a piece of French toast and dropped it on the plate. I added a serving of salad and grabbed the lavender honey. Custer scooped out the fruit. "We're getting low on cantaloupe."

"Okay. Let's get these orders out, and I'll get on it."

He cracked some eggs into a bowl and whisked them with finesse. "Do I still have a job?"

"I'm giving you a raise."

FORTY-SEVEN

At eleven thirty we were back in our groove. I was making coffee drinks again and seating patrons. I checked on Custer and was amazed how he had organized the food.

"You have a system."

"Yes, boss."

"How is your nose? It looks painful."

"I'll get it checked out after work." A cantaloupe fell open as he sliced it down the middle with a large knife.

"Custer?" I rolled my shoulders back. "The sheriff said he found your dad's truck out in the country. It was empty." I hesitated. "Can I ask?"

"You already know I started going after my dad last night. I had to. I still can't believe what he did to Annie."

"Oh." I crossed my arms, containing the fear rising up my throat. "What happened?"

"He was long gone. I went to a few places I thought I might find him, and then I just started to ride. Got all the way to the Delaware shore. Sat on the beach and smoked all night."

"And?"

" 'Let it be still, and it will gradually become clear.' " A peaceful smile appeared on his face. " 'If you want to accord with the Tao, just do your job, then let go.' "

"That's lovely."

"I realized sitting there on my own that you people are important to me. You've done nothing but treat me with respect. And I was about to leave you in the lurch."

"What's important is that you came back."

He looked up at me. His green eyes glistened. "You all are better than any family I've ever known."

When I returned to the dining room I noticed Jackson at the bar. I walked over and said, "Hello, stranger. How have you been?"

"Couldn't be better. And I'm looking forward to this brunch you got going on here. I don't suppose you have any Bloody Marys?"

"I do indeed. Old Bay Bloody Marys. Sound good?"

"What are you waiting for?"

I filled a glass from the pitcher and added a celery stick. I set the glass in front of Jackson and watched as he took his first sip.

"Mmm. Pepper vodka?"

"Yes. I had to do a lot of research on how to make a good one. But I'm open to suggestions."

He munched on the celery. "Let me think on that. Although this one here is pretty perfect."

"So where have you been? Did you get tired of the food here?"

He rolled his eyes. "No way. But I was stressing pretty bad about not having any work, so I took some R and R."

"You and your wife?"

"Ah, Rosalie, you heard what Butch said the other day. Yeah, I tried to defend her honor—or maybe I was defending mine—but the wife and I don't really get along all that well. She really does call me a dog. She's been doing it for years. She put me out of the bedroom one night, and I haven't been back since." He finished off the celery. "Not sure I deserved it but"—he shrugged—"then again, maybe I did."

I studied him. His face was tanned. I noticed a solid-gold chain around his neck I had never seen before. He picked up his drink with his left hand. A brand-new Rolex encircled his wrist. "Well, the rest seems to have agreed with you. Is that a tan I detect?"

"Yeah. I got me a little color. Hides the rosacea a little, don't you think?"

"Absolutely. Where did you go? Ocean City?"

"Even better. I got a friend who keeps his boat down in the Caribbean. He let me stay down there for a few days." He drummed his thumbs on the bar. "Do you know how blue that water is?"

"I think the right word is *azure*."

"Yeah. That's it on the button."

Crystal appeared. "Can you hand me three champagne glasses?"

I picked up the glasses and set them on a tray. She lingered for a moment, then gave her head a quick shake and walked away.

"You must be happy to have your job back."

"Heck yeah. I got the e-mail yesterday. It's been a good week." Jackson wiped his mouth with a napkin. "Did you hear CJ Fiddler is the one who stole the money?"

"I did. And the sheriff is pressing charges against Lori Fiddler for killing him. Seems all the mysteries in this town have been solved at last." I narrowed my eyes, watching him closely.

He frowned, deep in thought. "Now that, I did not know. So the sheriff has enough evidence to convict her?"

"Enough to press charges."

"Who would have thought? Little old Lori Fiddler. You know what, Miss Rosalie? I think I'll switch to the sparkling. I got lots to celebrate. Right? I'll be getting my job back. And when you get a minute, I'm ready for some grub. I'll take one of everything. Charge me triple."

A loud *pop* resounded through the café as a cork ricocheted off the ceiling. "Heads up," Crystal shouted. The diners cringed until it landed in a young girl's water glass with a *plop*. The girl began to giggle and covered her mouth with her small chubby hands.

"Oops," Crystal said, looking sheepish. "That one got away."

"Brava!" an older gentleman called out. He lifted his hands

and began to clap, his palms slapping together enthusiastically. The ovation was contagious, and soon the café thundered with applause. When the raucous celebration at last died down, Crystal pulled out the edges of her apron and curtsied.

Glenn approached, a wide grin on his face. "The girl is a crowd pleaser."

I was smiling, too. "It had to happen sooner or later."

Glenn stood before the computer and punched in an order. "I've just received a text message from Gretchen. She and Annie are doing a jigsaw puzzle."

"Oh," I said. "That's absolutely perfect, Glenn." I warmed at the idea of them together, just like my Aunt Charlotte and me.

"Therapeutic, don't you think?" Glenn tapped his index finger on the screen.

"What a relief to have Gretchen there with Annie. She misses my mother so much."

Glenn finished typing and looked over at me. "Everyone is grieving in one way or another, trying to heal and carry on. How did I have the audacity to think it was worse for me?"

"Sometimes it feels unbearable. But it's not a competition."

"No, it certainly isn't. And it helps to let others in. You've taught me that, Rosalie."

"Thank you, Glenn. Say, you and I have some work to do."

"Oh yes. We need to get cracking."

FORTY-EIGHT

On Monday morning I rose early, gave Annie a kiss on the cheek, and went downstairs. I hadn't seen Tyler since Friday night and had lain in bed most of the night wondering what our next encounter would be like.

Bini was at the kitchen table. She looked up. "Hear about Butch?"

"Yes," I said. "Do you know if he's shown up anywhere?"

"No word."

I folded my arms tight against my chest. I hadn't been anticipating a conversation with Bini. I had been hoping it would be Tyler standing in my kitchen greeting me with a warm smile. And maybe even a kiss.

Bini dusted crumbs from her hands. She had grown fond of the leftover muffins I brought home from the café. "They'll find him, dead or alive." She picked up her plate and carried it to the sink. "I don't think the Wells family will care much either way."

I was about to go look for Tyler when I heard the front door open.

"Hope the coffee isn't gone," Tyler said, and walked over to Mr. Miele. Dickens sauntered in after him, stopped briefly by my knees for a quick pat, and flopped on his bed. "I know you ladies like your morning brew." He stood next to Bini while filling his mug. "How did he get in there?"

"It's crazy," Bini said. "But I think he dug under the fence with his talons."

"But how did he get the hen out of there?"

Bini looked up at Tyler, and said in a logical, emotionless voice, "I think he ate her right there in the pen. We're lucky he didn't eat more than one."

So much for something between Tyler and me. All my anticipation of this moment was dashed. He hadn't even made eye contact. I'd been hoping to gaze into his eyes and feel a dazzling connection between us. "Did the hawk get another chicken?" I said, trying to shake the feeling of invisibility.

"He did," Bini said.

"Show me where you're talking about," Tyler said.

"Tyler," I said, "I'm sorry about your brother."

He looked over at me. No smile. No razzle-dazzle. Rats.

"Yeah," he said. "Can't say I'm surprised." He started to walk away. "He'll show up eventually."

"At least Annie's okay," I called after him.

He stopped. "Annie? What's wrong with Annie?" There. Eye contact.

"Butch tied her up on Saturday and wouldn't tell us where she was."

"I'm sorry, *what*?"

"Yes. It was pretty traumatic."

Tyler combed his hands through his hair. "Why didn't you tell me?"

"I haven't seen you. It's been a little crazy around here."

"Tyler," Bini said, "come on. We've got to fix this before the hawk comes back."

Tyler was deep in thought. I willed him to look at me, but instead he popped his cap on his head and said, "I'll talk to Annie when she wakes up. I'm real sorry this has happened. She must be pretty shook up." He picked up his coffee and headed out the door with Bini.

"So many predators," I said under my breath.

I spent a little time on Facebook while waiting for Annie to rouse and learned Jamie Fiddler was in Las Vegas. It was clear from his photos that he was drinking and gambling and spending time with a lovely young woman. Why do people go to Vegas? To get away. To get drunk. And to spend money. Money. Did Jamie have the money?

Jamie was working through some serious emotional turmoil. Doris had said he'd learned CJ wasn't his father long before finding the yearbook. Cops have access to health records. How would that have impacted his relationship with CJ? Glenn had learned Jamie and CJ were both at the tavern the night of the murder. Had Jamie confronted CJ with news of his paternity?

We were narrowing it down. Four suspects were in the lineup: Jamie, Butch, Jackson, and Jake. It would have to be a process of elimination. Although I had no idea how to get more evidence from Butch now that he had disappeared.

I picked up my phone and texted Glenn.

Did you ever talk to your mail carrier?

I waited. The bubbles appeared.

Purple tips was there the night CJ was murdered.

Did Jamie and CJ get in a fight?

She said she got pretty drunk that night. Stayed until closing. She confirmed CJ went on a rant. She said she told him to shut the, well, you know, up and sat somewhere else.

If you see her today, ask her about Jamie. K?
He's in Vegas. He may have the money.

Interesting. How is Annie?

Just coming down the stairs.

I set my phone down and looked up. Annie was showered and dressed. "Do you mind if Custer comes over?"

"Of course not. How are you?" I stood and pulled her into a hug.

She patted my back and stepped back. "I'm pretty good." She turned around and retied her ponytail. "Is it possible for an experience like I just had to make a person stronger? I mean, all my life I've wondered how I would react in a crisis. Would I fight or flee? You never really know until you're tested."

"And you fought."

"I sure tried. Have they found him?"

"Not that I've heard. Just his empty truck."

"I'll feel better when they do," Annie said, and rubbed her wrists.

"Breakfast?"

"I'm starving."

Custer arrived just as we finished our doctored-up scrambled eggs. He and Annie embraced as if one of them had been away at war. And perhaps they both had, in a way.

They settled out on the porch. Tyler and Bini were working with the chicken fencing, so I asked Annie if it was all right if I checked in with Doris.

"Okay, Mom. Tell her I said hi."

"Any news?" Doris bent over and picked up my paper, looking stiff and older than her sixty-five years.

"Did you know Jamie is in Vegas?" I said. "There are photos of him on Facebook."

"The whole world knows Jamie is in Vegas. It's as if he's advertising it. Why would he do that, Miss Rosalie?"

"I'm not sure. Maybe he's hurting? People handle hurt in many ways."

"Jamie is aggressive that way. He doesn't like not being in control." Doris rolled her eyes. "I mean, you see how he is. He's a police officer. He worships his body. Never a hair out of place. And then it turns out his entire life has been one big fat lie."

"Doris, is there any way he has the money?"

"Ah, Rosalie, I can't think of anything but that. It's as if he wants them to catch him."

"Is he protecting Lori? Would he take the fall for her?"

"It appeared to me that he hated Lori last Thursday afternoon."

"It's hard to hate your mother. You can have a lot of feelings, but hate?"

"Can the sheriff see those pictures?"

"He should at least try if he's doing his job. If you want to understand the Millennials, you have to become familiar with social media." I dug through my purse for my wallet. "Did Lori make bail?"

Doris nodded. "She said it was pretty perfunctory. I think the good sheriff has lost his verve." Her forehead wrinkled up. "Is that the right word?"

"It is the perfect word." I handed her the money for my paper.

"I'm afraid I'm losing hope." Doris accepted my money. "Gum?"

"Yes." I selected a pack of wintergreen from the display.

"Say," she said as she dropped the change into the cash drawer, "how's Annie?"

"Resilient."

"Just like her mama."

I popped a piece of gum in my mouth and picked up my paper. "Annie is inspiring. She's already realizing what she's learned from this experience. Adversity can make you stronger. Please don't lose hope. Besides, I have an idea."

"You do?" Doris looked at me, her eyebrows arched.

"It's fuzzy, but I think it's coming into focus." I clicked my heels together. "I have no idea how, but I'm going to figure this out. Whoever it is, we have to know. It could be a friend, a family member, or, well, anyone."

"You just gave me a little flicker of hope. God bless you, Miss Rosalie Hart."

FORTY-NINE

I tossed my paper into my car and locked the doors. I texted Annie while I walked to the café. By the time I had filled a basket with muffins, she replied to say she and Custer were on a walk and I should take my time. I emerged into the bright sun, slipped on my sunglasses, and headed toward the square. I crossed the street and walked along the diagonal sidewalk through the park in the center of town. I admired the annuals Kevin had planted. Pink and lilac impatiens surrounded the fountain, lined the walkway, and spilled out of terra-cotta pots. He did it all on his own, wanting to beautify the town he loved.

I passed the library, the post office, and a few historic houses. A Victorian with gables and authentic dark green and magenta paint stood majestically on a corner. I took a right and entered the John Adams College campus. Summer students were enjoying the good weather, sunbathing here and there, tossing lacrosse balls, and reading under trees. I noticed the new dorm rising from the ground like a phoenix. Traditional John Adams College red brick was progressing up the sides. Hammers pounded from within.

As I neared the construction site, I felt someone following me. My instinct was to pick up the pace. But I channeled Annie's inner tiger and turned around abruptly.

"Cal," I said.

"Where are you going with that basket?"

"Nowhere now."

He placed his hands on his hips. His white tee was filthy, his yellow hard hat askew. "Are you responsible for this?"

"Your dirty shirt?"

"Somebody figured out who took the money. And something tells me it wasn't the private investigators."

"Sometimes things fall into your lap." I picked the paper bag out of the basket and handed it to him. "There probably aren't enough to go around now that everyone is back to work."

"You think I share these?" He smiled.

"I really appreciate your help," I said. "I thought I needed more information from you, but I think I know what I need to do."

"Does that mean no more treats?"

"I didn't say that. Wish me luck?"

"Always."

I continued down the sidewalk and stopped at a three-story brick building. A sign outside said LIBERAL ARTS. Jake was a literature professor. I was pretty sure he taught creative writing and American lit. Hopefully he was in his office.

The tip tap of my shoes on the marble floor resounded in the hallway. I read the directory and found Jake's office number: 204. The building was quiet and cool. I climbed the stairwell, one hand on the large banister, the steps worn down from the many students who had ascended and descended the steps over many years.

The door to 204 was partially open. I rapped lightly on the oak door. "Hello?" I called.

"Come in," Jake's deep, resonant voice replied. I stepped in, and he looked up from a laptop, wire glasses low on his nose. "Rosalie. What a pleasant surprise."

"Am I disturbing you?"

"Not at all." He was wearing a gray John Adams Lacrosse T-shirt with faded blue letters, the lower half of his face darkened by stubble. "Just perusing Facebook. Your café is doing well." He smiled. "I'm a fan."

I stepped inside and looked around. The bookshelves were loaded with trophies and team photos; one, stuffed with books, filled an entire wall. Framed diplomas and awards lined the others. Overflow volumes were stacked on the floor haphazardly.

"Can you sit for a minute?" Jake said, and removed his glasses.

"I would love to." I perched in one of two wooden chairs facing his desk and crossed my legs. "I was just taking a walk and noticed this building. I was hoping you'd be here so I could say hi."

Jake closed his laptop. "It's good to see you. I've been feeling a little sheepish about my behavior the other night."

"Please don't. I love those conversations, when friends are being honest and forthright. Don't you find when you're having those talks you're often surprised what comes out of your mouth?"

He leaned back in his chair and folded his hands behind his head. His biceps bulged. "Well, I'm sure I surprised you."

"Have you thought more about what you're going to do?"

"Every minute. It's the biggest decision I've ever had to make."

"If you leave Kevin, will you go back in the closet?"

"I think I've lost that option, for a whole lot of reasons."

"What does your heart say?"

"Ouch?"

"Mmm," I said. "I get that."

"What about you? Will you ever marry again? Or have you given up on that institution?"

I smiled. "No one's ever asked me that before." I gazed out at the lawn below. A breeze blew in the large window and rustled the papers on Jake's desk. My hair fluttered around my face. I looked back at him. "It's been a long time, but I remember really enjoying being in love. And I was very happy being married. So, yes, I hope to love again and remarry. When the right guy comes along, of course. Not sure if that's going to happen while I'm working in a café on the Eastern Shore all day."

"There's the Internet."

"True. But for now I'm too busy." I tried to ignore the small ache in my stomach. Ever since feeling rebuffed by Tyler, I had lost the urge to eat. For days I had deluded myself that maybe we had a thing.

"Hello?" Jake called softly.

"Honestly? There is a guy. I thought we might be working toward something, but I've just learned I was wrong."

"Ouch."

"Yes, another ouch. Seems we have that in common too. But I guess he and I will still be friends. Goodness, now who has the loose lips? I've never told anyone that before."

"I'm honored. Now we're even."

"Jake, I keep wondering why you are wiling to let CJ impact your future."

"Because CJ happened. And it probably won't be the last time a guy like him gets so closed up in his own small mind that he lashes out."

"So the last incident was the eruption at President Carmichael's office. Did he do anything else after that?"

"No. He ran out of time."

"Jake?"

"You're wondering if I killed him, aren't you?"

"Did you? Because I won't judge. My daughter was just abducted for a short time, but if I encountered that man, I would consider doing him harm."

"Is she okay?"

"Yes. She wasn't physically harmed, but he abducted her. He was using her to get to someone else. I think she's pretty shaken up, but she seems to be handling it okay for now."

"I would do anything to protect Kevin. But I knew better than to go after CJ. You see, people who attack out of a deep loathing have a terrible force behind them. It's as if they feel justified, so the impact is over the top. If I took CJ on, he would up the ante so high I would have to retaliate with equal force. Guys like him dehumanize people like me, which can make them justify any sort of behavior."

"So you left him alone?"

"I thought about going after him. He was going to continue to escalate. There was nothing stopping him. But to answer your question, I didn't."

"And Kevin?"

"No." Jake shook his head. "He doesn't have it in him."

"He sure loves you."

"I get what you're saying about your kid. But honestly? I don't think you would have killed the guy who used your daughter. There aren't a whole lot of 'love' crimes. Hate crimes, oh yeah. But I don't see people killing because they love someone with their whole being."

"And Kevin loves you."

"There's a lot of hate in this world, Rosalie. A lot of prejudices and single-minded bigots who feel obligated to rid the world of people who aren't like them. People they feel better than."

"So they win?"

"Sometimes."

"Maybe not this time?"

Jake leaned forward, his forearms on his desk. "I haven't made any decisions."

"I will never know what it's like to be a gay man in this world. Or black, or Muslim. I am a woman, and I have certainly faced adversity as a result, but I will never walk in your shoes. I can only admire you for stepping out the door every day and being true to yourself. That's huge."

"Wow." Jake shook his head. "Thank you."

I smiled over at him. "I still would have understood if you had gotten in an altercation with CJ that ended badly."

"You would have. But don't you see? As much as that guy stirred me up, on a rational level I know that when a gay man is pleading self-defense, there are going to be a whole lot of folks on the jury who think, well, buddy, if you weren't gay, this never would have happened. *Boom*. Prison doors close, and Jake Willows's life is over."

"Well, then, I'm really glad you didn't kill CJ. Okay, thanks for the talk. This was lovely, as always." I slapped my hand on my thighs. "I'm really glad I wandered by here."

Jake stood and rounded his desk. "I'm glad, too. And I'm glad your daughter is okay. Kevin and I will have you over, and you can tell us all about it. No, better yet, bring her, and *she* can tell us all about it."

"Hmm." I raised an eyebrow. "You and Kevin entertaining? I like the sound of that."

"Listen to you." Jake smiled. "I'm not sure what just happened here, but I enjoy talking to you, Rosalie Hart."

FIFTY

I dropped the basket in my car and texted Annie again as I walked.

You ok? Mind if I make one more stop?

np. I'm helping Bini with a project. It's fun. Take ur time.

I wondered what on earth that could be.

Tyler is really sorry about what his brother did to me. We had a really nice talk.

Good. I love you. xo

I slid my phone in my purse and hitched it up my shoulder. I believed Jake. And I was extremely relived to cross him off the suspect list. I walked back into town and headed for the sheriff's department. I had three more suspects left. My body resonated with the feeling that I was close. Really close.

I waited at a light, although there wasn't a car on the road. I could see the sheriff's department at the end of the block. It was housed in an old train depot that had to be at least two hundred years old. A large, sloping patinated copper roof made it a landmark in Cardigan.

Delilah sat behind a desk, her dyed red hair glowing in the sun streaming through the dimpled windows. She had been the secretary at the sheriff's department for the last forty years. Her cat-eyed glasses protected a pair of wide blinking blue eyes.

"Afternoon, Miss Rosalie."

"Hi, Lila. Is the sheriff in?"

She nodded enthusiastically. "I just typed up Lori's interview. Hearing's tomorrow."

"So soon?"

"State's attorney is ready to move."

"Can I go on back, or should you announce me?"

Lila looked over her shoulder. "Joe—Rosalie Hart's on her way back." She looked at me and smiled. "It's a small space."

I poked my head into the sheriff's office. "Mind if I come in?"

"Yes."

"Okay," I said and walked in the door. I sat in a gunmetal gray chair opposite his desk. "Can I ask you a few questions?"

He leaned back so far I thought his chair would topple over. "I thought I told you I had a case. And I also told you I'm tired. Spent. Kaput."

I set my purse on the floor. "Sheriff, where is CJ's truck?"

"Impound lot."

"How did you get it there?"

He frowned. "We had to tow it."

"Was the money inside?"

"No."

"Were the keys on his body? Pockets, maybe?"

The sheriff sat forward. "No. But they could have fallen out."

"You said the body wasn't moved. That whoever shot him left him the way he landed."

He lifted his chin. "So maybe Mrs. Fiddler has them. Maybe she wanted to keep her house key."

"If it was a crime of passion as you suggest, she certainly was thinking clearly enough to remember to get the keys."

"Doesn't have to be about passion. I'd be just as happy accusing her of having planned the whole thing."

"And the gun. Whoever shot CJ tried to wipe it clean but didn't do a very good job. Is that right? I mean, the woman cleans houses for a living. She certainly would know how to dust."

"Maybe she was in a hurry to get out of there. Wouldn't you be?"

"There were more than Lori's prints on it, though, am I right?"

He pinched his fingers together and zipped his lips.

"Sheriff, if I told you there is someone else who might have killed CJ, would you at least check to see if there were unknown prints on the gun?"

"No need."

I sat back, trying to regroup. "Oh, Sheriff Wilgus, is there someone in town who keeps a boat on one of the Caribbean islands?"

"Say what?"

"Sorry. Subject change."

"Fred Banks. Down in the Caymans. Why do you want to know that?"

"Fred Banks? I don't know him. What does he do here in Cardigan?"

"Retired. His wife left him a bunch of cash." He crossed his hands across his stomach. "Now he thinks he's Jimmy Buffet."

"I think I know who killed CJ and took the money. I'm very serious about this."

"And I'm laughing while you get the hell out of my office."

I stood. "Thank you for your time."

"What are you up to, Hart?."

"I'm just being me, and you are back to being you. But if I ask, will you please check for prints?"

"Get out of here. You're giving me a headache."

"Maybe drink some water. You may be dehydrated."

"Get out," he roared, and I skedaddled out of there as fast as I could.

"Thanks for stopping in," Lila called after me.

I checked the time and headed for my car. If I took the long way home I would pass the Cardigan Tavern. I had a favor to ask Chuck, and I prayed he would agree to do it.

FIFTY-ONE

I found Annie and Bini by the henhouse. Bini was on a ladder, and Annie was on the ground surrounded by pie tins and old CDs. "What's going on?"

"The hawk came back, so Bini and I are going to hang this stuff in the trees," Annie said. "Bini did some research, and apparently the noise and reflection of the sun will confuse the hawk."

"Wow," I said as I looked at the strings of aluminum foil Bini had looped around some branches. "Yard art."

"You want your eggs, don't you?" Bini said without turning around.

"She put that fake owl on top of the coop, too," Annie said.

Bini climbed down the ladder and brushed her hands together. "Hawks are solitary hunters. If they think another bird of prey is in their territory, they'll stay away."

"Whatever works," I said. "Is Tyler gone for the day?"

"He's talking to one of your suppliers," Bini said. "Can you do anything with pastrami?"

"That's sounds delicious. Same guy I get the bacon from?"

"Yup."

My mind was already coming up with ideas. I had recently

discovered an amazing creamy Dijon mustard from France. A breeze rustled the aluminum. A pie tin took flight, and I ran after it. When I brought it back I said, "Do you need some help?"

"Sure," Bini said.

I settled into the grass next to Annie, and she handed me some string and a pair of scissors. "There's something about scaring off predators that's therapeutic," I said. "Right, Annie?"

"I'm all about the fight." She grinned.

Bini was about to ascend the ladder again but stopped and turned to look at us. She blinked a few times. "So, you said that because of Butch. Is that right?"

"Yes, exactly," I said.

"Hmph," Bini said, and went back to work.

Later that evening, Annie and I sat at a card table and worked on the jigsaw puzzle. The doors were open, and we were accompanied by a nighttime symphony of chirps, yips, and hoots, punctuated with an occasional deep croak. Aunt Charlotte's table was torn in spots. The batting puffed out of the vinyl surface like little clouds. Rust crusted the joints of the chairs. But it was the only place I could imagine doing a puzzle in this house.

I'd stopped by the tavern on my way home that afternoon. Chuck had agreed to help by letting me know the next time Jackson showed up. Apparently he had been there every night so far this week drinking a very expensive whiskey. I hoped he wouldn't end his streak now. His visit to a Caribbean island made me think he had come into some cash. If CJ had been keeping the money in his truck to prevent Lori from giving it back, Jackson could have taken it after he killed him. Glenn agreed my scenario had some potential. But how would I get him to confess? I flipped a five-pronged jigsaw piece between my fingers and frowned. This was a process of elimination. Just as I had done with Jake, I had to learn whether or not Jackson was a murderer. If he wasn't, my next conversation would be with Jamie.

"I told Dad what happened," Annie said as she tapped a piece in place.

"What's that?" I eyed her over my reading glasses. "What did he say?"

"He was really nice."

"He was?"

"Instead of telling me what I should do or what I'd done wrong, he asked what he could do to help."

I set the oddly shaped piece down and selected one with a flat edge. I looked over at Annie. "That's wonderful."

The savory aroma of rye bread filled the living room. I checked the timer. Five more minutes before I would remove it from the oven. I noticed Annie reading something on her phone. "Are you going to see Custer tonight?"

"Would you mind?" She eyed me tentatively, her eyebrows arched. "I know we're doing the puzzle and all."

"Of course I don't mind."

Annie typed with both thumbs.

Ten minutes later, Custer's motorcycle was propped in the drive and he and Annie had settled on the porch. The bread was resting on a cooling rack, golden brown on top. My idea was to make paninis with the pastrami, adding some mustard and Swiss cheese. What else . . . red onion? A spicy relish? Maybe both.

I jumped when my phone signaled I had a text message.

He's here.

Custer had his arm around the back of the wicker love seat. His fingers twisted a lock of Annie's hair. His eyes were brighter, his nose still bandaged, the tape making an ex across his nose. "Hey, boss. Cops found my dad."

"Is he okay?"

"He got beat up pretty bad. He's in a hospital near DC."

"Oh, how awful. Is he in police custody?"

"For certain." Custer gave his head a definitive nod. "They charged him with kidnapping, among other things."

"I hate that word." I hugged myself. "It's terrifying."

"Agreed," Annie said, and snuggled in closer to Custer.

"Hey, I brought you something." Custer reached into the back pocket of his jeans, jostling Annie, and removed an index card. He held it out to me. "I don't know if you're interested, but my grandmother has offered you one of her secret recipes. It's been in the family for generations."

"Your grandmother on your mother's side?"

"That's the one. She lives down on the water in Oxford. Has her whole life." Custer drummed his fingers on Annie's shoulder.

The recipe was scratched out in a light pencil. "Shrimp and grits?" I looked up. "That's one of my favorite dishes."

"There's a secret ingredient."

I reread the card. "Scrapple?"

"That's it," Custer said. "She doesn't give it out to anyone. But when I told her how you've been helping me, she came up with the idea. It's her way of saying thanks. Maybe you could serve it as a special someday. I mean, only if you want to." He peered up at me.

"Oh, my goodness, Custer. This is a fabulous idea. It's like with Crystal's teas. We can do a little write-up about your grandmother. Maybe add a map of the Eastern Shore with a star for Oxford's location." I smoothed my thumb over the card. "I need to do some research on scrapple."

Custer tried in vain to suppress the smile on his face.

"Hey, you two, I need to run out again. I shouldn't be long. You okay?"

"No worries," Annie said as Custer kissed the top of her head. "Especially now that Butch isn't on the loose anymore."

FIFTY-TWO

I called Glenn as I drove into town. "I'm on my way to the tavern. Glenn, can you call the sheriff and tell him I'm going to confront the killer?"

"That won't be good news for him," Glenn said. "What do you want me to tell him?"

"Ask him to check the prints again and if there is a set that doesn't belong to either CJ, Lori, or Jamie, to please consider coming to the tavern."

"I will call him right away."

"Thank you. I'm still trying to figure out what to say to Boone. How on earth will I get him to confide in me?"

Glenn exhaled into the phone with a loud whoosh. "Rosalie, I don't know if you notice this kind of thing, but Jackson is a little sweet on you."

"He is?" I stopped at a light a little abruptly. "Really?"

"Um, yes. Very much. Why do you think he's been at the café every day, seated at the bar?"

"He likes the food?" I said, trying to take in what Glenn was saying.

"I know this goes against your nature, but maybe you could play that up."

"Glenn," I said, "I don't know how. I'll make a fool of myself."

"If Jackson is our man, do you want him to walk away?"

I continued down the road and turned into the tavern parking lot. "I've got to think about this for a minute. But I know one thing. Blue Point will be involved."

"Whatever it takes. But I don't think it will be as difficult as you think. Jackson has already bought an expensive watch and a gold chain. My guess is he's busting at the seams to tell someone he's rich. Who better to tell than you? A woman he wants to impress."

"I'm listening."

"Watch his alcohol intake. Gauge your timing. Let him get inebriated, but not so drunk he can't think straight."

"And if I'm close to getting a confession?"

"I'll wait in the parking lot, hopefully with our good sheriff. You text me when it's time to come in."

I turned off the car. The engine ticked and then fell silent. "The sheriff won't do it, Glenn. And he'll be very upset if I have him come here but can't get any results."

"Upset is not a new emotion for him. But I honestly don't believe he wants to convict an innocent woman, even if he is furious with her. If you don't hear from me, he agreed to come."

"Okay." I sunk my teeth into my bottom lip. "Glenn?"

"Yes, dear?"

"If Jackson did murder CJ, well, what if he regrets telling me everything?"

"I'll be there," Glenn said, "as will the sheriff. But you be careful, Rosalie. Please don't put yourself in harm's way. It's not worth it."

Dusk was settling in as I walked toward the tavern. Neon beer signs glowed in the high, narrow windows. When I stepped inside it looked as if the gray had crept right on into the bar.

Chuck was jiggling a martini shaker like a maraca. His arms pumped up and down as he signaled with his head. I squinted, adjusting my eyes to the room, and there was Jackson seated at the bar. I left several empty chairs between us when I sat down, folded my hands together, and squeezed them as if in a desperate prayer.

The Blue Point sloshed over the sides as Chuck set it in front of me. "Do I do that every time?" he said as he wiped the counter with a damp rag.

"No worries. You wouldn't believe how much coffee I spill in a day." I took a small sip. "Thank you for helping me, Chuck," I said in a hushed voice. "I know you like to stay neutral, but this is the only idea I could come up with."

"Even Switzerland has to take a stand now and then." He rubbed the top of his shiny head and whispered, "Just don't let it get around that I helped. Okay?"

"Indeed." I checked to ensure Jackson was still engrossed in his drink and nudged my phone across the counter. "I have my text to Glenn already written. All you need to do is hit send. Oh, and the password is *t-o-d-d*."

Chuck dropped my phone in his pocket. "Got it."

I clutched my glass and looked down the bar again. Jackson was hunched over his drink. I gazed at him, willing myself to pull this off. I was surprised when he looked up. I gave him a little wave.

"Rosalie," he called. "What the heck are you doing here?" He picked up his drink and walked over to me. I pressed my spine against the back of the chair.

"I think I'm becoming a bit of a regular." I hesitated. I had to play this just right. "I get lonely in that big old house all by myself."

"Well, that's certainly good news." He eased himself onto the chair next to me. His face was ruddy despite the tan. "But I must say, I never expected to see a pretty lady like you hanging out at the tavern."

"Hey, watch it," Chuck said. "Maybe she likes the company."

Jackson laughed. "This here Chuck's a good guy, ain't he? He's the trustworthy type. Good quality in a bartender."

"Yes," I said. "I agree."

"I'll have another, old buddy."

"Another Gold Label?" Chuck said. "You sure?"

"Why not?" Jackson said. "Life is short. Life is good."

I took a long drink. "You must be happy to finally be back to work at the college, Jackson."

"I'm there, but I need to undo the lame job those other guys did. Some people around here assume getting help from the city means the workmanship will be better. But they don't recognize the talent we have here in Cardigan. We're a hard-working lot. Doesn't get any better."

Chuck set a glass in front of Jackson and stepped away. He started adjusting the vodka bottles, turning them so the labels faced forward. It was clear by the way he kept his head motionless that he was listening intently to our conversation.

"You must be relieved Lori confessed about CJ stealing the money," I said. "I wonder where it is now."

Jackson took his first sip of the new pour. "It's probably still in the back of his pickup."

"How do you know that, Jackson?" Slow down, I thought. He has to warm up to you. "Or have you already figured this out on your own?" I crossed my legs and smoothed my skirt over my thigh. "I know you're very clever."

He glanced down at my legs. "Didn't have to figure it out, although I'm sure I would have. Dumb sucker told me. Sitting right at this very bar. He couldn't keep his mouth shut. Never could. He said his wife was pressuring him to give it back. He was worried she'd do it, so he kept it with him."

I took a another long swig of my beer. I didn't have a clue

what to say next. Jackson was looking at my legs again. I cleared my throat. "He must have really trusted you if he told you such a private thing."

"He offered me ten percent if I could find a way to get him out of the country."

"That's a pretty good offer." I smiled and finished my beer. I put my fingers over my mouth and stifled a dainty burp.

"Say, Chuck," Jackson said, and polished off his whiskey. "How's 'bout another round for me and Miss Rosalie."

"Good idea," I said. "But I think I'll have what you're drinking. What's Gold Label?"

"The good stuff." He winked. "You sure look pretty tonight. Nice skirt. So you're a drinker, then."

"I grew up on a farm," I said. "I had my first beer when I was twelve."

Jackson's eyes widened in surprise. "That right?"

I tried to hold his gaze while Chuck set our drinks in front of us. "So did you take CJ up on his offer? Or at least try?"

"Nah. Sounded messy. CJ was a sloppy guy. In everything but his profession." Jackson sipped his whiskey.

I studied his eyes. The pupils were slightly dilated. No slurred speech yet. But this was his second drink since he'd sat down next to me. I had no idea how many he'd had before I arrived. I had to nudge this along. I took a sip and almost spit it out. My throat burned. I steeled myself and took another. "You know, it's kind of sad, Jackson. CJ died and never got to spend any of that money."

"Oh, I don't know. If you ask me, he wouldn't have known how to spend it. CJ just wasn't cut out for being rich. You see what I'm saying?"

"Unlike you." I felt a little nauseous. "I bet you could handle it."

"I've been told I have very good taste." Jackson sat a little straighter.

"So where is that money? Did anyone else hear CJ tell you he had it?" I took another sip, eyeing him over the rim of my glass. "Maybe that's who killed CJ."

Jackson shrugged. "Could be. Hey, Chuck," he said. "Remember that night CJ got shot?"

Chuck loaded a blender with a heavy dose of tequila and some margarita mix. "I'm not going to forget that night for a while, Jackson."

"Was anyone sitting near us?"

Chuck shook his head. "After CJ went on his antigay rant, I think he pretty much cleared out his end of the bar." He fired up the blender.

Jackson's eyebrows dipped as if he was considering something. The blender went silent.

"Maybe CJ should have just skipped town on his own," I said. "Maybe gone to the Cayman Islands or something. If he had any brains, that is."

Jackson looked over at me. "Say what?"

One more sip. "This stuff is pretty good. I'm getting a little woozy." I braced my hands on the bar. "Liquor is quicker, right?"

"I like the quicker part." Jackson had started to slur his words. I thought about Glenn's advice. It was time.

"I think the Caymans would be a fabulous place to live out your days. That's always been my fantasy." I spun my glass around. "Just the idea of it makes me feel warm inside."

Chuck froze mid-pour.

"That right?" Jackson smiled at me.

"If that kind of money fell into my hands, I would get on the first plane out of here."

"I like the way you think, missy." He patted my hand.

"You know, Jackson, even if the money was stolen, there's no need to bide your time before you leave. I mean, someone has already been charged with the murder *and* stealing the money. Why would they come after you?"

"I didn't steal that money."

"I know. CJ did. Everyone knows that now."

Chuck reached for my phone in his pocket. He turned away and looked down at it.

"I had a lousy husband, Jackson. I really did." I dipped my head closer to his. He was wearing some very strong cologne, but not enough to mask an underlying body odor. I was beginning to doubt very seriously that I could pull this off. I squeezed my eyes shut. Alessa. She could do this. And she was older than me. I used to feel attractive, I thought. There was a time Ed found me sexy.

There. That was my problem. I still saw myself through Ed's rejecting eyes. But Ed didn't get to decide if I was attractive anymore. And there was a really good chance I still was. Every woman is attractive, I thought. We just have to tap into that inner passion that makes us glow.

I rolled my shoulders back. "Just imagine it, Jackson. Warm sun on your skin every day of the year. Sand between your toes." I looked up at him. "Flowers in your hair."

Chuck dropped the phone in his pocket and finished filling the glasses with margaritas.

Jackson studied me. "You would run away, just like that?"

I gazed up at him with the most soulful eyes I could muster. "Yes." I searched his face and whispered, "In a nanosecond."

Jackson shook his head a little, as if trying to bring me into focus. His eyes narrowed. "What if I could do that for you, missy? Get you out of here. Take you someplace tropical."

"Don't tease me, Jackson." I heard the door open and close. I had to keep Jackson's eyes on me. If he saw the sheriff looming behind us, this was all a wash. I touched his arm and ran my finger over the face of his watch. "That's beautiful."

"There's more where that came from. You like diamonds?"

I nodded enthusiastically. "I think they look especially sparkly on tanned skin." I was close and yet felt miles away. I might get this man to proposition me, but how would I get him to tell me what he'd done? Stroke his ego, I thought. Just like Glenn said. He's proud to have the money. Bursting at the seams. I slid the toe of my pump over his calf. "So you would buy me diamonds?"

He leaned in closer. "Whatever you desire." His breath smelled of whiskey and a trace of old socks.

I caught Chuck's eye. His brow was furrowed. Maybe I was closer than I thought. I faced Jackson and fluffed my hair. "What are you saying?"

"Come with me," he purred, a hungry look in his eye.

"Where?" I whispered.

"The Caymans, just like you said. Maybe it's fate you wandered in here tonight." He leaned in so close his face blurred. "I'm leaving in two days." He draped his arm around my chair possessively. "Anything you want is yours."

"You sure I won't cramp your style?"

"Oh yeah." His hand slid down to my bottom. It was all I could do to not sock him in the gut. "You won't need no surfer boy if you got Jackson Crawford in your hut."

"Really?" I said. "Two days? I guess I won't need to pack much." I scooted back in my seat. "Tell me, Jackson." I swallowed, willing myself to not look at Chuck and break Jackson's trance. "How did it all go down? Come on, I love this stuff. It's like a movie. You must have been amazing. I'll bet you were just like George Clooney."

Jackson puffed out his chest. "I waited for him outside. CJ always parked in the back, because he didn't want anyone to take the money. When he stumbled out of the tavern I told him I wanted it. He said he would give me half to keep me quiet. But you see, there was no reason for me to agree to that. He could either give it all to me, or I would turn him in. Next thing I knew, CJ reached in his truck and took out a shotgun. He locked the doors and faced me. I tried to calm him down, but he pointed it right at me. Guy was so drunk I got it from him, although he put up a pretty tough struggle. But I'm a whole lot stronger." Jackson tightened his bicep muscle. "Next thing I knew, he lunged at me. It was self-defense, pure and simple." Jackson finished his drink and gazed into my eyes. "You got a bikini?"

"No," the sheriff said. "But I got me some prints."

FIFTY-THREE

Annie returned to work on Wednesday, and I was glad to have a day at the café where I could massage recipes and tap into my creativity. I had asked Janice where I could find some high-quality scrapple, and she replied that high-quality scrapple was an oxymoron. But I was intrigued by Custer's grandmother's recipe. Scrapple was purportedly an Eastern Shore staple made with pork scraps, different kinds of flour, and spices. The finished product was a congealed log of sorts. After coming up short with Janice, I knew exactly who would be able to direct me to the proper source for good scrapple: Bini. And sure enough, the very next day she brought me a pound of freshly made Eastern Shore scrapple.

I left my grocery bags in the kitchen and went out to the dining room. The tables were scrubbed clean, the floors polished, the menus stacked. A large pile of mail was spread out on the bar.

I clicked the remote and turned on the stereo system in the dining room. After flipping through the CDs, I decided *The Best of Andrea Bocelli: Vivere* would be the perfect accompaniment to inspire me. I cranked up the volume and put the wedge under the swinging door so I could hear every evocative note while in the kitchen.

A breeze blew in the door as I spread the ingredients out in front of me. I scrubbed a red pepper and placed it on a rack in the oven to roast. I was glad the investigation was over, freeing me up to focus my energies on the café again. Doris's sister was safe and sound and trying to rebuild her new, and very different life. I was sorry to see Jackson go to jail, but then again, he did kill a man. I had been worried about the health of his heart when he saw the sheriff standing behind us, the light from the windows enlarging Joe's presence to feel almost godlike. Jackson's mouth had fallen open as he looked at me in confusion. I felt wretched, a familiar feeling when solving a murder. CJ Fiddler was dead. And Jackson had killed him. Glenn nailed it when he predicted Jackson would have wanted to tell me what he'd done. And maybe Jake was more right than he realized about human nature. Boone had convinced himself CJ was nothing but a loudmouthed fool. Dehumanizing him in that way must have made it easier to take his life.

The music reached a crescendo, as I continued to work, sautéing the crumbled scrapple, peeling the shrimp. I was in my café, and it grounded me. My father had walked the perimeter of his farm like a rooster protecting what and who he loved. I was beginning to understand him now, because I too felt a fierce protectiveness for the people and places I cherished. There it was—our similarity. Thank you, Bini. Why hadn't I realized growing up how content my father was with his life? He didn't need more. I was his little girl with her own eccentricities and he loved me for who I was. I once saw a saying, *happiness is loving what you have.* My father could have written it and he certainly lived it. I smiled to myself. Understanding him in this way gave me a sense of peace.

Bocelli kept me company as I worked. Custer's grandmother's aged index card was propped against the salt shaker. The grits were simmering in butter and cream. The pepper had blackened and I put it to rest in a brown bag. I dipped a shrimp in buttermilk and dredged it in some cornmeal mixed with Old Bay seasoning. Once all the shrimp were coated, I dropped them in a frying pan with a little vegetable oil and butter. The shrimp were fresh, and they pinked up in no time. The scrapple was draining on a paper towel.

I peeled the charred skin from the red pepper, diced it and added it to the grits along with some aged cheddar cheese and seasonings. Next came the crumbled scrapple and I stirred it all together. I rubbed my hands together. Time for the taste test.

After scooping some of the grits mixture in a bowl and topping it with the shrimp, I grabbed a napkin and headed out to the bar. As I walked through the open door, I wondered what the side should be. Roasted corn on the cob? Maybe sliced in thirds, slathered in butter, and dusted with Hungarian paprika? I wondered if Custer's grandmother had a signature coleslaw recipe.

I perched at the bar, dipped in my fork, and took a bite. "Whoa," I said with my mouth full. It was delicious. Normally I would be already thinking of ways to tweak a new creation, but this wasn't my recipe to tamper with. And my guess was this one had been honed and adjusted for generations.

I finished the entire bowl and was so excited I wanted to share it with my friends. Maybe I would drop some off at Glenn's place on my way home. And Doris Bird might be needing a little something for dinner. And I should definitely take some to Jake and Kevin. I could bring them a bottle of wine, maybe coax them together a little more.

Next I made a batch of medium-roast coffee, my afternoon go-to, and sat at the counter sorting through my mail. I sipped my coffee and flipped through a brochure I'd ordered last week, excited it had arrived. I startled when I heard a knock at the door. I turned to see the sheriff peering in.

"Hi," I said as I opened the door. He was in civilian clothes, khakis and a short-sleeved polo shirt, a rarity for him. "You're just in time for coffee."

"No coffee. I'm on my way to the airport."

"You're taking a vacation?" I smiled. "It's about time."

"I'm going to Las Vegas to get Jamie."

"Oh my gosh," I said. "You are? Did Lori ask you to do that?"

"No. This is something I'm doing on my own. What do you think? No," he said, shaking his head. "I don't want to know what you think. I'm not even sure why I'm here telling you."

"Come and sit down. Just for a minute." I preceded him to the bar where we both perched on the high-backed chairs. The sheriff seemed preoccupied and combed his hand through his hair several times. It was unusual to see him hatless. "Sheriff, what will you do when you get there?"

"I'm not really sure. First I have to find him."

"That shouldn't be too hard. After all, you are the law."

"Yeah, I know." He looked up at me. His crow's-feet intensified as he narrowed his eyes. "I keep telling myself he must have told me about the paternity results for a reason. If he didn't want anything to do with me, then why let me know?"

"That's a very good question. I agree, he wanted you to know."

"Thing is, I can't stop thinking he got it from me. The drinking, that is." His forehead was deeply lined. "Maybe I can help him stop before it gets out of control."

My heart warmed. That had never before happened in the presence of this man. "Go after him," I said. "Forge that connection. I think it could be very good for both of you."

He studied me. "I don't know how to do that, but . . ." He checked his watch. "But I have to at least try." He stood and removed his sunglasses.

I couldn't contain the wide grin I felt bubbling up from inside. "Godspeed."

He gave his head a stiff nod and walked out the door.

I sat back at the bar and sipped my coffee. I flipped through the pages of the brochure. The photographs were stunning. Breathtaking landscapes. Ancient buildings. Italy. I longed to go to there. The Italians seemed to know the secret to living, relishing everyday pleasures: food, wine, love. Love. I propped my chin in my palm. There it was again. My missing piece. I thought about Tyler. Did I love him? I rolled my eyes. I'd loved him for a long time. And it had grown stronger every day I'd spent with him. Having thought so much about my father, I had gained some insight into who I had been in my marriage—a placater, pleaser, waiting for direction from someone else on how to live my life.

I gazed around the café, admiring the ochre walls and floral toppers, the gleaming Mieles and the chalkboard waiting for the next special. I was different now. I was ready to relish life like an Italian. I closed the brochure. Maybe I could learn the language. Maybe I could—I startled when I heard a noise in the kitchen. "Hello?" I called out. I could see the shadow of someone moving about. I heard cabinets opening and closing. "*Hello*?" I said again. The kitchen door opened and Dickens trotted through. "Oh my goodness." I hopped up and ran over to him. "Look at you." I scratched his ears enthusiastically. His tail thumped against the floor. "You're out and about."

Tyler's head appeared in the doorway. "Busy?"

"No." I wrapped my arms around Dickens. "Tyler, he seems better."

"Steroids. Doc said it could slow down the cancer for a couple of years if it takes, and it sure seems to be."

"Oh my goodness. That's wonderful news." Dickens perched on the floor and rested his head on my knees.

"I brought you something," Tyler said. "It's a little belated. But I can't find the champagne glasses. Don't you serve champagne now?"

I set Dickens's head gently on the floor and stood. "They're out here, on the shelf."

Tyler walked behind the bar and picked up two glasses. I noted he didn't need to stand on his tiptoes. The scent of sandalwood met my nose. He was in clean, faded jeans and a T-shirt that was a little more snug than I was used to seeing him wear. His sandy blond hair was loose about his head, his ball cap stuffed into the back pocket of his jeans.

"Punch out early?" I watched as he set the glasses next to each other on the marble.

"Bini's letting the chickens free range, then I think she'll call it a day, too."

"Mmm. Champagne." I spun the bottle around. "Moët and Chandon? Nice."

"Read the entire label."

I leaned in closer. "Dom Perignon? Oh my gosh, Tyler, did you win the lottery or something?"

"Let's just say I got a good deal on the spinach this spring." He peeled off the foil surrounding the cork, unwound the wire, wrapped the towel around the top of the bottle, and eased out the cork stopper. After a quiet pop, a cool mist rose out of the opening. Alessa would have approved.

He filled the glasses and raised his in a toast. "To the Day Lily Café. Long may she live."

"Thank you, Tyler." We clinked glasses. I smiled up at him and took a long, luxurious sip. The bubbles tickled my throat.

He studied me. "You know what I realized this afternoon?"

"What's that?"

"I've missed seeing you."

"You have?"

"I'm used to having you around the farm every day."

"I've been feeling the same way. I miss talking with you."

He leaned back against the counter. "I also want to apologize for the other night."

"Why?" I took another sip. "Tyler, did you only kiss me because you'd been drinking? Do you regret it now?"

"What? That's not what I meant. I was worried I had crossed some sort of boundary because the wine had freed me up to do so. I told you that night I'd wanted to kiss you from the first day I met you."

I inhaled deeply and focused. I wanted to be fully present for this moment. No fears, no old worries. I was Rosalie Hart, the owner of the Day Lily Café. "It was a lovely kiss."

Tyler came around the bar and sat down. He put his hands on either side of my chair and turned it so we faced each other. "I said that about the wine because it gave me the courage to kiss you. I didn't regret it in the morning." He lifted my chin and kissed me with his soft lips. Every dormant nerve ending responded, and a delicious warmth ignited my body. When he finished I looked into his eyes. He met my gaze. "How was that one?"

"Even better."

"You sure?" He had a playful grin on his face. "'Cause I really like kissing you."

"I like kissing you, too."

He handed me my champagne glass. "It might get weird. How are we going to play this?"

I took a long sip. The bubbles were so tiny and numerous they made me giggle. "You know, maybe what seems weird to our friends is that it's taken us this long."

"Maybe," he said. "But you and I needed to learn to trust again. Otherwise it never would have worked."

"And are you ready now?"

"Honestly? I've been ready for a while. But I wanted to make sure you were, too."

I put my hand on his and played with his fingers. "You're very astute."

"So we can do this, right?"

"Yes. We will still do what we do. Only now we get to kiss and stuff."

"And stuff?" His eyes danced.

My face warmed. "Maybe we shouldn't overthink it."

"Agreed." He topped off my glass. "You like this champagne."

"Very much."

Tyler looked around the room as he sipped. "This place is amazing. I didn't really get a chance to see it when there were so many people here last week."

I studied his profile. His straight nose, dimpled chin, long lashes. "Thank you for celebrating with me."

"You know, Rosalie, I have a few ideas of my own."

Wow. He so rarely said my name. It sounded as beautiful as the note Bocelli was singing in the background. "Tell me, Tyler."

"I'm talking about the farm. I know we've already done a lot, but it could be so much more. Not just organic crops, but organic animals, and flowers that attract the right insects, all keeping the ecosystem stable. Global warming is snowballing." He stopped, his brow furrowed. "That metaphor didn't quite work."

I laughed, kicked off my shoes, and tucked my legs beneath me.

"We could establish a humane slaughter system," he continued. "That way we could raise some cattle. They've done studies about animals and stress. And if we decide to do it, we wouldn't have to stuff them into trucks and send them to feedlots. We could do it right there on the farm. We're forming the co-op, and I've got a lot of interest from other farms."

"Cattle?"

"Grass-fed beef. I've been trying to decide which field I'll put them in. I may forgo the soybeans this year and plant grass. I'm not sure what kind is the best, but Bini will do the research."

"I like the idea a lot, actually. I love cows."

"Don't tell me you're going to name them."

"Of course I will. I've already got some ideas. Will they be Black Angus?"

He grimaced. "Yes."

"There will have to be a Midnight. Oh, and Shadow."

"At least they'll be original."

"I've got one, Cocoa Chanel, *c-o-c-o-a*." I nudged him. "Come on, that's pretty good."

"You go ahead and think up your names, but I've got a lot to do to make it happen." He eyed me. "So you're okay with this?"

I nodded enthusiastically. "More than okay. I love it. And I'll help you in any way I can."

"We'll learn together." He pointed at me and then himself. "You and me."

I lifted my glass. "Another toast?"

"Always."

"Here's to you and me being sustainable, too."

He smiled. "Yes, Rosalie. I like the sound of that." He clinked his glass against mine, locked eyes with me, and drained his champagne. He set the glass down. "Actually, that raises another question."

"Really?" My heart fluttered with anticipation.

He reached over to the stack of mail and picked up my brochure. "Any particular reason you were reading this?"

I swallowed hard as he held it up.

Casa Bianca. A villa set high in the hills of Tuscany offering two-week-long cooking vacations.

"Oh, that. Just a little somethin' I was thinking about doing."

Recipes

Grand Opening Egg Bake

This dish serves six and can be prepared in one large skillet or it can be prepared in a large skillet then dished into six oval ramekins before baking.

¼ cup olive oil
1 medium onion, chopped
1 green pepper, chopped
1 red bell pepper, chopped
4 garlic cloves, finely chopped
½ to 1 teaspoon Rosalie's aromatic salt (see recipe below)
1 teaspoon dried oregano
1 28-ounce can crushed organic Italian tomatoes
½ can chopped ripe olives or 1 small can sliced ripe olives
12 to 14 fresh mozzarella pearls
6 eggs

½ cup shredded whole milk organic aged white cheddar cheese
4 to 6 basil leaves, chopped

Preheat oven to 425°

Pour olive oil into a large skillet. Add onion, both peppers, and garlic. Sauté over medium/high heat for 15 to 20 minutes or until peppers and onions have softened, stirring occasionally.

Pour in tomatoes and add the olives, oregano, and salt. Stir together and cook until mixture has begun to thicken. Remove from heat. Fill ramekins if using at this point. Scatter the mozzarella over the top. Push the pearls into the sauce with a spoon. Crack an egg over each ramekin or crack six eggs over mixture in the skillet spacing them evenly. Top with basil and shredded cheese.

Bake in the oven for 10 to 15 minutes or until the egg whites are solid but the yolk is still slightly runny.

Serve with a side arugula salad, thick crusty bread, and a potato cake.

Variation: Replace mozzarella and basil with feta crumbles and fresh oregano.

Potato Cake

4 to 5 Yukon gold potatoes
1 small yellow onion

1 egg
3 tablespoons flour
¼ teaspoon Rosalie's aromatic salt
2 small chive stalks, snipped into small pieces
2 tablespoons butter
vegetable oil

Peel potatoes and boil until softened but not mushy, 10 to 20 minutes depending on the size of the potatoes. Let cool. Grate the potatoes and onion and drain in a sieve, compressing them with your fists to induce drainage. Cover with a dish towel and let them sit for ten minutes. Pour off additional fluid. Place potatoes in a bowl and combine with remaining ingredients.

Form the potatoes into patties and prepare either of the following ways:

Fry: Melt butter and oil to coat the bottom of the pan. Patties should be partially immersed. Place the patties in the skillet and cook on medium to medium/high heat flipping frequently until the outsides are crispy.

Bake: Brush a baking pan generously with oil. Place cakes on the pan and brush tops with oil. Bake 10 minutes at 350° then broil until crispy and browned, flipping once.

Easy Arugula Side Salad

I know arugula leaves are usually served whole, but when dining out or with friends at home, I always appreciate a chopped salad. It is much easier to eat and you aren't caught with a lettuce stem sticking out of your mouth or your salad falling onto the table while you try to toss it.

1 small bag organic arugula, coarsely chopped
1 lemon
⅛ to ¼ cup olive oil (to taste)
½ to 1 cup freshly grated or shaved parmesan cheese
Rosalie's aromatic salt to taste
Freshly ground pepper

Squeeze the lemon over the arugula. Add olive oil, parmesan, salt, and pepper and toss. Serve immediately and enjoy!

Caramelized Onion Grilled Cheese and Ten-Minute Tomato Soup

Although the pesto mayonnaise grilled cheese offered by the Day Lily is a crowd favorite, I recently traveled to New York to visit my brother, Oliver, and had the most incredible grilled cheese made with sweet caramelized onions. I came up with my own version and although it takes a little time to caramelize the onions, it's well worth the effort.

Caramelized Onion Grilled Cheese

For one sandwich:
Crusty roll or 2 slices of deli bread
4 slices organic Baby Swiss cheese
4 slices organic aged white cheddar cheese
Chipotle mayonnaise (available in most grocery stores)

6 tablespoons caramelized onion or more if you have room on the bread (see recipe below)
Butter for the bread

Slather the mayo over the inside of both slices of bread. Spoon onions over the bottom slice. Top with both types of cheese. Cover with second slice of bread. Butter outside of sandwich and grill in a panini maker until cheese is melted and bread is toasted. Slice in half diagonally and eat with the soup. I particularly enjoy dipping the edge of the sandwich into the soup before taking a bite. This sandwich can also be grilled on a stove top.

Caramelized onions
4 to 5 yellow onions, sliced
1 large shallot, sliced
3 tablespoons butter
½ teaspoon sugar
1 teaspoon salt

Melt the butter in a large sauté pan. Add onions and shallot and cook on medium heat, stirring frequently. Cook until onions are soft, about 20 minutes. Stir in sugar and salt and increase heat to medium high. Cook onions until caramelized, stirring frequently. Remove from heat. Store in refrigerator until ready to make the grilled cheese. Warm to room temperature before making the sandwich. Leftovers are perfect for a bowl of French onion soup.

Ten-Minute Tomato Soup

2 tablespoons butter
1 shallot, diced

2 cloves garlic, pressed through a garlic press
1 28-ounce can whole Italian tomatoes
2 cups broth or stock
½ teaspoon Rosalie's aromatic salt
1 tablespoon tomato paste (Buy it in a tube and nothing goes to waste.)
2 small sprigs of each: basil, oregano, and thyme tied together with a clean string
½ to 1 cup heavy cream or half and half

Sauté the shallot and garlic in melted butter on medium heat until aromatic. Add the tomatoes and their juices, the stock or broth, tomato paste, and salt. Stir together and bring to a boil. Reduce heat to medium low. Using an immersion blender, puree ingredients until the soup is smooth and creamy. Drop in herbs and simmer 5 minutes or longer. Remove herbs and swirl in the cream.

If you don't have time to make the sandwich, add some garlic croutons and/or freshly grated parmesan cheese. Serve with a small salad of chopped romaine lettuce and a good Italian vinaigrette.

Kevin's Key Lime Bars

Crust
6 tablespoons chilled butter
3 tablespoons sugar
½ teaspoon salt
1 organic egg yolk (save the egg white for the filling)
½ teaspoon Mexican vanilla

1 cup flour

Preheat oven to 350°

Blend the butter, sugar, and salt on low speed in a mixer until creamy. Add the yolk and vanilla and blend until combined. Add the flour and mix again. Spread into an 8 x 8 baking dish and tamp down with your fingers and the palm of your hand until it is evenly spread and firm. Bake for 20 to 25 minutes or until starting to brown a little around the edges. Remove from oven and let cool completely.

Filling

1½ cups sugar
¼ cup flour
4 organic egg whites
Juice from 3 to 5 key limes (enough to make 6 tablespoons of juice)
Powdered sugar

Sift flour and sugar together. Add egg whites and lime juice and whisk for a minute or two. Pour over crust and bake at 350° for 20 minutes. Remove from oven and allow to cool. If filling isn't quite set, refrigerate for up to 2 hours. Sift the powdered sugar over the cooled filling and slice into squares.

Aromatic Seasoned Salt

A good friend introduced me to homemade seasoned salt a few years ago and I have been making it ever since. I use it in just about every dish I make. I've gifted salt cellars to friends and family over the years and when the holidays roll around I replenish their stores. The best way to make it is with a group of friends and a bottle of wine (or two). We each contribute bunches of fragrant herbs and chop and snip together while the hostess is in charge of the food processor. The warmth from the wine, the heavenly scents, and the hearty laughter are stimulating to the senses and soothing to the soul.

2 small sprigs of any of the following herbs (the first four are my favorite): thyme, basil, oregano, chives, rosemary, or cilantro
1 cup coarse sea salt
3 to 4 cloves garlic, peeled and chopped
zest of one lemon

Put all of the ingredients in a food processor and blend. Spread the salt out on a baking dish and let dry for two days, stirring frequently. Your kitchen will take on the aroma of an Italian cucina.

Roasted Cumin Seed Salt

This is something I just started to make and it is perfect for Mexican, Cuban, and Spanish food. I also use it in stir-fries and curries. It was one of the key ingredients for the black bean soup special at the Day Lily.

1 tablespoon cumin seed
3 to 4 tablespoons coarse sea salt

Place the cumin seed in a nonstick frying pan and toast over medium heat, stirring frequently. When the seeds are aromatic and beginning to change color, remove from heat. Place in a food processor or mini chop with the salt and blend. Store in a sealed container.

Black Garlic Salt

I recently discovered black garlic and am only scratching the surface of ways to work with this exotic delicacy. When I used it to flavor sea salt, I was wowed by the results. The flavor is rich and smoky. It is definitely worth making and takes less than five minutes to prepare.

3 to 4 cloves black garlic
1 cup coarse sea salt

Process together until thoroughly blended. Spread onto a baking sheet for a few days, allowing the salt to dry the garlic. Stir frequently. Black garlic can be found in the larger grocery chains and specialty food stores, and ordered from the Internet.

More recipes are available at www.wendysandeckelauthor.com.

Acknowledgments

Thank you to the talented people at Thomas Dunne Books. Most importantly, to Anne Brewer, Shailyn Tavella, and Jennifer Letwack, for your support, enthusiasm, and insights.

Thanks to Ken Atchity, the best agent ever, for first believing in me and for your ongoing wisdom and guidance. And to Michael Neff for getting the ball rolling.

Thank you to my immensely gifted critique group: Jon Coile, Denny Kleppick, Mary Bargteil, Terese Schlachter, and Susan Moger. You are my brilliant North Star when I am at the helm of a novel.

Thanks to all the wonderful people who read *Murder at Barclay Meadow.* Meeting you at events, book clubs, signings, and via the Internet has been one of my favorite parts of being a writer. Thank you for making the muffins, falling in love with Tyler, getting scared at the scary parts, and looking forward to my next book.

And, thanks to all of you who sent me your favorite family

recipes. They were inspiring. Check them out at www.wendysandeckelauthor.com.

Love to Elizabeth Piotrowski and Madeline Eckel for enriching my life in every way. And to my sisters, Chris Sand-Ashley and Stacy Sand, for being my rocks.

And to MBR. A big fat thank-you, baby.